{JUST LIKE FAMILY}

JUST LIKE FAMILY

A Novel

KATE HILTON

HarperCollins*Publishers*Ltd

Published by HarperCollins Publishers Ltd

First edition

HarperCollins books may be purchased for educational, business,
or sales promotional use through our Special Markets Department.

HarperCollins Publishers Ltd
2 Bloor Street East, 20th Floor
Toronto, Ontario, Canada
M4W 1A8

www.harpercollins.ca

Library and Archives Canada Cataloguing in Publication
information is available upon request.

ISBN 978-1-44345-145-1

Printed and bound in the United States
LSC/H 10 9 8 7 6 5 4 3 2 1

For my parents

{JUST LIKE FAMILY}

CHAPTER 1

Monday, July 10, 2017

I can tell you with absolute precision the moment my life begins to come apart.

At the time, it isn't a grand unravelling. It's a small tug from the nail that catches the yarn of your sweater and leaves a tiny imperfection that you can see in direct light; but then it morphs into a hole, and then into a rip, so that you can only wear the sweater under a coat running errands; and then before long you have to downgrade the sweater's wardrobe status to Not Outside the House (but you aren't ready to part with it because you paid a lot of money and the colour brings out your eyes); and eventually, the absence of structural integrity is the defining feature of the whole garment, but still, you love it; and then one day you catch it on another nail, and it's no longer a sweater at all but a hole, the absolute absence of a sweater in fact, and you can't even give it away to charity. It's like that.

I'm standing in the gallery, watching Peter present his plan to city council for the new waterfront development. The plan is visionary. It's transformative. I mouth the words along with him as he stands under the seal of his office, arms outstretched, looking magisterial, majestic, even—

dare I say—messianic. Probably I don't dare. Probably that last one is only my impression. I've bought into this whole project in a big way, and I have to remind myself sometimes that not everyone sees it the way I do. Politics is like that. You always have better information than everyone else.

They're my words, by the way, the ones Peter is saying right now. They are always my words. I write them, he speaks them, people believe them. That's our system. He's the mayor of Toronto, I'm the chief of staff, and together we run one of the great cities of the world.

I've known Peter all my life, was in love with him for a significant chunk of it, and worked with him from the day I graduated law school. There was no question that I'd take a leave of absence from our law firm to work on his campaign, and even less question that I'd come to city hall with him. You could say he is my work husband, and people do, but if so, we have a notably traditional relationship. I make sure that he eats properly and that the office staff is properly recognized at Christmas with a boozy lunch, and I straighten his tie before he walks out into the media scrum. When we practised law together, I did the research and argued the minor motions and took the phone calls from clients suffering either the trauma of litigation or the trauma of paying our bill for their litigation. I stayed up late before major court appearances and stuffed facts into Peter's brain, wondering how on earth he would manage to convert his complete ignorance of the case into a winning argument. And then he would. Watching Peter when he is on his game is beautiful.

And that's why I traded a lucrative career in law for public service. I care about this city—I was born here, and it has never entirely loosened its hold on me, no matter how far I run—but the move to city hall wasn't entirely altruistic. I'm here for Peter. I'm not in love with him now, obviously; I haven't been in love with him since my late teens. Push hard, and you might get me to admit to a lingering fantasy or two into my early twenties.

But now we are both happily partnered with other people, as we were meant to be. Which doesn't change the fact that Peter remains the most charismatic person I've ever known. He has that addictive quality that's carried so many others into public office: you feel better, happier, prettier when you get a hit of Peter's attention, and just a little edgy and desperate when he moves on to someone else. I'm immune now, but I recognize the lost look of a Peter junkie when I see it. It takes one to know one.

The afternoon session starts well. We've been working on the waterfront plan for three years now, a year in advance of the election, and for two years since we came to city hall. We've negotiated public-private partnerships and tax breaks and rezonings. We've got the support of the women's groups and the environmentalists, the save-the-waterfront people and the create-jobs people, the animal rights activists and the seniors. We have four developers and reams of architects and consultants. And we have a coalition of city councillors prepared to vote for our plan. It's nothing short of a miracle. I am a miracle worker, a modern-day Annie Sullivan leading Helen Keller to fame and fortune. I allow myself a rare, precious moment of self-congratulation. We are going to rescue the scarred, abused waterfront from the ravages of neglect and turn it into something they would be proud of in Chicago. Chicago!

And then Roger Wozniak lurches to his feet, and I realize my first mistake. I should have taken the meeting with Rick Wozniak, Roger's son, last week.

Roger Wozniak is a big bear of a man. I don't mean to suggest what people often do when they say that, which is to say gruff and large but cuddly on the inside. I mean he is beefy and hairy, and that he'll turn on you and eat you if he is hungry and it suits him, because he is concerned about one person: Roger Wozniak.

I tune him out as he yells about process and wasted taxpayer dollars; I ignore the camera crews filming every sound bite of misinformation. I'll correct the record later. The press knows by now that Roger doesn't often have the facts right. But isn't that part of his charm? He tells it straight! He's an outsider, a little guy!

He isn't, in fact. The Wozniaks have been major players in political backrooms for three generations. And they certainly aren't short of money.

The shouting, the lying: these are the cultural norms of city politics, the ones that Peter and I are trying to break down. Lawyers get a bad rap. We, at least, understand that there are consequences to being an asshole on the job. But here, at city hall, we celebrate ignorance over insight, bellicosity over reflection, hyperbole over accuracy. Stand up and yell in court and you get a reprimand. Stand up and yell on the floor of city council and you get a spot on the evening news, and an army of fans who find you "relatable."

"Consultation!" he bellows. "Where was the consultation?"

Of course, taxpayers *were* consulted. They were consulted so often, in fact, that the word "consultation" gives me an unpleasant shivery sensation, the way you feel when someone offers you a glass of whatever alcohol caused you to have your first bad drinking experience back in high school (peach schnapps, in my case; I still can't touch the stuff).

"My constituents deserve to know where their money is going!" yells Roger. "Mayor Haines is asking them to approve a plan that has been made in secret! Between the mayor and his developer friends!"

Booing erupts across the floor. My eyes drift to the other side of the viewing gallery in time to see our lead developer, Adam Rothman, sliding out of the room.

"That's right," yells Roger. "We won't be silenced!"

The booing grows more fevered. Some are booing our plan, but many are booing Roger. I wonder if he realizes this.

"Colleagues," Peter says. "Friends. Please." He looks tired and annoyed, and I know we're done. "Councillors! I invite you to come to the central microphone and I'll answer your questions in order."

"You see?" says Roger. "Now he wants process! Now that it's useful to him! What a joke."

Councillor Judy Mendelson stands up and walks over to the central microphone. She is close to eighty, has been elected ten times, and is getting slightly wobbly in thought as well as in gait. "I just want to say how much I appreciate the good work that Mayor Haines has done on this project," she says. "For too long, our waterfront has been sold off to the highest bidder. It is a public treasure. This project will give it back to the taxpayers." She steps back. It is all she can manage by way of a show of support, but we'll take what we can get.

I have to watch the tape later to figure out exactly what happens next. Judy steps back from the microphone at the same moment that Roger bounds up. They are, neither of them, steady on their feet, and they collide. But Judy is a third the size of Roger and the laws of physics apply here, even if the principles of good behaviour do not, and Judy goes flying, really catching air, which you can see if you pause the video in the right spot, and she lands with an audible crack—a crack heard throughout the council room, which signifies the end of Judy's political career and my political idealism.

I haven't always been idealistic. I started that way, but I took a break from worrying about the collective good for a few years to focus on self-actualization. Self-actualization sounds better than old-fashioned selfishness, but it isn't, particularly. Or it wasn't, in my case.

Many would say as much about their own teens and twenties, of course. But still. I haven't always made the best choices. I've hurt people. I've drawn down my karma. In this job, though, with Peter, I'm giving back. I'm reversing the damage. Idealism, the belief that we can change ourselves and, in doing so, change the world around us, is now my drug of choice.

I walk back to my office, slowly, after the paramedics have cleared the council chamber. I want to let Peter blow off some steam before I get there.

I push my way through the media scrum that has gathered, ignoring all of them, until I am safe in the outer office. Bonnie Heller, the office manager, looks up from her desk, which is really more like the command centre on the starship *Enterprise*. She is in her late fifties, perfectly groomed in a linen suit. But even from where I'm stand-ing, I can see that she is holding her irritation at bay. She has an intern answering the phone and taking messages. The intern looks exhausted.

"The mayor is unhappy," says Bonnie. I glance over at Peter's office door. It is closed. "He's on the phone with the developers. They are also unhappy."

"I think it's fair to say that everyone is unhappy," I say. "Especially Judy Mendelson."

"We've sent flowers," Bonnie says. "I've arranged for regular updates on her condition. Also Aidan Clarke is try-ing to reach you. And your husband called." Matt isn't my husband, but I don't correct her. We've been together for fifteen years and lived under the same roof for fourteen, so he's the closest thing I have to one.

Aidan Clarke is persistence personified: the city beat reporter who is always on the trail of the Big Story. Some-where along the line, I must have given him the impression that I could be his Deep Throat in the right circumstances. I leak him information when Peter agrees, which isn't often, and he tries to get quotes from me that suggest a juicier subtext, which isn't often.

"Where's Gloria?" I say. Gloria is my assistant, and she is much nicer to me than Bonnie will ever be.

"She's on lunch," says Bonnie. "She couldn't get away any earlier. It's been mayhem around here." Her expres-sion leaves no doubt as to whom she blames for this.

There is a loud noise from behind Peter's door. "I wouldn't go in there just yet," says Bonnie. But the door opens, and Peter emerges.

"You," he says, pointing at me. "In my office."

I make my way inside. Peter has been throwing things. He does this sometimes. Law books usually, as he's learned to throw objects that won't break. I'm not sure when this habit started. Peter wasn't a thrower of tantrums, let alone objects (breakable or otherwise), when I first knew him. But people change, and not always for the better. Believe me. I should know.

I sit. I've learned to let him speak first. We've both come a long way since our earliest days in this office.

"That was a serious fuck-up, Avery," he says. Now that he's exhausted his heat by throwing things, a frost is setting in. "How the hell did we get blindsided by that? You told me Wozniak was contained."

Of course, I'd said no such thing. No one in her right mind would ever claim to have Roger Wozniak contained.

"We did extensive consultations," I tell him. "We spent extra time with his constituents. I had his staffers review the proposal and invited them personally to the town hall meeting. They assured me that Roger was comfortable with our strategy."

"Did you show it to Rick?"

This is the crux of my error. Roger is a self-serving, socially conservative, uninformed loudmouth, but he's loyal, at least to the one person he trusts: his son. In his late forties, Rick is a Harvard-educated former investment banker who took over the family's auto parts business fifteen years ago when his father decided to run for office. He's the unelected brains of the operation, and I sit in at least ten meetings a year that have been called for the sole purpose of persuading Rick to persuade Roger to do what we want him to do.

"No," I say.

"No?"

"I don't work for Rick Wozniak," I say. "I'm sick of this, Peter. If Roger Wozniak can't think for himself, that's his business. Rick is outside the process. He's a citizen. If he wants to call the shots, he can run for election."

Peter tilts his head slightly to one side. In this moment I'm not the most powerful woman at city hall; I'm the law student, now on probation, having forgotten to mention a major case in a research memo. "That citizen is the reason our proposal didn't pass today, Avery. So you are going to take a meeting with that man, tomorrow at the latest, and show him how much this administration cares about his opinion. And once you've fixed this fucking mess, you can put us back on the agenda."

"Peter," I say, but he puts up a hand.

"Fix it, Avery," he says. "That's your job."

Sometimes I think I'm in the wrong business. This is a game for the thick-skinned, the sly, the blamers and not the pleasers, the beaters and not the cringers. Everyone here has some deep, clawing desire, barely hidden beneath the skin, but those who want power survive much longer than those who want love. Love is in short supply in politics, and it always comes with conditions.

Bonnie is waiting outside, expectant. She tolerates me, and sometimes, although not today, I think she might like me, but she's Peter's ally, not mine. We both know that.

"I need a meeting with the Wozniaks," I say. "Both of them."

"I'll set that up right away," says Bonnie. "First thing tomorrow?"

"That would be delightful," I say.

Bonnie casts an eye over her command centre. "Your phone is ringing," she says. "I'll put it through." Obviously, I've taken up enough of Bonnie's time.

I walk over to my section of the office, waving off various members of my staff milling around Gloria's empty desk, gliding (I hope, but it could be read as ducking) into my office and closing the door behind me. I realize that I hope it's Tara or Jenny, so that I can tell them what a day I've had, just like I used to do over drinks at the hotel bar near my old office. But Jenny isn't speaking to me, hasn't been since I came to city hall, and come to think of it, I'm not sure Tara is either. Is it two months since I've called her? Three?

Or maybe it's Matt calling. That would be nice. I'd like to think that we are thinking of each other at exactly the same moment. This is the reason people get coupled, so that they can subject someone else to the details of a bad day at work. But Matt is in another time zone. Zurich. Or is it Paris? I've lost track. At this point in his day, he'll be sleeping or in a meeting that started early or went late. And if he were on the phone, he'd say, "Remind me, what's happening on the waterfront project?" or he'd say, "Avery, you know you don't have to take that shit from Peter, right?" and it wouldn't make me feel better at all.

But it is not Jenny or Tara or Matt. It's my mother. If it weren't for Bonnie, I wouldn't pick up the call. But Bonnie is in a mood. I've let Peter down today, and Bonnie will punish me if she can. She'll pick the line back up, say, "Goodness, Martine, I know she's there. Let me try again," and put the call back through. And if I don't pick up the second time, she'll say, "Just hold the line, Martine, maybe she stepped into the ladies'. I'll find her for you."

I pick up the phone. "Hi, Mom."

"Hello, darling," says my mother. "Avoiding me?"

"Actually, yes," I tell her.

She laughs. "Honestly," she says. "I can hardly complain. I did raise you that way." She pauses. "You know why I'm calling."

And I do, because she calls every year at this time and says, "You know why I'm calling."

I say, "It's been wild here, Mom. Peter and I have been working around the clock on the waterfront project. Matt's been out of town. I'm not sure it's going to work out."

There is a quiet huff of air as my mother decides on her next move. When she speaks, her voice is soft. "I'm going to sell the cottage."

"No," I say. "Don't do this again. Enough with the threats, Mom. You aren't going to sell it."

"It's the middle of July, Avery. You haven't been up once this year. You came for one weekend last August, after I nagged you for the entire season. Ethan and Tara stay with her mother when they come, which is rarely. There is no reason for me to keep the property."

"Mom, stop it. Seriously."

"I mean it, Avery. This isn't your decision. The cottage is worth a lot of money now, and the taxes are outrageous. But we can discuss it further when you arrive. Let me know when to expect you." And she hangs up.

I take a long breath in through my nose and exhale through my mouth to a count of five. My yoga instructor contends that this will calm me, more than a glass of pinot noir or a tablet of lorazepam, although I subscribe to the combination method. As my mother herself taught me, you shouldn't put all of your eggs in one basket.

I breathe in and out. I try to visualize a place of calm and quiet. A beach, an ocean, palm trees waving. But Berry Point elbows its way in instead: dock, not beach; lake, not ocean; pines, not palms. In place of calm, a crush of personalities jostles for space like subway riders at rush hour. In place of quiet, the noise of three families in three cottages on a rocky point of land, and of three girls growing up side by side, just like family.

Later, when this day is dissected and analyzed by others for other reasons, I'll wonder: Was it really the day that my life started to unravel, or was it merely the day I noticed the rip spreading across the centre of my life? And if it only marked the moment I opened my eyes to the destruction already long at work, when did it all begin? How far back would I have to go to find the nail that brushed up against the fabric and caught, how many choices would I have to undo, how many versions of myself would I have to recast, in order to avoid what was to come?

By the time Peter arrived that summer, a shift was already underway.

"Everyone's so boring this year," I said to my mother. "No one wants to help with the Olympics." The Berry Point Olympics in July and the Berry Point Theatre Festival in August *were* summer to me, and I filled many grey winter hours planning Berry Point entertainments: composing teams and devising events for the Olympics, and drafting scripts and casting roles for the annual play. Tara had always been an enthusiast, if not an instigator. But this year, Tara's appetite for sunbathing seemed insatiable. Jenny, as usual, was prepared to humour me if it suited her, but not if it didn't.

"Try not to force it," said my mother. "Chances are that the other girls will get tired of lying on the dock at some point."

I rolled my eyes.

My mother sighed. "You did say I'd get my own back eventually," she said, speaking to the ceiling.

"I'm over here," I said.

"I'm not talking to you," said my mother. "I'm talking to Grandma."

I huffed out of the kitchen. I heard my mother laughing to herself, and I let the porch door slam, hard, behind me. I had a plastic baggie full of quartered lemons, a beach towel, and a book, and I ran down the staircase to the lake.

Tara and Jenny were already on the dock, and had laid their towels in the best spots, the ones with full sun. I rolled out my towel, making sure my head was in the sun, and started squeezing lemon juice into my hair and finger-brushing it through.

Tara stood up, stretched, and adjusted the yellow fabric of her bikini, considering her reflection in the boathouse window.

"Is it working?" she asked.

"I think so," I said. "What do you think?"

Tara pursed her lips. "I think you should try Sun-In."

"Really?"

"Sure," said Tara. "We can get some at the store later."

"Okay," I said. "Do you want to talk about the teams for the Olympics?"

"Let's do it later," said Tara. "The sun's perfect right now."

I opened my book.

"Where's Ethan?" asked Tara.

"He's out with my dad running errands," I said. It was a mystery to me why anyone would want to know where Ethan was. My older brother was a complete pain.

"I'm going in the water," said Jenny.

"I'll come," I said. "Tara, do you want a swim?"

"I'll come in when I get hot," said Tara.

Jenny and I swam without speaking. We were allowed to swim without adults now, as long as there were two of us in the water and we stayed close to shore. We swam until we were breathing hard, and then we stopped and floated.

"Tara's like a bump on a log these days," I said.

Jenny looked straight at me, but she didn't answer.

"What?" I said.

"It's a free country," said Jenny. "She can do what she wants."

"I guess."

"Okay," said Jenny. "I'm just saying."

I ducked underwater and swam a few strokes. When I came up for air, Jenny said, "I think I see something on the bottom."

"Are you diving?" I asked.

She nodded, sucked in a huge lungful of air, and dove straight down. She was down for a long time before her fingers appeared, rising up from the bubbles on the surface, pinching a white triangle. The rest of her arm emerged, then her head, blonde hair dark and glossy from the water. She threw her head back, gulped a deep breath, and said, "Find!"

"Let me see."

"Don't drop it."

"I never drop it, Jenny," I said. I circled my legs in a lazy eggbeater kick and examined the shard. "It has flowers on it!"

"Let's swim back," said Jenny. "I want to look at it properly."

I handed it to her. "Why is Tara so interested in Ethan all of a sudden?" I asked.

"You know why," said Jenny.

"But it's *Ethan*," I said.

"There's no accounting for taste," said Jenny.

I started to giggle, began sinking.

"Swim!" said Jenny.

I did. We climbed the ladder and put Jenny's find down on her towel so it wouldn't fall between the boards. It was fantastic: a thick piece of platter, edged with a pattern of blue flowers.

Tara, distracted for once from her tan, agreed. "It should go in the box," she said. The best treasures were stored in the birchbark box that Jenny had made last summer when it rained for a week. Jenny was always making something. She had turned the spare bedroom of her cottage into a studio. It had an easel, and a shelf of paint and glue, and boxes of beads. She was working on a little table now, which she had rescued from the dump. She had refinished it and was slowly painting the entire surface with vines and flowers.

"Girls!" It was my mother's voice. "Can you come up, please?"

"It's early for lunch," said Jenny.

"Maybe she wants to discuss our hormones again," I said, and all three of us laughed, united against the general idiocy of mothers.

We wrapped ourselves in our towels and ran up the long wooden staircase to my cottage. Everyone had gathered in the parking field: Mom, Dad, and Ethan; Tara's parents, Kerry and Bill; and Jenny's parents, Greta and Don.

Peter was here.

"We're so glad to have you here," said Mom. "We were getting sick of each other."

"You'll probably get sick of me, too," said Peter.

16

Mom looked over at the three of us and smiled. "I doubt that," she said.

"You never said he was so cute!" I whispered to Jenny. I couldn't believe it. Peter, Don's son from his first marriage, was the most handsome person I'd ever seen in real life. He could have been on the cover of *Tiger Beat*.

Peter came over to us. "Which one of you is Jenny?" he asked.

"I am," said Jenny.

"It's good to meet you," he said. "I mean, I did meet you once, in California, but you were little."

"Three," said Jenny.

"And now you're?"

"Twelve!" I said.

Peter smiled at me. He had perfect teeth. "And you're . . . ?"

"Avery!" I said.

"Avery," he repeated. "Nice to meet you." He reached out a hand and I grabbed on, but he was already turning to Tara.

I felt cool hands on my shoulders. "Settle down, sweetheart," said my mother. "He's here for a month. Give him some space."

I pulled my shoulders forward, shook her off. I was struck by the great unfairness of life in that moment, that Tara should look so brown and pretty in her yellow bikini.

"Let's get you something to drink," said my dad. "We'll all go down to the dock."

"Thanks, Brian," said Peter.

"I'll take your bags down to our place," said Don. "We've set you up in the spare room."

Jenny froze. "Jenny," said her mother, "can I speak to you privately for a moment?" Greta put her arm around Jenny's shoulder and walked over to the edge of the field with her.

"Is it true that he's staying a whole month?" I asked Tara as the rest of the group headed down to the water.

"That's what my mom said," said Tara. "He graduated from college, and he's taking the summer off before he starts law school."

"Why wouldn't he take the summer off in California?" I said. California was cool. Rural Ontario was not.

"He wanted to spend time with Don," said Tara, and shrugged. Don was by far the most boring adult on Berry Point. He didn't even join in on Games Night, let alone the Olympics or the Theatre Festival. He liked collecting stamps, and obsessing over seasonal water levels.

"I've never seen Don smile like that," I said.

"I hate Dad!" Jenny shouted from the edge of the field. We turned, and saw her push Greta away. "And I hate you!" She ran off into the woods.

Greta stood and watched her go, and then walked slowly over to us. "She's just upset," she said. "We've moved her studio into the shed while Peter stays with us. She'll be fine. Where is everyone?"

"They've gone down to the dock for a drink," said Tara.

"I'll join them," said Greta. "You girls come too. Jenny needs some time to herself right now."

Down by the water, Peter was getting the third degree.

"The University of Toronto," said Dad. "Good for you. It's the best law school in the country."

"I'm looking forward to it," said Peter.

"You're moving here?" I said. This was huge news, and I couldn't believe I was hearing it for the first time. "I thought you were here for a vacation."

"I get my apartment on September first," said Peter.

"Where are you going to be living?" asked my mother.

"In the Annex," said Peter. "On Huron, south of Dupont."

"Oh, you'll love it there," said my mother. "Brian and I had our first apartment on Brunswick. It was adorable."

"It didn't have air conditioning," said my dad. "It was a hot box. Attic apartment. We couldn't sleep for the heat."

"Oh, stop it," said my mother. "We loved it."

My dad smiled at her. "Yes, we did," he said.

"So, Brian," said Bill, Tara's dad, "have you decided on this year's project?"

My dad was famous for his projects. There was usually a big one every summer.

"Well," said Dad, "I was wondering about a raft. But I'd need some serious help."

"A raft would be amazing," I said.

"I like a project," said Peter. "I'm game."

"All right, then," said my dad. "A raft it is."

Peter, Ethan, and Dad took a trip to the hardware store for advice and supplies. They returned with a delivery truck full of lumber and fifty-gallon barrels, and a little book called *Afternoon Project: Floating Raft*. After dinner, Peter came over, and he and Dad made notes from the book.

"We'll have to do it on the dock," said Dad. "This sucker's going to weigh a ton."

19

"No kidding," said Peter. "I think we should build the frame and attach the barrels on the dock first, and wait to do the decking until it's already floating."

"Good plan," said Dad. "What do you figure this'll take, time-wise?"

"Hmm," said Peter, "If we're ambitious? Maybe four hours."

"Are you ambitious?" asked my dad.

"I'd have to say yes," said Peter.

In the morning, Dad rang the dinner bell at seven and I rolled out of bed. Ethan was already downstairs. Peter showed up with Jenny and Tara in tow a few minutes later, and Mom put an enormous pancake down in front of each of us. "You don't want to get hungry," she said.

When we finished breakfast, we gathered in the field for our assignments. "You four are going to carry all the lumber down," Peter said. "Jenny and Avery, you're Team One. Ethan and Tara, you're Team Two. See how quickly you can move the wood. Starting now: go."

We hauled lumber in pairs for an hour at least, pausing only to wipe sweat from our eyes and slap mosquitoes from our arms. Dad and Peter measured and sawed and hammered, and a frame started to take shape, almost as large as the dock itself. Dad and Peter took their shirts off. Mom brought sandwiches and drinks.

"I'm going home for lunch," said Jenny, who had barely spoken to anyone all morning.

"Are you coming back after?" I asked.

"Maybe," she said. "I don't like being Peter's slave as much as you do."

Mom examined the raft. "How's it coming along?"

she asked. There was a hint of doubt in her voice. I could understand why. The raft still looked like a random collage of window frames of varying sizes inside a gigantic box. Peter was staggering the framing to balance the weight. But I didn't need to be persuaded. I could see exactly how amazing it would be when it was finished.

"It's going to be the finest raft on the lake," said Dad.

"Time for the barrels," said Peter. "Teams One and Two, two barrels each. Martine, do you want to help Avery? Jenny's disappeared."

"Sure," said Mom. "I wouldn't want to say I missed the Great Raft Project of 1987. Lead the way, Avery."

The barrels were light but unwieldy. We half-carried, half-rolled them to the construction zone. Mom and I won the competition. Mom said winning didn't matter, we were all making an important contribution, but she was laughing. "I've still got it," she told Dad.

"Without question," he said, and kissed her.

Peter and Dad drilled holes in the frame and fed rope through the holes. They lashed the barrels to the raft at each corner with multiple loops and fearsomely complicated knots.

"Are you sure those will hold?" asked Mom.

"Positive," said Dad. "Peter knows his knots. Now, let's see if this beauty will float."

"Where's Ethan?" asked Mom.

"He went back up to the cottage," said Tara. "He was tired."

"He's going to miss the best part," said Dad.

We clustered around three sides of the raft. On Peter's count, we strained and lifted and moved as one to shift the structure toward the edge of the dock. "Steady," said Peter. "Put it down." He stepped back, assessed. A third of the raft protruded off the dock. "I think we need to put a few strips of decking on now, Brian," he said. "It'll give us a platform to work from."

"Have you done this before?" asked my mother.

"Not this exact thing, no," said Peter. "I've always liked building things, though. I had a summer job on a construction crew in California. It was sweet money."

"Well," said my dad, "you're certainly a welcome addition here. California's loss is our gain."

Peter instructed us on how to hold the planks and Dad secured them with the nail gun that he had rented from the hardware store. When half the planks were attached, Peter tied the raft to the dock with one of the anchor lines, and on his count we all heaved. With a mighty splash, and waves that travelled right across the lake, the raft was launched. We all applauded, all of us remaining: Mom, Dad, Peter, and me.

"Where's Tara?" I asked.

"She went up to check on Ethan," said Mom.

Peter jumped onto the raft. "Come on, Avery," he said. "Let's do this."

Mom and Dad passed the final boards to Peter, hand over hand, and I held them in place, just where he told me to, while he nailed them down. When the whole deck was finished, and the ladder was attached, Peter told me to go and get two paddles from the boathouse. "I need your expert advice on placement, Avery. Once the anchor is down, this raft is going nowhere. We have one chance to get it right."

I ran and got the paddles while Dad and Peter measured the anchor lines and tied a cinder block to each of them. Mom and Dad stood on the dock while Peter and I paddled out into the lake. It was a calm day, but still, the raft was heavy and I was breathing hard as I drew the paddle through the water with all my strength. "All right, Avery," said Peter. "Let's assess."

We put the paddles down and stood up. "How's this?" Peter called to my parents on the dock. We watched them confer, and then both of them gave us the thumbs-up. We did the same.

"First anchor," said Peter. "Ready?" We both bent and picked up an edge. "On your count, Avery," said Peter.

"One," I said, and we lifted. "Two," I said, and we swung it back. "Three!" I said, and we released it over the side. The splash hit us both in the face, and I laughed. My parents waved. I waved back.

We did the second anchor and the third, and then we were done. Peter lay down in the middle of the raft and I did the same. I felt the raft rocking and heard the pine trees creaking in the wind. My arms were aching. It was the most perfect day. I loved everything. I loved the raft, and the sky, and the water, and my family, and Berry Point, and Peter.

"That was so fun," I said.

"You hung in," said Peter. "I'm impressed."

"I like projects," I said.

"You are your father's daughter."

"Is that a good thing?"

"Definitely," said Peter. "Your parents are great."

"They're okay."

"They're a lot livelier than my dad and his wife," said Peter.

It wouldn't be hard to be livelier than Don, but I didn't say so.

"Are you looking forward to law school?" I asked.

"I'm more looking forward to being a lawyer," said Peter. "The program is pretty intense."

"Have you always wanted to be a lawyer?"

"As long as I can remember."

"I have no idea what I want to be," I said.

"You've got time," said Peter. "But first things first. What are we going to do for the rest of the month now that we're finished the raft?"

"Want to help organize the Berry Point Olympics?"

"Sure," he said. "Why not? Let the Games begin."

CHAPTER 3

Tuesday, July 11, 2017

It's already steamy when I step out of the doors of city hall into the plaza. I feel the sweat beading under my suit and my hair frizzing. I feel unprepared for my role as the star of the Avery Graham saga today. It is too demanding in this heat. I need a makeup trailer. I need personal staff: a stylist, a script coach, an agent to take care of pesky conversational skirmishes like the one I'm about to have.

I don't need any extras, though. I have plenty of those. I have the Sad Smoker, outside the doors, wafting clouds of cigarette smoke like dry ice, weeping angrily into her cellphone. I have Jesus on Rollerblades, who glides through the plaza at least twice a day, hair trailing behind him. I have the Grill Sergeant, who operates the hot dog truck on the northwest corner, barking commands at his customers while wearing a wardrobe consisting entirely of camouflage. I have the Narcoleptic Babysitter, who sits in the shade and dozes while her charges run around city hall plaza, dangerously close to the street, chasing pigeons. And I have the Bandwagon Objector, who has never, ever missed a protest in city hall plaza.

I would like to tell the Sad Smoker to quit smoking and find a nicer boyfriend. But I don't even know her name, and anyway, who am I to give anyone advice? I am, after all, on my way to see the Wozniaks, which is all the evidence anyone would ever need to conclude that the main character in my show has made some bad choices somewhere along the way. I'm hoping for catharsis before the final frames, but it won't be happening today.

We are meeting at Rick Wozniak's office, only a few blocks from city hall. Roger's constituency office is in a leafy suburb an hour away, where people drive cars to go to big box stores three blocks from their homes, so I'm not complaining. Not much, anyway.

When I arrive, Roger and Rick are already seated in Rick's conference room.

"Avery," says Rick, rising and clasping my hand as if we are old friends. "Thank you for fitting us into your busy schedule." Rick makes an effort to be a gentleman in the small matters; I'll give him that. Roger remains seated.

"Well," I say, "obviously the mayor is anxious to understand your thoughts on the waterfront development. We were, candidly, surprised by your objections, Roger."

"Were you?" says Roger. "You seem smarter than that."

"Dad," says Rick.

"Fine," says Roger.

"First things first," says Rick. "How is Councillor Mendelson?"

Roger's face is redder than usual. "Mendelson's too old for this game," he says. "She should think about retiring."

"I'm sure she is," I say. "She's fractured a hip. A return to work is unlikely at this point."

"A remarkable career," says Rick. "My father and I so admire her dedication to the city. I hope you will let us know if there is a celebration down the road. We'd be pleased to contribute to a gift." Roger nods his head in agreement.

"I'll make a note of that," I say. "We'll be sure to include your family in any plans."

"Excellent," says Rick. His assistant comes in with a tray, and a few minutes are spent on the pouring of coffee and the offering of cookies. There are always cookies here, no matter what the hour, and I never eat them. It feels dangerous, and possibly disloyal. The cookies are famously delicious. People whisper about them at city hall.

"To business, then?" asks Rick.

"Sure," I say. "Why don't we start with you bringing me up to speed on your current objections to the plan."

"The neighbours are pissed, and so are we," says Roger.

Rick takes over. "You can tell the mayor that we remain committed to the basic concept of the redevelopment, as we told you several months ago," he says. "But in the past week, it has come to our attention that the neighbours had not received full information about the plans. The mayor had given my father his absolute assurance that the neighbours would have full and complete input into the uses in the development."

"As I understand it, the neighbours were consulted fully," I say. "Is there a specific issue?"

"Let's call it a concern," says Rick. "A legitimate concern, about the women's shelter."

Now I'm honestly confused. A modest, discreet, non-intrusive, architecturally attractive, and politically popular women's shelter has been part of the design plan from the beginning. There are a few new additions to the project, compromises here and there, including a home improvement store that looks like an airplane hangar and a hunting and fishing supply store with a gigantic stag's head rising from the top of the building, but until this moment I have believed the women's shelter to be unassailable, both in purpose and design.

"As you know," says Rick, "the development will result in the demolition of affordable studio space for artists in the city."

"Yes," I say. "And that is why the mayor has created an equal number of new rent-controlled studios in the development plan."

"Exactly," says Rick. "And those studios are located above the women's shelter."

"Forgive me, Rick," I say, "but this isn't news. We haven't moved any of these elements in the project."

"No one is suggesting that you have," says Rick. "This issue is inadequate information. The neighbours were not informed that there would be children in the shelter. And now they are deeply concerned that the noise of the children will interfere with the creative process."

"Of course there are children!" I say. "Women leaving abusive situations take their children with them."

"Avery," says Rick, "no one is suggesting that these women should be separated from their children, merely that more needs to be done to consider the needs of the artists."

"Would you pass the cookies?" I say. I need some fat and sugar to absorb this outrageous political play. Roger Wozniak is Public Enemy Number One for the intelligentsia in this city. The idea that he is now styling himself as a friend to artists is too rich by half. The cookie is not, though. It is exactly rich enough. It is perfect. I take another, which doesn't count, because I'm burning a lot of calories right now by suppressing my rage.

"You want my vote?" says Roger. "You need to get the artists onside."

"What we'd like," says Rick, "is for the mayor to meet with the neighbours, specifically with the Artists' Cooperative, and work out a solution to the noise issue. I'm sure there are a number of ways in which this could be resolved. And when the artists are satisfied with the process and the outcome, my father will vote for the plan."

"Right," says Roger. He looks at his watch. "Are we done? I have a lunch."

"We're done," says Rick. "Thanks, Dad." Roger pushes his chair back and is gone in seconds.

I make a move to rise, but Rick speaks. "I apologize if my father appeared rude just now."

"Don't worry about it," I say.

"He may lack a certain finesse, but he truly wants the best for this city."

"Of course."

"Did you know that he'll be seventy this year?"

"I didn't," I say. And, in fact, I'm surprised. There is a boyishness in Roger that appeals to those who want their politicians to be exactly like them and no better. I would have put his age at least five years younger, and I'm struck by a wonderful thought. "Is he considering retirement at all?"

"I tell him he should slow down," says Rick, "but he loves the work. It puts the fire in his belly."

"Retirement can be a daunting prospect for a man of that generation," I say.

Rick's face relaxes into a smile. "Exactly!" he says. "And on that topic, I wanted to ask for your help with something. I hope you won't mind."

"I'm sure not," I say.

"You may not know that my father is a poet," says Rick.

"I'm sorry," I say, "I thought you said 'a poet.'"

"Let me back up," says Rick. "I've been going through my father's papers recently. The family is throwing a party for his seventieth birthday, and we wanted to have a display of photos and other memorabilia. It turns out that Dad's quite the pack rat. Anyway, I came across a file of poems that he wrote in his twenties. I asked him about it, and he told me that it was quite a passion for him when he was younger."

"How fascinating."

"Isn't it?" says Rick. "I had no idea. And it struck me that I might be able to give him a surprise birthday present, and at the same time, remind him that he once had hobbies outside of politics. Maybe inspire him to take up his pen again."

"He's lucky to have you as a son," I say.

"That's kind of you to say," says Rick. "I owe my dad a lot. There is no one more generous or supportive. Truly. So it would give me a lot of pleasure to do something special for him. And I was hoping you might help me do that."

"If I can."

"I hear that you were a writer yourself."

"Only for about five minutes," I say, "a long time ago."

"Like riding a bicycle, I'm sure," says Rick.

"Not in my experience," I say.

"I was hoping," says Rick, "that you might agree to look over one of his poems and give me your opinion on it. Ideally, I'd like to figure out how to have it published for his birthday."

"Rick, I was never a poet, and barely a writer. You must know dozens of people more qualified than I am to critique your dad's poetry."

"None of them are connected to Hugh Crane," says Rick.

"Oh," I say. "Yes. Well, in that case."

Rick opens a file folder and hands me a single typed sheet. I read it, and then I put the page down in front of me.

"How . . . unexpected," I say.

"Can you help?" he asks. "A publication would mean a lot to us."

I think of Peter, and all of the work I've done for the past three years, and the fine people of our city who deserve a beautiful waterfront. I paste a cheerful expression on my face and think of Toronto. And I say, "I'll do what I can."

He beams. "I won't forget this," he says. "Please tell Mr. Crane how very much I admire *The Beak*."

"I will," I tell him.

"My father will be over the moon."

"Let's keep it to ourselves for now," I say. "Until we hear back from Hugh. Publication can be a long road. I wouldn't want to get his hopes up."

He nods. "Yes," he says. "I see your point. In the meantime, I'll see what I can do at my end to move my father along on the waterfront plan."

"That would be much appreciated," I say.

"I can't work miracles, Avery," he says. "Get the neighbours onside, and we'll go from there."

"The mayor will be pleased," I say, extending my hand to shake his.

"I'm indifferent to his pleasure or displeasure," says Rick. "I wouldn't want to mislead you. I have genuine respect for you."

"Okay," I say. "Thank you."

"I grew up in a political family," he says. "My grandfather, my uncle, my father—they were all close to the leaders of the day. We ate politics for dinner every night. We were, I guess you would say, connected."

I nod. "And you still are."

"Yes," he says. "And when you are connected to many different people, information finds its way to you. Lately, I've been receiving information about the mayor."

"What kind of information?"

"I can't say," he says. "It's only gossip, and I dislike gossip."

"What *can* you say?"

"There aren't many surprises in this business when you've been at it long enough. And you learn, after a while, that most rumours are at least a little bit true."

"I don't know about that," I say.

"I know you don't," he says. "That's my point. That's why I'm telling you what I'm telling you."

"You're not telling me anything," I say.

"We'll talk again," says Rick.

I walk back into the office, sending texts as I go. I still haven't shaken the imposter syndrome that goes along with having staff whose role it is to make you look and feel competent. *Find out everything you can about Jim Crawford,* I type, and people spring into action. *Book lunch with Tara Gillespie.* It's a marvel, it really is.

And then there are the people who have no interest in making me feel competent. "Peter wants an update," says Bonnie as I walk in, and points to his door.

He's on the phone as I enter, but he smiles at me, a good sign, and points to the chair opposite his. I sit.

"Avery has been hard at work on the problem this morning," says Peter into the phone. "I don't want you to worry, Adam. Everything is well in hand. Last-minute posturing is normal. The project is going ahead as planned. You have my word." He hangs up.

"How's Adam?" I say. Adam Rothman, last seen exiting the viewing gallery with unseemly haste, is our largest development partner. His company is building all the residential units at a miraculously low price, and donating the playground and the boardwalk. A great deal hinges on Adam's happiness—the waterfront, Peter's next election, my mental health. And, judging from the expression on his face yesterday, he needs a happiness intervention of epic proportions.

"That depends," says Peter. "What do the Wozniaks have to say for themselves?"

"There are some complaints from the neighbours," I say.

"Really?" says Peter. "You told me you had that covered."

"I thought I did," I say.

"That's politics for you," says Peter. He's in a remarkably even temper today. "What kind of neighbours have we got this time? Seniors? Families?"

"Artists," I say. "A group led by a sculptor-slash-multimedia-artist named Jim Crawford, who is also a self-described urban activist. They call themselves the Artists' Cooperative Council, or ArtCo for short."

"Catchy," says Peter. "Artists. Good. The lefties belong to us. Did you tell the Wozniaks to drive back to the suburbs?"

"Rick seems to have a relationship with the ArtCo folks," I say.

"Ate a cookie, did you?" says Peter.

"No," I lie.

Peter laughs. "Was it the double chocolate chip?" he says. "Fucking delicious, that one." He has the design concept plan on his desk, and he flips a page and points. "We could eliminate the women's shelter entirely if we had to," he says.

"No, we couldn't," I say. "We got three councillors on board because of the women's shelter, and we'll lose their votes if we take it out."

Peter shrugs. "Fair enough," he says. "Then I guess you'll have to go see the art people and figure out how to move them. There's always a lever." Peter is never a detail person, until he is.

I, on the other hand, am a perennial detail person. "Usually," I say. "Not always."

He laughs. "You know, Avery," he says, "I was thinking about your dad today. Brian would have loved this project."

"Yes, he would have," I say. My dad had been a lawyer who cared more about urban planning than he did about the mechanics of real estate deals, and he'd loved the files that gave him a window into city politics. Like

Peter, he was the sort of person who could see unrealized possibilities. I want to believe that I have his gift, but, in truth, I am the sort of person who borrows vision from others.

"There was something else, Peter," I say. "Rick mentioned a rumour about you. And I've been dodging calls from Aidan Clarke."

"Which rumour, Avery? There are ten reporters in this city who get paid to circulate rumours about me. You know that."

"Rick didn't give me any details. But he seemed to *know* something."

Peter shifts his reading glasses to the end of his nose, raises his eyebrows, and watches me over the rims. "Go ahead, Avery," he says. "Let's play *West Wing*."

I hesitate here. It's no secret that Peter is a hard dog to keep on the porch. I know it, his staff knows it, the press knows it, and his wife, Hannah, knows it. I don't pretend to understand Peter's relationship with beautiful, articulate, remote Hannah, the perfect political wife. If I were a man—Leo from *The West Wing*, for example—I suspect I would have insisted on some details by now, but I can't bring myself to do it. It is one of many lurking anxieties that I have about my job performance.

"Is there anything I need to know?" I ask.

"You've known me for twenty-five years, Avery," says Peter. "If there were something to know, you'd know."

"Everything fine at home?" I ask.

"Seriously?" he says.

"Yes, Peter," I say, "seriously. I'm doing my job. It's my responsibility to remind you that the Wozniaks are watching your every move. The waterfront project is in a delicate place. The mayor's office must be above reproach."

"Message received, Avery," says Peter. "You can stop now." He pushes his glasses back up, turning his attention back to the drawings.

I raise my hands in the universal sign of surrender, but he isn't looking at me any longer. "What do you want to do next, Peter?" I ask. "Do you want to meet with the artists personally?"

"Not unless you think it absolutely necessary," says Peter. "Can't you handle it yourself?"

This is Peter's favourite trick for getting out of unpleasant assignments. "Seriously, Peter?"

He grins. "Thank you, dear," he says.

"I'll handle Tara, too," I tell him. "You're welcome, by the way."

"Tara?" he says. "You lost me. Were we talking about Tara?"

"No, because I was handling it by myself," I say.

"And doing it beautifully," he says.

"You are such . . ."

"A pleasure to work for. I know. I feel the same way," he says.

I smile in spite of myself. It's impossible to stay irritated with Peter. Or at least, it's impossible for me. "You're going to love this," I say. "It turns out that Roger Wozniak writes poetry."

"Did you say 'poetry'?" says Peter.

"I did. Prepare to be amazed," I say. And I read:

Bar Girl
by Roger Wozniak

She moves her hips from left to right,
Her shoulder bears a tattooed star.
Her waist is bare, her skirt is tight,
The girl who dances on the bar.
She comes here every Friday night,
Collecting money in a jar.
She floats above us like a kite,
The girl who dances on the bar.
I wish I may, I wish I might
Love her near and not afar,
And pull her close and hold her tight,
The girl who dances on the bar.

"It goes to show," says Peter, "you never really know anyone."

"I see some Leonard Cohen influences in the piece," I say.

"The man is spinning in his grave right now," says Peter. He points to the couch. "Go sit over there. I don't want to be caught in the crossfire when God strikes you down for blasphemy."

"You don't believe in God," I say.

"I believe in Leonard Cohen," says Peter. He shakes his head, as if to clear it. "And Tara Gillespie? I'm having trouble connecting the dots here."

"Tara's dad is one of Hugh Crane's best friends," I say. "He's like family to her."

"A dirty uncle?"

I give him a look. "More like a cousin," I say sternly. He grins. I continue. "Rick told me that it's his father's dream to have his poetry published. Hugh is the editor-in-chief of a magazine that publishes poetry."

"And you can't ask him yourself because . . ."

"Because I can't. As you well know," I say. "But Tara can, so I'll ask her to ask him."

"No need to get snippy, dear," says Peter. "Sounds like you have a plan. Go make it happen."

"I have lunch booked with her tomorrow," I say. "Oh, and I'm going up north on Friday for the weekend. I have to show my face at the cottage before the end of the season."

"It's a bad time," says Peter.

"When is it not a bad time?" I say. "It's a command performance. But why don't you come too? Bring Hannah and the kids? You'd be welcome."

"No," says Peter. "I wouldn't be."

I wish I could knit up all the strands that unravelled when Peter's father left Jenny's mother. But I can't, because Jenny's childhood resentment of Peter has hardened into an impenetrable, incomprehensible antipathy, no matter what she says about moving on and letting go. Berry Point is Jenny's home now, and Peter isn't welcome. I drop the subject.

I want to shake off the mythology of childhood friendship, the idea that the bonds of our youth are the closest ones we'll ever form. Best Friends Forever: we repeated these words to each other so often, Tara and Jenny and I, that I'll never completely disbelieve them, even though I know, rationally, that they promise the impossible. How can it be otherwise, when all we do is change?

"So, to return to the business at hand," says Peter, "if we solve the neighbour problem, we have the Wozniak vote?"

"It would help if we could grant Roger's wish to be a published poet, but yes."

"It's a modest request, as wishes go," says Peter.

"You've obviously never tried to get published," I say.

"Fair comment," says Peter. "I forget that you were a writer."

"I try to do the same," I say.

CHAPTER 4

September 1998 and January 1999

There was a brief period in my late teens and early twenties when I decided to take a break from being responsible, organized, and goal-oriented. My mother refers to these as my "lost years," or "the years you took off my life." Occasionally, she also says, "I'm going to have a word with Brian about *all that* next time I see him." "All that" is my dad's decision to leave a substantial chunk of life insurance money outright to Ethan and me without considering how mature, or not, we would be at the age of eighteen; "next time I see him," is, obviously, when she, too, dies.

My father wasn't expecting to die when he did, and he didn't think through all the details. He'd made Ethan and me beneficiaries, along with our mother, of his life insurance policy; our portions were held in trust until we turned eighteen.

My first year of university was a disaster. I'd gone to the University of Toronto—my dad's alma mater, and Peter's too—but it was a huge school, and in my hometown. I needed an experience that was both new and comforting, and I got neither. I knew I was grieving, but I didn't know how to heal. So I ran away.

For the next four years, I was more often in Europe than not, on some internship or exchange, trying to cobble together enough credits for a degree. During this period I antagonized registrars at several institutions of higher learning; honed my advocacy skills petitioning for extensions, independent studies, and extra credit; irritated friends and family by extolling the virtues of "studying at the University of Life"; and spent a great deal of money.

By the end of the summer of 1997, though, it had begun to dawn on me that I wasn't the sort of person who was going to marry a European and spend the rest of my life teaching something to do with literature at an ancient university while raising multilingual children. I'd spent a month backpacking with Tara and Jenny that summer, and they'd reminded me, persistently, that I had a life back in Canada that I could resume if I returned. I suspected that my mother had given them a secret mission to brainwash me into coming home with them. But she didn't really need their intervention. The other travellers I met were getting younger, and my conviction that personal tragedy had matured me far beyond my cohort was beginning to waver. There were moments now when I wondered if, in fact, it had done the exact opposite. And I was gratingly, achingly homesick.

Jenny and Tara, having graduated, had returned home with purpose. Jenny was doing research for a professor in the art history department, which was going to look fantastic on her graduate school applications. Tara was starting a one-year public relations program, but more importantly, she and Ethan were getting married in December, and planning to use Dad's insurance money to buy a house. A *house*.

It would be hard to overstate how much this information undid me. Disconnected from the day-to-day progress of life back home, I found myself, for the first time, trailing the pack. I wanted, suddenly, desperately, to catch up. I wanted to hit a milestone. And the only one within striking distance was a master's degree.

That Christmas, back home for Tara and Ethan's wedding, and sentenced to serve my last semester at my degree-granting university—which had told me in no uncertain terms that it would not be granting my degree if I didn't show my face on campus—I lolled on the couch listening to Alanis Morissette and writing in my journal and watching old videos of *The Breakfast Club* and *Say Anything* and weeping. My mother's only comment on all this was to come down to the rec room one afternoon, hand me a box, and leave.

The box was full of admissions materials from schools all across North America, for master's programs in every subject I'd ever mentioned with enthusiasm: English, art history, psychology, sociology, social psychology. There were applications for law schools, too, which I set aside for the fireplace. And then there were applications for MFA programs in creative writing.

I have no idea what deep maternal insight had prompted my mother to include them, but it was inspired. I was hooked. I went through the brochures, thumbing them, folding down pages, annotating them. I hadn't done any creative writing since high school, but I liked the idea of being a writer, and I thought, with a kind of tuning-fork clarity, that it was something I could do well if I set my mind to it.

The one thing I had that differentiated me from other applicants, I believed, was material. I put my mind to distilling it into a single short story, twenty pages in length, with more focus than I had brought to any academic assignment since high school. My mother, again, made no comment when I handed her ten completed applications and asked her to mail them for me, other than to say, "Sure, honey. I was going to the post office anyway."

And NYU, by some miracle, admitted me.

The miraculous nature of my admission was confirmed when I arrived on the first day of classes in September 1998. The line of students awaiting course schedules snaked down the corridor, and most of them were dispatched inside of two minutes. But the registrar pulled out my file, flipping through each page. She asked for my letter of admission and examined the entire file a second time, much more slowly. I could feel tension rising among the waiting hordes behind me.

"What happened here?" she said, apparently rhetorically. "You're missing several prerequisites," she added, the first question obviously addressing a broader issue of suitability than mere course requirements.

"I know," I said. "I'll make them up."

"You will if you want to graduate," she said. She'd met the likes of me before. She handed me a package. "This is a very unusual academic record, Ms. Graham," she said. "You have a lot of work ahead of you."

"I understand," I said.

"You've been assigned Professor Crane as your advisor. Go and see him during his office hours on Friday and arrange a weekly meeting time. Here is your class schedule and course handbook." She slid a heavy envelope across the counter. "Next!"

I stood on the steps of the administration building and tapped my last cigarette out of the package. I'd been saving it for either emergency anxiety abatement or celebration. This was a bit of both. I knew I didn't deserve to be here, at least not by virtue of my academic achievements. But this was an MFA, and artistic potential mattered; it could, and had, in my case, created a loophole in the system.

A blonde girl sat down on the steps nearby, smoking. She looked as though she belonged. I asked her for a light. She flicked her lighter, held it for me.

"Horrible habit," she said, taking a long pull of her cigarette.

"Disgusting," I agreed. "This is my last one."

"Mine too," she said. "Are you new?"

"Fresh off the plane," I said. "Is it that obvious?"

"The orientation package is a dead giveaway," she said, pointing to the fat envelope sitting on the step beside me. "Where'd you fly in from?"

"Toronto, most recently," I said. "But I've been in England and Italy for most of the last four years."

"Nice," she said. "Why on earth did you come back?"

"Time to grow up," I said. "Well, sort of grow up, I guess. I'm in the creative writing program, so maybe that's debatable."

She laughed. "Completely debatable," she said. "Wait until you meet your classmates."

"Worldly, mature, and sophisticated?" I said.

"Only in their own minds, alas," she said. "I'm Liz. Second year of the program. Aspiring poet, future waitress."

"I'm Avery," I said. "Aspiring novelist, attempting to avoid thinking about the future in any respect."

"Welcome," said Liz. "Who's your advisor?"

"Professor Crane," I said.

She crinkled her nose. "Too bad," she said.

"What's wrong with him?"

"He's old school," she said. "He has a hard-on for anything written by a man before 1965."

"You talking about Crane?" An extremely tall woman with a nose ring sat down next to us. "I'm Cara," she said.

"Avery," I said. We shook hands.

"Our friend Craig had Crane last year. Craig said he doubted that Crane had read any post-colonial theory at all."

Liz nodded. "Stephanie said that he was completely dismissive of her paper on intertextuality," she said to Cara. "I read it. It was good. She argued that literature could only be understood intertextually in the digital age."

"Interesting," said Cara.

"Crane didn't think so," said Liz. "He made her spend the next three weeks writing about a single paragraph in *Anna Karenina*. About a *ball*."

"Brutal," said Cara. "Sorry, Avery. That sucks."

"You win some, you lose some," I said. I had absolutely no idea what they were talking about. "Listen, I've got to go and meet my roommate, but I'll see you guys around, okay? It was great meeting you."

"You too," said Liz. "Good luck."

I took the subway home to the Lower East Side and walked up three flights.

"Jenny?" I said.

"How'd it go?" asked Jenny.

"Not bad," I said. "The registrar admitted me, but it sounds like my advisor is an asshole."

"You can't have everything," said Jenny.

"True words," I said. "How about you? How was your day?"

"Meh," said Jenny. "I had more fun decorating the apartment. Check it out." Jenny was doing a master's degree in decorative arts and design at the New School, which was a compromise with her ex-stepfather, Don, who was funding it as part of the conditions of her parents' divorce. He wouldn't pay for art school, and Jenny wouldn't do a traditional program in art history. The compromise appeared to please neither of them.

The tiny front hallway was now decorated with small cardboard boxes in various colours, each hanging from a ribbon, and each with a tiny object glued to the inside. There were beads, coins, feathers, scraps of fabric, a medal, postcards, and fragments of maps. "What do you think?"

I hugged her. "I think you're a genius," I said.

She hugged me back. "What did your advisor do that made you think he's an asshole?" she asked.

"I haven't met him yet," I said. "But apparently everyone hates him."

"Who's everyone?" said Jenny. "You need to stop worrying about what other people think and make up your own mind. What's his name?"

"Hugh Crane," I said.

"Hugh Crane?" said Jenny. "From Berry Point?"

"Berry Point? What are you talking about?" I said.

"That friend of Tara's dad's. The one who comes up every year. Brown hair? Bermuda shorts?"

I shook my head, drawing a complete blank.

"I'm sure it's him," said Jenny. "Don't you remember? Tara said to look him up last time we saw her. That he was a prof at NYU."

"It's all somewhat hazy," I said. "Did she mention it after the vodka shots?"

"Quite possibly," said Jenny. "Anyway, Hugh was okay. He was old and had bad taste in shorts, but otherwise he seemed fine. It's not like you have to sleep with him."

"Very funny," I said. "As if I'd sleep with someone who wears Bermuda shorts. Give me some credit."

Hugh wasn't wearing shorts the first time I slept with him, in his office, on his leather couch. And we didn't sleep, although I was exhausted.

I'd spent too much time over the past few years not sleeping enough or eating properly and having sex with men I didn't know and generally being aimless. I'd been adrift for so long, actually, that I felt like a complete foreigner (though of no country in particular) with a better ear for European languages than for the cadence, vocabulary, and politics of liberal arts department-speak. I wanted to be reinvented.

According to the guidelines for advisors and students, Hugh and I were supposed to be working on a plan to turn the short story I'd submitted with my application into a novella. But Hugh thought it was more important in the short term to cure the deficiencies in my reading history. He had designed a reading list for me, and we spent our weekly session together studying the craft of other writers, ones that Hugh admired: Cheever, Hemingway, Munro, Nabokov, Woolf.

How I anticipated those weekly meetings. The conversation was intense. I prepared for those sessions as if they were final exams. I did extra research, scoured the secondary sources for critical tidbits with which to impress him, carrying them back in my mouth like a cat with a field mouse. I arrived early. I chose my clothes carefully, put on makeup. I accessorized. And really, I didn't have much else going on, aside from the occasional glass of wine or cup of coffee with Liz and Cara. In addition to my reading for Hugh, I was taking four other courses, one of which (my fiction seminar) required me to produce original writing each week. Over one September, I had transformed from a hedonist into an ascetic.

Hugh was worldly. He'd lived in Berlin and spoke German fluently. He had read everything of significance. He'd seen tragedy, too: he had lost both his parents in a car accident in his twenties. He wasn't stylish—Liz and Cara had been correct about that. But he was kind. Until I met Hugh, I hadn't understood that hard experiences could make you gentle.

In Hugh's office that fall, I felt myself click back into place. I felt smart again. I felt energetic. I felt lively and funny and focused.

And I wanted Hugh. Desperately. I wanted all that kindness and gentleness for myself. I needed him to see me not as a student, but as a woman. What if I hadn't been lost all these years, but instead on a preordained path that led to Hugh? Fiction and solitude had made me dangerous.

The day I seduced him, we were talking about writers' retreats. Hugh had written his second novel in a pension near the beach in Cirali, Turkey, and still believed it was the best writing he'd ever done.

"Weren't you lonely?" I asked him, regretting immediately the way my question made me sound: young and terribly unsophisticated.

"I wasn't, no," he said, smiling. "There were other writers there, and a good bar on the beach. And a steady stream of backpackers looking for interesting life experiences."

"Like sleeping with published writers?" I said, trying to right myself in the conversation.

"Occasionally," said Hugh.

"I was there last summer, on Cirali beach," I told him. It was true. I would have lied, if necessary, to keep the conversation on a more personal footing, but as it happened, I'd been to see the turtles before moving home.

"What did you think of it?" he asked.

"I thought it was one of the most beautiful places I'd ever seen," I said. Again, truth. "I had to leave before the turtles hatched, though." I wondered why I was telling him this story. I could feel a blush rising, could see myself through Hugh's eyes as a naive student, in over her head.

"What happened?"

"I wanted to visit a *hammam*. Some other travellers I met suggested one that was popular with tourists. But I went at the wrong time, and there weren't any other women there. I got a male masseuse. Masseur?"

"He must have thought it was Christmas come early," said Hugh.

"I'm pretty sure he didn't celebrate Christmas," I said. "But he was . . . excited, yes. I don't think he'd seen a Western woman, or maybe any woman, naked before. It wasn't very relaxing. And then he showed up at my hotel the next day."

Hugh looked fierce, reached out, pulled his hand back. My skin prickled where his hand had almost been. He had wanted to touch me. I knew it. Good sense and propriety had overridden it, but I'd seen the desire in him. I felt incandescent with power. I could have him. I could take him.

"Nothing bad happened," I told him. I moved slowly, and put my hand on Hugh's knee, left it there. "I was fine, really. But it seemed like a good time to leave." I stroked my thumb back and forth. His breath caught.

"The turtles are amazing," he said. "I'm sorry you missed them."

He slid his hand over mine, linked our fingers. Our eyes met and held. His eyes were brown, a steady, warm brown, with laugh lines at the edges that crinkled when he smiled. His hair was brown, too, no grey. He had a strong jaw that was clean-shaven, with only a hint of shadow in the later afternoon.

"Avery," he said, "I can't. This isn't . . . you're lovely. It's not that. I'm your supervisor. I'm way too old for you." But he didn't let go of my hand.

"I think I should get a vote," I said, and I closed the distance between us and touched my lips to his, just the tiniest touch, barely a whisper of contact.

Hugh stood and walked away. I was stunned, mortified at having so badly misread the situation, until I heard the lock turn. Hugh returned and sat with his hip touching mine. "What was I saying?" he asked.

"It wasn't important," I told him. I kicked off my shoes, tucked one leg under the other, faced him.

"No," he said. "Not important." He cupped my cheek with his palm, then slid it down the side of my neck, stroked my collarbone, cradled a breast. "So beautiful," he said. "God. What have you done to me?"

"Nothing you didn't want me to do," I said.

He sighed. His hand continued its slow descent, brushing the curve of my waist, hip, thigh, before coming to rest on my knee. "Every man has his limits," he said. He gave me a wry smile. "So," he said, "how did you like the reading this week?"

I laughed, and so did he. I said, "I think I'm ready for something more hands-on."

"Experiential learning," he said. "They tell me it's all the rage." He looked at me, serious, intent. "This isn't the kind of thing I do, Avery. Sleeping with students. I'm not that guy. I want you to know that. I want you to be sure. We can stop right now and not mention it again."

"That's not what I have in mind," I told him, lying back, drawing him down with me.

Months later, whenever I thought of our first time together, I would still be surprised at how hungry we were for each other. It wasn't tender, the way we came together; it wasn't playful. Nor was it the best sex I'd ever had: it was cramped and awkward to undress each other on that old couch, and eventually we stood up and tore our own clothes off in frustration; and the conversation about protection was far from smooth ("Are you . . . ?"

"No. Do you . . . ?" He did); and the sofa squeaked each time one of us shifted our weight, and we worried that someone might hear us out in the hallway.

But Hugh paid attention, took his time. He asked again, "Are you sure?" and waited for my answer before he pushed into me. He kissed me as I came, ladies first, and I was renewed in that moment with the possibility of a future stretching beyond that couch, that room, that physical act, a future in which I made sense to myself.

The next few months were heady. It was cleansing to feel purposeful again. I was doing well in school, too, and working like crazy. My professors (not only Hugh) were generous with their praise. I joined a writing group and helped organize a conference. And I was wildly, recklessly in love.

"I haven't seen her in ages," I said to Jenny as we waited for Tara at the train station that January. Tara was coming for the weekend.

"I haven't seen *you* in ages," said Jenny.

"I'm sorry," I said. "I know I haven't been around much. It's easier to write at school, at the library."

"How stupid do you think I am?" said Jenny. "I know you're practically living at his apartment."

"That is completely not true," I said. We had to be very careful, Hugh and I, not to be seen together too often.

"It wasn't the deal, Avery," said Jenny. "I didn't plan on living in a shithole by myself."

"I still live there," I said.

"Whatever," said Jenny. "I'm not doing this for another year. Spend more time at home or I'll find another roommate."

Tara came through the gates. Jenny and I grabbed on to her, and the three of us nearly toppled over Tara's suitcase, but caught our balance just before we fell.

"Oh my God, you guys," said Tara. "I missed you so much!"

"We missed you too," I said.

"I'm so glad you're here," said Jenny.

We rode the subway down to our apartment and dropped Tara's things before heading out to dinner. There was an inexpensive Italian place around the corner that reminded me of the trip we'd taken together to Rome. We ordered a carafe of wine, and poured it generously.

"Tell me everything," said Tara. "You first, Jenny. How's the program?"

"I hate it," said Jenny. "I should never have let Don talk me out of art school."

"Are you making anything?" asked Tara.

"I'm painting," said Jenny. "There's free studio space at the school. Too bad it isn't for credit."

"Is it safe there?" said Tara.

"Safer than it is in this neighbourhood," said Jenny.

"I would worry about you if you didn't have each other," said Tara. "I love it that you're roommates. Oh my God, you guys, how long has it been since we had a sleepover?"

"Tara," I said, "I was planning on staying at a friend's house tonight. You know, so you wouldn't have to sleep on the couch."

"But I don't mind," she said. "Not at all! Please don't go on my account."

"Seriously?" said Jenny. "You're seriously going to do this tonight?"

"Our place is tiny, Jenny," I said.

"Is that why you never bring him over?" she said.

"Bring who?" asked Tara.

"My boyfriend," I said.

"Didn't you know she had a boyfriend?" asked Jenny, who knew the answer perfectly well.

"No!" said Tara. "Tell me now. Who is he? I want to meet him!"

"I don't know if he can do that this weekend," I said.

"Why not tonight?" said Tara. "I don't mind if he crashes our reunion."

"It's not that," I said. "He's a bit shy."

Jenny snorted. Tara looked confused, and worried.

"You have to preserve your friendships when you're in a romantic relationship," said Tara. She'd been married for over a year at that point, which apparently qualified her as an expert. "Ethan was totally supportive of this trip. He encouraged it!"

"That's great," I said. "You seem really happy."

"You're changing the subject," said Tara. "What's this guy like? What's his name?"

"Hugh," I said. "His name is Hugh."

"And?" said Tara. She turned to Jenny. "Have you met him?"

"Not exactly," said Jenny. "I know who he is."

"I don't understand," said Tara.

"She's having an affair with her supervisor," said Jenny. "So it's a secret."

"Fuck you, Jenny," I said.

"Back at you," Jenny said.

"What's going on?" said Tara.

"You know him, too," said Jenny. "It's Hugh Crane."

"I . . ." said Tara. "I don't know what to say. Isn't he married?"

"No," I said. "He's divorced. He's been divorced forever."

"Just like you'll be together forever?" said Jenny.

"Stop," said Tara. "Stop. Please. I'm sorry, Avery. Obviously, this is a big deal for you."

"It is," I said.

"It's only that . . . isn't he kind of old for you?"

"You think?" said Jenny.

"Age doesn't matter," I said, with some heat. "Hugh is experienced and mature."

"Hugh's a very nice man," said Tara, "but a secret relationship? Doesn't it bother you?"

It did bother me, in fact. I was sick of living out of a weekend bag and watching videos in Hugh's apartment. The clandestine thrill had passed and a gnawing irritation had taken its place. A secret affair was inconvenient, even stifling at times, but I could hardly tell that to Tara or Jenny.

"Don't be so uptight," I said. "It's exciting. Not everyone wants to get married and have babies, Tara. I want to live."

"By hiding in your father figure's apartment?" said Jenny. "Yeah, you're living the dream."

I looked at my watch. "I should go," I said. Neither of them tried to stop me.

Later, curled against Hugh's side, I said, "Is it really such a big deal? We're adults. It's a graduate program. There's no power imbalance here."

"Avery, I know you're frustrated," said Hugh. "So am I.

Don't you think I want to show you off to the world? But you have to be patient. I love you. But I also love my career. And I can't give you the life I want you to have if I ruin it."

"I could request a new advisor," I said. This was not a new conversation.

"I don't think that would be good for you," said Hugh, as he always did. "I want you to be taken seriously, which you wouldn't be if you were caught up in a departmental scandal. And anyway, I don't think any of my colleagues would be willing to take on additional supervision in the middle of the year."

"We're living in the greatest city in the world and we barely leave your apartment except to get takeout and buy condoms. We can't go on like this forever," I said. It was as close as I ever came to crying in front of him.

"We won't," said Hugh. "I promise you." He smiled, his face full of love. "Forever is a long time, darling."

CHAPTER 5

Wednesday, July 12, 2017

I choose the restaurant carefully. Tara may be my oldest friend and my sister-in-law, but she doesn't owe me anything. You could say that entering politics is like joining a religious organization, where you renounce worldly connections and possessions to serve a higher purpose. You could also say that politics is an echo chamber where already self-absorbed people become even more so. Tara, I suspect, would take the latter view.

We go to Malachite. It's the gorgeous, newly renovated wine bar and bistro at the art gallery. It's almost impossible to get a lunch reservation, unless you are Bonnie. So now I owe her, too.

I'm there early, another gesture of supplication. Tara walks in right on time, her chestnut locks looking as Middletonian as they always have. She slides in across from me and orders tap water, a bad sign. She's all business today.

"So," she says, "what can I do for you?"

This is positively frosty for Tara, and it takes me a second to get my bearings. I've clearly screwed up, badly and recently. But admitting that I don't know what I've done will only make things worse. So instead I play it cool. "What do you mean?" I say.

"Avery," says Tara. "We've been friends for our whole lives. I'm married to your brother. I know you. This isn't a girls' lunch. So what do you need that's such an imposition that you couldn't ask me over the phone?"

Busted, I decide to go with the unvarnished truth. "I need you to ask Hugh for a favour," I say.

"Hugh Crane?" says Tara. "Cousin Hugh?"

"Yes, that Hugh," I say.

"Remind me why you can't ask him yourself?"

"Tara."

"Fine, Avery," says Tara. It's always been difficult for Tara to be mean for any length of time, or to hold a grudge, however merited. Jenny and I left her in the dust in that department. "I'm listening."

"Roger Wozniak is an aspiring poet," I say. "His son got the idea that it would be nice to have his poetry published in *The Beak* as a birthday present."

"Roger Wozniak," says Tara. "Huh. Wouldn't have called that."

"People are complicated," I say.

"No shit," says Tara. Tara never swears.

"So anyway," I say, "Hugh isn't going to publish it."

"You've read it?"

"I have."

"And it's terrible?"

"It doesn't have emoticons in it," I say. "But yeah. It's bad."

"Hugh doesn't owe me any favours," Tara says. "And especially not where you're concerned, as you know."

"That's why you can't tell him it came from me," I say.

"And why would I be helping the Wozniaks?"

"I don't know," I say. "You're in PR. You're creative. You can make up something convincing, can't you?"

"Maybe I could," says Tara. "But I've got a few other things on my plate, actually. To recap: I'm running a division at a PR firm, raising two kids, managing a household, and trying to keep my marriage together. Oh, and I was just elected class parent. Please, don't congratulate me."

"He's the next Leonard Cohen," I say.

"If you think I'm going to have a sense of humour about this, you'll be sadly disappointed," says Tara.

I've been warned. It's time to grovel.

"Tara, I really need your help. I will do whatever you ask me to do."

We both know what I'm offering here. There is only one thing Tara wants from me, the one thing I've steadfastly refused to do for the past three years. There is a pause as we both acknowledge the moment that has come.

"I understand that you're coming to the cottage this weekend," says Tara.

"So I'm told."

"I want you to talk to Jenny," says Tara. "I want you to try to make it right with her."

"I can talk to her, but I can't promise miracles."

"I said 'try,'" says Tara.

"Fine," I say.

"Then you have a deal."

"Thank you," I say.

"You're also buying lunch."

"Peter's buying lunch."

"Even better," says Tara.

We place our orders, and with the menus gone, there is nowhere to hide.

"So," I say.

"So," says Tara, "I hear that Martine has decided to sell the cottage."

"It's not going to happen," I say. "It's classic attention-seeking behaviour. Mom doesn't want to sell."

"No?" says Tara. "That's not what I hear. You know she has a boyfriend, right?"

"Of course," I say. This is not true, and Tara knows it.

"She's been internet dating," says Tara.

I take a long drink of water. "I know," I say.

"She's taking pole dancing for fitness class," says Tara.

"Yes, I hear she's enjoying that," I say.

Tara eyes me. "I can do this all day, Avery," she says. "How about you let me know when you're ready to stop lying?"

I slump in my chair, defeated. "Is she really taking pole dancing?"

"No," says Tara. "But the internet dating part is true. She's seeing a retired archaeologist named Bernard. He's an expert in Mayan civilization. They want to do some travelling, maybe live in Mexico in the winters. Martine wants to free up some capital."

"Not the cottage," I say.

"Not your call," says Tara.

"Let's talk about you," I say.

"Well," says Tara, "it was my birthday on the weekend, so Ethan and I went to the Inn on the Bay."

"Fuck," I say. "Oh fuck. Tara, I forgot your birthday. Oh my God."

"Yup," says Tara. Her eyes are shiny and she doesn't look at me as she takes a long drink of her tap water.

To be clear, I forget most people's birthdays. But Tara's birthday is special. Because it fell in the summer, we celebrated it at Berry Point every year. The rest of us didn't mind that Tara was singled out; we all knew that summer birthdays are a bad draw, basically, because you can't do anything with your school friends. And Tara is fundamentally so sweet and generous that it is a pleasure to do nice things for her.

So we'd do it up. My mom would roast a turkey with stuffing, because that was Tara's favourite meal. And Greta would bake one of her famous layer cakes. And Kerry would cut a gorgeous bouquet of flowers from her garden. All three families would arrive at five, for drinks, and Dad would make Shirley Temples for us. The moms wore lipstick and the dads (well, not Jenny's dad, but the others) told stories, and it was the highlight of the summer. And I've never forgotten Tara's birthday once, not once, in my whole life, until now.

"I feel sick," I say. "I'm so sorry. I've been running in circles at work, but that's no excuse."

"It happens," says Tara.

"It shouldn't," I say. "It won't again."

"It's just that I feel distant from you since you went to city hall," said Tara. "I miss you. I miss the three of us."

"I know," I say.

"I tried so hard to fix you and Jenny," she says. Tears are running down her face now. "I thought I'd accepted it. But every birthday, it breaks my heart not to celebrate it with my two best friends."

"I'll talk to Jenny," I say. "I'll try again. I promise."

"Okay," says Tara, mopping her face with a napkin. "That's all I can ask for."

I wave the waiter over. "Could you please bring us two glasses of sauvignon blanc?" I say. He nods and glides away.

"Tell me about your weekend away," I say. "That sounds fun." Inn on the Bay is an hour out of town, and has an award-winning spa and restaurant. It caters to busy people who can't take more than a night or two away but want to have a nice meal and an opportunity to have sex with each other. It does a brisk business in birthdays and anniversaries.

"It was fine," she says.

"Just fine?" I say. "That place is stunning."

"It is," says Tara. "But I think my expectations were too high, you know? I wanted to spend the weekend bonding with Ethan, but something blew up at work, and he was on the phone the whole time. And I sat around reading romance novels on my Kindle and thinking, *I'm one of those women.*"

"One of which women?"

"One of those women whose sex life consists of reading dirty books on her Kindle."

"Ignoring entirely the fact that we are talking about my brother," I say, "there is no way that Ethan isn't attracted to you. You're gorgeous. He's been crazy about you forever."

"Maybe I just chased him until he gave in," says Tara.

"You chased him until he got his head out of his ass and noticed girls," I say. "And then he realized what an unbelievable catch you were and he never looked at anyone else." I love my brother, but in truth, this is the mystery of their relationship to anyone looking in on it: that Tara chased after Ethan for years before he even noticed her, and that she never seriously looked at anyone else. From adolescence, Ethan was it for her. There's nothing remotely surprising about the fact that Ethan fell hopelessly in love with Tara; men often do. The waiter, for example, appears smitten as he tops up her water glass with obvious care.

"But I worry about that," says Tara. "What if he's having a midlife crisis? What if he's wondering what it would be like to be with other people?"

"What if he's having a busy stretch at work?" I say. "That's by far the most likely scenario. When you hear hooves, think horses, not zebras. Have you talked to him about any of this?"

"Not really," she says. "We never get a quiet moment, and when we do, it seems like a mistake to turn it into a hard conversation."

"You shouldn't worry so much," I tell her. "If Ethan says he's busy, then he's busy. He's the most predictable man in the world." Tara gives me a look. "I know that I don't usually mean that as a compliment, but in this case, being boring and reliable is an asset, right?"

"Sure," says Tara. "Unless you only appear to be predictable and reliable, but are instead poor at communication and incredibly repressed until one day you can't take it anymore and run off with your sexy young associate, which is what my neighbour did last month."

"Jesus," I say.

"I don't think Jesus had much to do with it," says Tara.

"It was more of an Ashley Madison thing than a Jesus thing. If Ashley Madison is still a thing." She sighs. "It's hard to keep up with the decline of civilization."

"But Ethan is a rock," I say. "You told me that yourself, remember?"

"I've consulted widely on this question," says Tara, "And it turns out that every woman who signs up to be a mother is also agreeing to be the rock. We are agreeing to be the people who don't freak out at the sight of blood or vomit, who eat the one burned cookie, who pretend that all they ever wanted for Mother's Day was breakfast in bed, a mess in the kitchen, and a homemade card. Men can go golfing for Father's Day and not know the name of the kids' teachers or how to work the new washing machine that you got three years ago. They are allowed to scream 'Oh my God, someone threw up,' and then spend a half hour finding the air freshener. That's just the deal."

"You used to be an incurable romantic," I say. And it's true. Of every Disney-princess-loving woman I know, Tara was the most starry-eyed of all. True love is her foundational mythology.

"Marriage is a great cure for romance," says Tara. "You should know that, speaking of Hugh."

It's a fact: I know how love can sour and curdle. But I still believe in it, and I will up until the day that Tara and Ethan can't make it work. Their union, for me, is the repository of that fragile possibility. They entered into marriage with the odds in their favour, which is certainly more than I can say about myself. If they separate, I will never again believe in love that can weather a lifetime. And I'm not letting the idea go without a fight.

"Maybe you guys should come up to the cottage this weekend," I say. "We could have a belated Berry Point birthday party. We'll invite Jenny over."

Tara mouth curves up: progress. "That would be nice," she says.

"Let's do it," I say. "Come up. I haven't seen Claire and Anna enough lately." I wince as the words exit my mouth.

Tara's smile disappears. "No," she says. "You haven't. They were really disappointed not to have Auntie Avery at their dance recital."

Shit. "I'll make it up to them," I say. I mean it, too. I adore Tara and Ethan's girls. They are beautiful and smart and strong and they love me. They haven't yet figured out that I'm unworthy of their adoration. "Come up to the cottage. We can hang out on the dock and paint our nails. It'll be like old times. We can take them for ice cream."

"I'll talk to Ethan," she says. "I'll try to make it work. I could come without him if he's too busy."

"It's a plan," I say.

Tara gives me a real smile now. "Persistent as always," she says. "Now, what's going on with you, aside from work? I haven't seen Matt in ages. How is he?"

"Fine," I say. "I haven't talked to him in a few days. We keep missing each other. He's in Paris, I think."

"You think?"

"It might be Zurich. I lost track."

"You lost track of your husband in Europe?"

"He's not technically my husband," I say.

"Uh-huh," says Tara. "So what did Peter have for breakfast this morning?"

"His usual," I say. "A carrot muffin and a smoo—" I catch myself. "We have a breakfast meeting on Wednesdays." I pause. "I know what you're doing," I say.

"The question is, do you know what *you're* doing?" says Tara.

"I'm trying to make the city better."

"And that's laudable. But it can't be your only priority. You deserve a bigger life than that. And so does Matt."

"It's temporary," I say. "The waterfront project is demanding. It's Peter's legacy, and it's at a critical point. It's all hands on deck at the office right now."

"Mostly *your* hands, I'm guessing."

"I'm the chief of staff," I say. "That's my job."

"And you're amazing at it," says Tara. "You're one of the most powerful women in the city. I'm very proud of you."

"It's all because of Peter," I say. "Without him, I'd be another miserable downtown lawyer."

"I think you give Peter way too much credit. He wouldn't be where he is without you, either."

"I'm sorry I missed your birthday," I say.

"I know," says Tara. "And this lecture has nothing to do with that. Well, almost nothing." She squeezes my hand. "I love you like a sister, Avery. You know that."

I nod. I'm close to tears, and I don't want to risk speaking.

"What does Matt say about the cottage?" asks Tara.

I clear my throat. "I haven't talked to him about it," I say.

"Let's try another question, then," says Tara. "If you're so keen on marriage, how come you guys aren't tying the knot?"

"Matt's never asked me," I say.

"He'd ask if he thought you wanted him to."

"Oh, I don't know about that," I say. "Why fix something that isn't broken?"

"Is that how Matt feels?"

"Yes," I say. "I'm sure it is."

"Because you've talked about it."

"Not exactly."

"Because you're phobic about marriage."

"Possibly," I say. "And this conversation hasn't helped, by the way."

"Hmm," says Tara. "Do you want my advice?"

"Not really," I say.

Tara shakes her head. "The truth at last," she says. "First: Marriage is hard most of the time, and it's more work than we were ever led to believe, and the sex gets more dutiful and less exciting, and you find yourself reading *Fifty Shades* for a little buzz, and the division of labour after you have kids is total bullshit if you are the girl. *Total bullshit*. But even on the worst day, it's worth it if you are both all in. My impression of Matt is that he is all in. Are you? I can't tell."

"Anything else?" I ask.

"Yes," says Tara. "You need to figure out why the cottage is so important to you. If you can explain that to your mother, you stand a fighting chance of changing her mind."

I have no idea how to answer Tara's first question, but the second one is easy. I already know why my mother can't sell the cottage.

It is the last place I know I was happy.

CHAPTER 6

July 2001

Certainly, I was not happy in the summer of 2001, which was when I met Matt. Those two facts are not unrelated.

I was still living in New York, though not with Jenny. Jenny wasn't speaking to me then. I'd told her I wanted to stay in the apartment, that I'd change my ways and spend more time there, and that she shouldn't advertise for a new roommate. I'd meant it. But I hadn't delivered, and Jenny had weathered another lonely few months before packing up my belongings in garbage bags and setting them in the hallway. Things were said.

After graduation, I had turned my attention to the only job I was now qualified to do, aside from waitressing or folding sweaters at the Gap: writing. I set up shop in a café near my new apartment, a kind of drop-in centre with lattes, where the regulars were all current students or recent graduates of the creative writing program. They were all demented in their own ways, all of them working on projects of great ambition and no commercial potential. They were tiresome and needy; they were deliberately, studiously, and even aggressively odd. It was becoming apparent to me, after a year in their company, that I had very little in common with them.

An added peculiarity was that the café owner, Melinda, had advertised on several popular tourist blogs, claiming that the café was a site of great literary significance and that visitors could watch important novels being written *in real time*. In return for serving as the attractions in this "unique New York experience," we writers could sit all day and never be asked to relinquish our seats.

This made us museum exhibits for tourists who wanted a cultural sweetener with their caffeine. They would whisper to each other, trying to figure out if any of us were famous. It was pathetic how much we all enjoyed their attention, even though we pretended to be above it. Since graduating, I'd had the sense that I was beginning to fade at the edges, and that I might disappear in this vast place full of hungry, ridiculously talented people. At the café I felt visible, at least.

I used to envy the vacationers for their unabashed enthusiasm and their manifest preference for personal comfort over fashion. I envied my fellow writers, too, for whatever buoyant combination of hope and arrogance kept them afloat in a hostile sea of poverty and obscurity. They were, all of them, sincere in their missions. I, by contrast, was a fraud.

It was unbearably hot that summer. The heat sucked the life out of me and made me fantasize about summers at Berry Point, the water lapping against the old dock, and the wind in the pines, and the loons calling to each other in the morning mist. Loons, for God's sake! I was half-mad with homesickness, but I hadn't allowed myself to understand that yet.

My mother was calling regularly, trying to persuade me to escape the heat and come up to Berry Point for a week or so, to work on my book there. Then, I attributed my

inertia to the oppressive heat. Now, I see that I was para-
lyzed with ambivalence, unable to take the next, necessary,
step on my own.

Then Matt walked in. Literally. Melinda, the café
owner, had taken a few days off, creating a vacuum in the
café universe. Matt, utterly without writing credentials or
ambitions, took a seat, made himself as comfortable as
a long, lanky man in a café chair could be, and stayed.
By the time Melinda returned, Matt had been there for
the better part of a week. He was also in a litigious frame
of mind, because he was studying for his New York bar
exams. Melinda had a polite word with Matt about the
culture and customs of the café, and Matt had a polite
word with Melinda about the laws of the state of New
York, and Melinda retreated behind the counter and got
him a latte on the house. And that was the end of it.

The next week, standing at the coffee bar at lunchtime, he stuck out his hand. "Matt Nathanson," he said.

"Avery Graham," I said.

"Avery," he said, "I could use some assistance. I'm
bored out of my mind right now. If a person can die of
boredom, I might be at risk."

I laughed. "That's terrible," I said. "I wouldn't want to
stand idly by if I could help."

"Have lunch with me," he said. I hesitated. "Please,"
he said. "You could save a life."

"All right," I said. "At least then I'll have done something productive today."

We carried our sandwiches over to Matt's table. He
moved his stack of books onto the floor. "Real estate
today," he said. "Bar admissions. Horrible."

"You're a lawyer?" I said.

"Not until I pass the bar exams," he said.

"When's that?"

"In three months," said Matt. "Assuming that I pass them on the first try. But you're supposed to be distracting me. How did you end up as part of Melinda's psychic family?"

I choked on my coffee. Matt patted me on the back while I coughed. When I caught my breath, I said, "Clever. Pretend to be in distress and then try to kill me. I never saw you coming."

He grinned. "It's the mild-mannered Canadian thing," he said. "They never see us coming. You should know. How long have you been here?"

I sighed. I'd been passing as a New Yorker for a few years now. This was more proof, it seemed, that I wasn't even a good fake.

"Three years," I said. "I came down for grad school. I'm a writer."

"That is very cool," said Matt. "Law school is full of people who wanted to be writers but didn't have the balls. What are you writing?"

"A novel," I said. I was going through a superstitious phase, and had convinced myself that the more I talked about the book, the less likely I was to finish it. In truth, I was expanding and revising the novella that I had submitted in my final semester of the MFA program, about a young woman's sexual awakening following the death of a parent; it was intensely and, I was beginning to realize, painfully autobiographical.

I was rethinking the project, changing the point of view, adding characters and subplots, and becoming increasingly magical in my thinking, which I suspected was common among writers upon finding themselves mired in a doomed book. Also, I liked the idea of retaining some mystery with Matt, so that he might imagine me as the sort of writer who would win awards and be sought out by obscure publications for her views on the future of the novel, and not as what I actually was: an unemployed and chronically miserable MFA graduate.

"What's it about?" said Matt.

"Do you read fiction?" I asked.

"Yes," he said. "Absolutely."

"What was the last thing you read?" I asked.

"I'm not telling," he said. "I bought it at an airport. You would judge me."

"I wouldn't," I said.

"You would," he said.

"Okay. I probably would," I said.

"How about this?" said Matt. "Let's go to a bookstore. You can recommend something for me."

"Now?" I said.

"Why not?" said Matt.

"I . . . can't," I said. "Not today. I've got to get some writing done."

"Tomorrow?" he asked.

"Um . . ."

"Sorry," he said. "I don't get out much these days."

"That," I said, "is a tragedy. You're in New York!"

"All I've seen of New York is the inside of my law firm, the library, and a bunch of restaurants."

"You *do* need saving," I said. "Bookstore tomorrow it is."

He beamed. "It's already the best part of my week," he said. He shook his head. "Conveyancing. Apparently, people do this for a living."

"Once you pass the exam, you never have to think about it again, right?"

"If I do, I'll have made some very poor decisions," he said.

"The only way out is through," I tell him. "My dad used to say that, and he was a lawyer." I stood up. "Back to work."

I walked back to my own table and stared at my screen. I found myself thinking about my favourite bookstores, wondering where to take Matt. There was the bookstore near campus with the carved ceiling, which had a great panini place around the corner where we could eat afterwards; or the one with the rare first editions, near the park with the huge chestnut trees where we could take a walk; or the one that played old Edith Piaf recordings and had a tiny bakery next door.

What could be more innocent than a trip to a bookstore? I closed the screen and rubbed my eyes. I rummaged in my bag and extracted a pad of lined paper. I had been experimenting with journaling, automatic writing, and various other forms of procrastination, which were supposed to dislodge my creativity from wherever it was blocked. The results were predictably dreadful, except with respect to my cursive, which was much improved.

My cellphone rang.

"Hello, darling," said Hugh. "How's it going today?"

"Great," I told him. "This section is coming along nicely."

"You see?" he said. "I told you that all you needed to do was to glue yourself to the seat and it would come. I'm so proud of you." I had, in a moment of intimacy that I now regretted, confided in Hugh that I was working on Cultivating Discipline, and I was finding the ground surprising hard and stony. Hugh had taken to calling me every day around this time, to boost my spirits and my resolve. I hated it.

"Thanks," I said. His pride made me squeamish. My career was important to him, more important, I was beginning to understand, than it was to me. And in lying to him about my progress and pretending to appreciate his calls, I understood, too, that I was protecting him from small-scale disappointments; it was all I had to offer.

"See you at dinner, then," he said. "I'm cooking that lentil and chickpea casserole you love. A reward for all your hard work."

"Wonderful," I said.

"I love you," said Hugh.

"Me too," I said. I disconnected the phone and put my head down on the table. Hugh exhausted me.

We had been married for less than a year.

Start as you intend to finish: another one of my dad's pearls of wisdom. Had I? It had been Hugh's idea to get married to make up for all the secrecy early on in our relationship. I would have been happy to live together in a more public way, but he was overcompensating. He wanted to celebrate us, he said. It felt like less of a celebration to me than a performance, and no one had given me the script. Hugh spoke obliquely about every marriage having an adjustment period, and I hoped fervently that he was correct. I was inclined to defer to his views on diagnosis. He had been my teacher, after all, and I tended to accept most of his opinions, supported as they generally were by well-researched footnotes. And, in any event, I didn't have an alternative theory.

I sat back up. Matt was looking over at me with concern. He mouthed the words *Are you okay?* and I nodded and waved him back to work. He was hard at it, two books open at once, and a stack of cue cards that he was scribbling on when he wasn't attacking his keyboard, and I could feel his energy sparking across the room; it was bracing. I thought, *He has the most perfect wrists of any man I have ever seen.*

I could remember, and it troubled me to do so, that there had been a time when Hugh's wrists made me weak with desire. I had sat, once, across a desk from him, watching him read an essay, and been transfixed by the sight of his wrist, the crisp cotton of his cuff, and the black strap of his watch. I remembered kissing him, the first time we had sex, right at the pulse point, where the buckle had left an imprint on his skin, and I remembered the shiver that went through him, and through me.

What I realized that day in the café, writing the book I would never publish and thinking about the man I would leave, and the man I would leave with, was that we don't understand memory at all. We believe that shared memories bind us together, when, in fact, they have the destructive power of the worm in the apple. When I thought of the early days of my affair with Hugh, for example, I could recall the dawning awareness of my ability to unsettle him, the crystallizing knowledge that we would end up in bed together, sooner rather than later, and that it would be very, very good when we did. I could appreciate that I had once felt that way, could reconstruct it intellectually, but I couldn't feel it again.

That's our first mistake, of course: the idea that any of our decisions are truly rational. Shear the emotions away and any choice looks peculiar at best. And then there's our second mistake: believing that memories are shared at all. We know that eyewitness testimony is unreliable, that everyone sees the world through a filter as unique as a snowflake, that the colour receptors in our eyes process *blue* in such a way that we see separate skies when we stand next to each other and look heavenward. But still, we can't quite believe it.

The sad fact is that the past, perhaps especially our own past, is mysterious. Lodged in the present, you move further away each day from the reasons why you took this path or that one. And you're left with only the story you've told yourself, the one with perfect lighting and a flattering angle. The one that even you know doesn't really look like you.

CHAPTER 7

Thursday, July 13, 2017

I wake up to the sound of the front door opening. I think about people who have keys. Have I missed a day? Is it Friday, which would make it the housekeeper? Has my mother officially lost her mind and driven down here to force me up to the cottage? Have I overslept so much that Peter has come to make sure I'm still alive?

This last seems most likely, so I call, "Peter?"

"That's a bad sign," says Matt, walking into the bedroom.

"Oh," I say. "It's you. What are you doing here?"

"That's even worse," says Matt.

"No," I say. "Sorry. I'm half-asleep." I smile at him. "Let's start again." I open my arms, and he comes over to me cautiously. I pull him into a hug, holding on tight. "I'm so glad to see you, you have no idea," I say. "But really, what are you doing here? I thought you were supposed to be in the air right now."

"I was," he says, into my hair. "The meeting finished early, and I'd had enough, and I was able to switch seats to the earlier flight. It only cost a small fortune."

"Worth every penny," I say. "Let me look at you." I lean away, hands on his shoulders. He reaches up, wraps his hands around mine, and levers them straight up until I lose my balance and flop backwards onto the bed. Matt rests on his elbows above me, his face close to mine.

"Aren't you tired?" I ask.

"Can't give in to jet lag," he says. "Best thing is to stay awake."

"Can I help?"

"I hope so," he says, and kisses me, a question.

I rest my hands on his waist for a moment, and then glide them up to his shoulders and down again, an answer. He deepens the kiss.

Later, with my head on his shoulder, I say, "Your heart is racing."

He says, "Does Peter have a key to our house?"

I sit up. "We don't really know the neighbours, and it made sense, with you away so much, for him to have one. Just in case."

"In case of what?" says Matt. "I don't think Peter would water the plants, if we had any plants."

"I don't know," I say. "If I were sick or something."

"I would discuss it with you before giving a key to anyone," says Matt.

"I should have," I say. "You're right. I'm sorry."

"I'd like you to ask for it back."

"Do you have any idea how awkward that conversation would be?" I say. "Why would you care one way or the other?"

"Because I don't feel comfortable with your boss having access to our home," says Matt. "I don't like him enough for that, and I don't want him here."

"What do you mean, you don't like him? You've never said that before."

"I'm saying it now."

I look away, catch a glimpse of the bedside clock, feel my chest seize with stress. "Jesus Christ," I say. "It's after nine. Why didn't the alarm go off?"

"Search me," says Matt.

"I had a meeting first thing this morning," I say.

"If Peter needed you that badly, he could have come to get you. He does have a key," says Matt.

"For God's sake," I say, rolling off the bed, crossing the room, and closing the bathroom door behind me with some force. I rush through the shower, run a comb through my hair, and pull it into a damp ponytail. I throw on a simple summer dress and some sandals and sprint downstairs.

Matt is making coffee in the kitchen, rumpled and adorable. He meets my eye, unapologetic. "I'm still annoyed with you," I say.

"And I'm still annoyed with you," he says. "But I love you anyway."

I sigh. "I love you too," I say. "I'll see you tonight."

At the office, Bonnie puts up a hand as I slink by her desk. "He's been asking for you," she says.

I pivot, and take the few steps to Peter's door, knocking as I open it. "Wait," says Bonnie. "He's in a meeting."

But I've already stepped through the doorway as I process that Peter is sitting on his sofa right next to a woman. They both turn.

"Avery," says Peter, rising. "Nice of you to drop by."

"Yes," I say. "Sorry about that. Matt arrived home early from Paris. I couldn't rush off without saying hello."

"No problem," says Peter. "You've got to tend the home fires every now and again." He turns to the woman, who stands. She is small and tidy, in a crisp new suit. "Melanie, meet Avery Graham, my chief of staff. She's the brains behind this operation. Avery, this is Melanie. She's a law student. She's going to be our intern for the rest of the summer."

Melanie steps forward, holds out a hand. "It's such a pleasure to meet you," she says. "This is a dream job for me."

I shake her hand, and shift my gaze to Peter. "I didn't realize we'd posted for an intern," I say.

"We didn't," says Peter. "But when I met Melanie at the event in Judy Mendelson's ward last week, and she asked about opportunities in our office, I realized that she'd be a perfect fit around here. And we could use some extra hands on the waterfront file."

"Terrific," I say. "Peter, could I have a word?"

"Sure," he says. "Melanie, why don't you head out to Bonnie's desk and ask her for the briefing notes for today's meeting."

"Right away," says Melanie. "And again, Mr. Mayor, let me say what an honour it is to be part of the team."

"Peter," he says. "Call me Peter."

"Thank you, Mr. . . . . Peter," she says, stepping out and closing the door behind her.

"There are already a lot of hands on the waterfront file, Peter," I say.

"What's the issue?" says Peter.

"We're taking hits from all sides, we've got the Wozniaks out for blood, and we're giving someone we don't know access to the inner sanctum. I don't like it."

"Melanie's the top of her class. She's exceptionally bright and personable. She deserves the chance to prove herself. I gave that to you, if you recall. And she reminds me of you. Haven't you been saying for months that we need to clone you?"

"You'd known me for twenty years when you hired me, Peter," I say. "She's an unknown quantity, however talented, and we're exposed."

"Unclench, Avery," says Peter. "We're not trusting her with our state secrets just yet. Take her to your meeting with Jim Crawford. After that, if your instinct is that we should keep her out of the fray, we'll get one of your staffers to supervise her for the rest of the summer, and we'll give her a stack of research memos to write on best practices in waste management or bike lanes. But give her a chance before you rule her out, okay?"

"Fine."

"How's Matt, by the way?" asks Peter. "Working hard, as always?"

"He's perfect, as always."

"Good guy," says Peter. "The four of us should have dinner soon."

"That would be nice," I say. Peter suggests this every so often and it never happens.

"I'll have Bonnie set it up," says Peter. "When's the meeting with Crawford?"

"I need to get going," I say.

"Off you go, then," says Peter. "You wouldn't want to be late for our artist friends."

"God forbid," I say.

Melanie and I pull up in front of a large warehouse on the west edge of the waterfront. It takes some effort, but we find an unlocked door that seems to be the entrance; at least, it is where the demolition notices are posted. Inside is a long, wide hallway, utterly deserted, with no sign of a central office.

"Do we have a unit number?" I ask.

"I'm so sorry," Melanie says, flushing. "I didn't think to ask Bonnie for one."

"Lesson one," I tell her. "Never assume that people will give you all the information you need." If I'd chosen Melanie myself, I'd probably confess to her that I'm still learning this lesson. But having had mentorship thrust upon me, I don't.

"Should we knock on doors and see if anyone can tell us where Jim Crawford is?" she asks. "Or do you want me to call the office?"

"Give it a minute," I say, and sure enough, we hear the sound of rapid footsteps. A woman appears at the end of the hallway, waving.

"Are you from the mayor's office?" she calls.

"Yes," I call back.

The woman breaks into a run. By the time she reaches us, she is out of breath and flustered.

"I'm Marla Kraft," she says. "I'll take you to Jim."

"Take your time," I say. "We're not in a huge rush."

"No, no," she says. "He wants to see you right away."

If Marla Kraft were one of the extras in the movie of my life, she would be the Magician's Assistant: long, very curly hair with more grey than brown, an abundance of draped layers and patterns, scarf over caftan over loose pants, purple eyeshadow that must be the product of a mid-eighties colours analysis. Marla is a Summer, obviously.

She leads us down the hallway and up a staircase to the second floor. "My studio is here, next door to Jim's. He's in the middle of a major commission, so I'm helping him with some of the ArtCo administration."

"That's kind of you," I say.

"We're like a family here, really," she says. "Everyone needs to pitch in."

She knocks on a door that is covered in stickers, and opens it. I register a few of the slogans as we are ushered in: "The Only Good War Is a Class War," "Occupy," "Democracy Is Nice but Revolution Gets Shit Done."

"Jim," she says, "I have our visitors from the mayor's office."

The man doesn't turn right away. He's holding a can of spray paint in his left hand. He's wearing coveralls, a long braid down his back. There's something familiar about the braid, I think, and then he spins and I realize immediately who he is.

Jim Crawford is the Bandwagon Objector.

"And so," he says. "The mayor's office comes slumming."

"Mr. Crawford," I say. "How nice to see you." Have we met before? I don't think so, but I'm not going to risk a "nice to meet you." "Thank you for alerting us to your concerns. The mayor would like to know more about them."

"Not enough to come himself, I see," he says.

"I apologize," I say. "I should have introduced myself. I'm Avery Graham, the mayor's chief of staff. This is Melanie . . ."

"Christie," says Melanie.

"Christie," I say. "Melanie is a law student who is

87

assisting us in our office this summer. I hope you don't mind having her participate in this meeting."

"Not at all," says Jim. "Students change the world more often than anyone else. Be welcome, Melanie."

"Thank you," says Melanie, beaming.

"Mayor Haines wanted me to tell you that he regrets not being able to attend this meeting personally, and that he is anxious to understand and address the issues that you have with the development," I say. "Shall we get started?"

I look around but see only one stool.

"I'll get some chairs from my studio," says Marla. "Back in a jiffy." She races to the door and out into the hallway.

While she's gone, I wander over to the canvas. "I understand you have a commission," I say.

"That's right," he says. "For one of America's signature cultural icons."

"Which one?"

"California Comix."

"Oh, well done," I say. "Congratulations." I have no idea why I should be impressed by this, never having heard of California Comix, but I have become a real proficient when it comes to polite social dishonesty.

"The oldest comic book store in . . . is it North America?" asks Melanie.

"In the world, actually," says the Bandwagon Objector.

"Incredible!" says Melanie. She moves closer to the artwork. "I love this," she says. "It's so Tim Burton meets Banksy."

"Exactly," says Jim. "Good eye." He looks at me. "People always underestimate youth."

I can sort of see where Melanie is coming from. The piece is a gigantic spray-painted portrait of a boy who bears more than a passing resemblance to Edward Scissorhands, without the scissor hands.

Marla comes in with a chair, sets it down, and heads out again. "Melanie," I say. "Why don't you help Marla with the chairs?"

"Oh," says Melanie. "Of course." She practically runs out the door after Marla, and returns moments later with two chairs, one balanced over her shoulder.

"Thank you, dear," says Marla, coming in behind Melanie. She arranges the four chairs in a circle, and we all take our seats.

"Mr. Crawford," I say. "I understand from Councillor Wozniak that you have concerns about the development that weren't raised at the public consultations. I look forward to hearing those concerns. But I wondered if you could help me understand why we are only learning about them now."

"Everyone knows that public meetings are a sham," says Jim. "Protests are one thing. There's safety in numbers. But they use those meetings to collect information about dissidents. Before you know it, you're on a watch list and being searched at the airport."

"Jim has a lot of experience in these matters," says Marla.

"Right," I say. "Well, I'm happy to receive your valuable input personally, then."

"As you know, Avery, this building—a home to artists for the past fifteen years—is being destroyed."

My research indicates that the only artists working here up until four years ago, when the city refurbished the building, were teenaged kids with spray cans, but I nod. "The city recognizes the contribution that artists make to our community, Mr. Crawford. I can assure you that the preservation of studio space has been a foremost consideration in the design of the new complex."

"Space, yes," says Jim. "But what kind of space?"

"Clean, safe, well-ventilated, bright, rent-controlled space," I say. "Space designed with reference to the highest international standards for artists' studios."

"Standards," says Jim, using air quotes around the word, "are politically negotiated crumbs that self-serving overlords dole out to the ignorant public. Roger Wozniak understands that."

"Are there other kinds of overlords?" I say, thinking, *The only standards Roger Wozniak cares about are allowable emissions for SUVs.*

"I beg your pardon?" says Jim.

"I understand that you have raised a specific issue about noise," I say. "Can you tell me more about that?"

"Yes," he says. "ArtCo, the Artists' Cooperative Council, of which I am the president and Marla is the secretary, learned recently that our downstairs neighbour in the new building will be a women's shelter."

"That is correct," I say.

"I'm a feminist, naturally," says Jim. "So I wouldn't want my comments to be taken out of context."

"Naturally," I say.

"We on the council were in favour of the idea of sharing space with abused women initially," says Jim.

"That was also the mayor's understanding," I say.

"But now we learn that children will be living in the shelter as well. And so the situation is quite a different one from what was contemplated when we first discussed it."

"It is quite normal for women escaping domestic violence to take their children with them," I say.

"We understand that," says Marla.

"I bloody well didn't understand it," says Jim. "People should say what they mean and mean what they say. This is sharp dealing."

"I don't think the mayor would appreciate that characterization of the negotiations," I say.

"If the shoe fits," says Jim.

"Mr. Crawford," I say, "Our interest here, as it has been from the beginning of these discussions, is in finding a sensible solution that works for all the parties involved. The issue you now raise is one that frankly didn't occur to anyone up until now. So we are trying to understand your objection and deal with it. There is no ulterior motive."

"The mayor wants his big shiny legacy at any cost. I'd call that an ulterior motive," says Jim Crawford.

Marla puts a hand on Jim's knee. "Jim," she says, "let's remember the rent-controlled studios."

"There's no point in a rent-controlled studio if you can't produce art in it," he says.

"Hang on," I say. "You obviously believe that you won't be able to work with children downstairs. Why is that?"

"Do you have children, Avery?" asks Jim.

"No," I say.

"Neither do I. And that is my choice. I choose to focus on my work without distraction. I should not be forced to cope with the consequences of other people's choices in my own studio."

I consider this a fair description of my own job: being forced to cope with the consequences of other people's choices. And as I'm trying to find a diplomatic way to say this to Jim Crawford, Melanie raises her hand.

"You don't need to raise your hand," says Jim. "We believe in free and unfettered speech here."

"I was wondering about the soundproofing measures in the building," says Melanie. "Have we explored increasing the soundproofing? That might be a simple solution to the problem. Maybe we could recommend that to the mayor?" This last question is directed at me.

"Excellent! That's the kind of action we need more of in politics," says Jim. "Less talking, more doing."

"Thank you for that suggestion, Melanie," I say. "Mr. Crawford, you have my word that I'll look into this issue and see what can be done to reassure you that the spaces in the new building will be at least as agreeable as the ones you have currently."

"I prefer what she said," says Jim.

"I understand," I say. "But I don't want to make promises I can't keep. Let me study the problem and I'll get back to you with a proposal."

"Mealy-mouthed double talk. I expected no better," says Jim.

"Thank you for taking the time to see us," I say. "We'll be in touch as quickly as we can."

Marla sees us out. She says, in a low voice, "The other artists here are looking forward to the new studios. We appreciate your efforts. It's just that Jim can be a bit of a bully, you know. It's always best to humour him."

We climb into the car, and as soon as the door closes, Melanie says, "Did I say something wrong? Isn't soundproofing a simple way to solve the problem?"

"It would be if it didn't add between $500,000 and $800,000 to the cost of the build, and if I weren't currently trying to cut $3 million from the total project cost."

"Oh," says Melanie.

"Melanie," I say, "It's great to have you, and I'm sure there are many useful things that you can contribute to our office. Shadowing me at meetings is a terrific way to learn. But that's what I need to you to be: a shadow. Watch and learn. And please don't make any suggestions unless you've cleared them with me first."

"Got it," she says. "I'm sorry. I shouldn't have said anything."

I soften. Peter's right. Melanie isn't so bad. I should lighten up on her, I know.

"Don't sweat it," I say. "You're learning."

"I can't wait to see Mayor Haines in action," says Melanie. "He's amazing."

"He is," I say. "But he's also incredibly busy. I hope you won't feel disappointed in your experience with us if you don't have a lot of direct access to him. You'll be working most closely with me and with members of my staff."

Melanie looks surprised. "But Mayor Haines, I mean Peter, said that we'd have a chance to chat at the end of each day."

My jaw tightens. "I'm sure he'd like to do that in theory," I say. "He's very supportive of young people. But the reality of his job is that he isn't often in a position to spend that kind of time with one staff member, even with me. And I'm his chief of staff." I place no emphasis on "chief of staff." I congratulate myself for this.

"I totally get it," says Melanie. "So should I mention

the soundproofing issue to Peter when I meet with him? Or is that something that you want to raise with him?"

God, I think. *I want to punch Peter in the face.* Not Melanie, really. It's not her fault that she's hopelessly young and inexperienced. In fairness to her, she's much more focused than I was at her age. I was wandering around Europe, finding myself, yet another project that didn't pan out as expected.

I feel myself aging in real time.

You are a mentor, I think. *This is a teachable moment.* "Let me ask you," I say. "Given what you've learned today, how should we handle the situation?"

Melanie looks genuinely puzzled. "I think I should mention the soundproofing issue to Peter when I meet with him this afternoon," she says.

"Right," I say. And I crank up the volume on the radio, and drive.

CHAPTER 8

July and December 1997, and May 1989

The train station in Rome was a sweltering human stew, garnished with fashionable shoes and handbags. I was worried that I wouldn't be able to find Tara and Jenny, and in the end they found me, tackling me in a clumsy group hug with backpacks.

"You're here!" I said. I clung to them. It had been so long since I'd seen someone from home, and we had a whole precious month planned, two weeks in Italy and two in Greece. "What do you want to do first? Do you want me to take you to the hotel?"

"Please," said Tara. "I'm dying to dump these bags."

"Food," said Jenny. "I'm starving."

"There's a spot you'll love, right near the hotel," I said.

"Lead on," said Tara. "I need to keep moving or I'll fall over. I barely slept on the plane."

"Is it too early to start drinking?" said Jenny.

"Not in Italy," I said.

"Picture!" said Tara.

"Now?" I asked. There were people everywhere, streaming past us on all sides.

"Yes," said Tara. "Now."

We asked another tourist to take the photo, and we returned the favour, and then we set off for the hotel. In six blocks, we almost died twice. A Fiat swerved at the last moment, and the driver swore at us. Five minutes later a moped did the same, but the driver raised the visor on his helmet and blew us a kiss. "That's Italy for you," I said.

Our room had three single, extremely hard, beds but it was cheap and convenient, and breakfast was included. It had a partial view of a courtyard festooned with laundry lines. I sprawled out on my bed while the others unpacked and filled me in on cultural and other developments from home.

"It works like this," said Tara. "You give me the name of a celebrity."

"Dead or alive?" I asked.

"Either," said Tara.

"River Phoenix," I said.

"River Phoenix was in *The Mosquito Coast* with Martha Plimpton, who was in *Parenthood* with Steve Martin, who was in *Planes, Trains and Automobiles* with Kevin Bacon."

"Kevin Bacon was not in *Planes, Trains and Automobiles*," I said. "That was Ethan's favourite movie. I must have seen it twenty times."

"He's totally in it," said Jenny. "He races Steve Martin for a taxi."

"It's an awesome drinking game," said Tara.

"We'll play it tonight," I said.

"We need to do some wedding planning," said Tara.

"Tonight?" I said.

"What have we been doing for the last six months?" said Jenny.

"Macro-level planning," said Tara. "Now we move into the micro-level."

"What's the macro-level?" I asked.

"Date, venue, dress, guest list, menu, music," said Tara.

"Bridesmaids," said Jenny.

"Bridesmaids," said Tara. "I have the best ones." She grabbed each of us by the hand and squeezed.

"No crying!" said Jenny.

"Has there been a lot of that?" I asked.

"You could say," said Jenny.

Tara laughed. "It's true," she said. "Everyone is so nice to you when you get married. It's overwhelming. There's so much *love*."

Jenny and I exchanged a glance. "And what's the micro-level?" I asked.

"Gift registry, invitations, cake, honeymoon," said Tara, counting them off on her fingers.

"Sounds urgent," I said. "We'd better get to it immediately."

"Okay, fine," said Tara. "Maybe it could wait until tomorrow."

"Maybe you could take a few weeks off, and focus on honeymoon research," I said. "Ethan would love Italy."

"They've narrowed it down to the Caribbean," said Jenny. "Europe is too cold after Christmas."

"Thank goodness she has you," I said. "I'm the weak link in the bridesmaid chain."

"Laugh all you like," said Tara. "You'll see when you get married."

"Not on the horizon," I said.

"Not in this lifetime," said Jenny.

"Don't say that," said Tara. "You can't say that. You'll meet the right person and you'll change your mind. You guys are romantics at heart."

"You're projecting," said Jenny.

"And you're revisionist historians," said Tara.

She wasn't entirely wrong. We'd all been hopeless romantics at one time. What girls aren't? We had gobbled down love stories all summer long, a new stack each week from the library in town. We loved Jo March and her Friedrich, and Anne Shirley and her Gilbert. And we were fascinated, most of all, by our parents' love stories.

We made the grown-ups at Berry Point tell us over and over again how they'd met and fallen in love. We tried to reconcile the young couples in the stories with the adults we knew. And as the summers passed, and we grew up, we came to understand that love stories didn't end happily all the time, or possibly ever.

Don and Greta's story was the most romantic one of all: *Cinderella* and *My Fair Lady* all wrapped up into one real-life version. Greta had been a single mom on a scholarship, working her way through university. Jenny's father had left shortly after she was born and moved back to Europe. Greta didn't know his address.

When Jenny was a baby, Greta worked the evening shift at the library, because the old lady in the apartment next door could watch Jenny then. Don, who was a professor, liked visiting the library late at night because he was less likely to run into his students. He was divorced, and had a son in California, who he missed a lot. One night, Don was looking for a book in the stacks, and Greta had that very book on her cart for reshelving! It was Fate, said

Greta. Don asked Greta out for breakfast, and within a year they were married. Don treated Jenny like his own daughter, and they became the family they were destined to be.

Except that Don was chilly and boring, and Greta was lonely. And when Peter moved to town, Don didn't need his new family anymore. And he left Greta and Jenny high and dry, as my mother said, and Greta had to sue him to make ends meet.

And there were Tara's parents, Kerry and Bill, who had met each other at summer camp when they were teenagers. They were the leads in the camp play, and they had to kiss each other onstage. Kerry was nervous, so Bill took her into the woods to practise where no one could see them. They liked kissing each other so much that they had never stopped, Kerry said.

Except that we rarely saw Bill kiss Kerry, and when he did, it was on the cheek. Kerry liked organic gardening and yoga, and Bill liked cars and golf. Bill ran an advertising agency in the city, and often he had to attend events on the weekends. So Kerry spent most of the summer at the cottage by herself. Neither of them seemed to mind. "Bill gets underfoot when he's here," Kerry would say.

My parents were different. They'd met on a blind date in university, where my dad was studying law and my mom was studying French history and literature. Until he met my mom, Dad had only had appetizers, and never hors d'oeuvres. Mom said that she'd never met anyone who made her laugh so much. You had to be careful not to burst into a room, or you might find them kissing each other. It was gross, but also nice.

And then Dad died and broke Mom's heart.

So we had our reasons for caution, Jenny and I.

"You'll love the bridesmaids' dresses," Tara said. "Won't she, Jenny?"

Jenny sighed. "Yes," she said. "Ladies, I am not going to starve to death in a city that is essentially a giant restaurant. That would be a little too ironic, even for me."

"Come on," I said. "Let's go." I'd learned enough about Rome in my travels to avoid restaurants on the main squares, as well as those that had English on the menu. I'd borrowed a Rick Steves guide from an Australian, who'd stolen it from a hostel in Portugal, and found a trattoria in an alleyway nearby that had reasonable prices, delicious pasta, and a lot of backpacking patrons flipping through the pages of Rick Steves guides.

"Seriously, Avery," said Tara as we walked. "You want to get married someday, don't you?"

"I don't know," I said. "I'm a long way from that right now."

I did want to get married someday, at least theoretically. And I was happy for Tara, and for my brother, Ethan. I was. But it was a lot to take in. At the end of our trip, Tara would return home to finish her micro-level wedding preparations, and start her certificate program in public relations. And Jenny would go home and volunteer at the museum, and do research for one of her art history professors, and work on her applications for graduate school. And I would do a term at University College London until I had to return home in December to squeeze into my bridesmaid's dress and into a final, structured, required term at the University of Toronto so that I could graduate and . . . that was the problem, of course. I had no idea, and I preferred not to think about it.

"So," I said, linking arms with Tara, "are you excited?"

"So excited," said Tara. "I'm getting nervous about the day, though. I hate being the centre of attention." Coming from almost any other bride on the planet, this would have been a bald-faced lie, but I knew it was true. Tara had always blushed furiously at her own birthday parties and tried to make other people blow out the candles on her cake.

"You'll be perfect," I said. "Ethan is ridiculously lucky."

Tara smiled. "We both are."

"Tara," I said. "How do you know?"

"Know what?"

"That you want to be with him forever. How can you be sure?"

She thought for a few steps. "You know Ethan," she said. "He's decent, kind, solid. I've known him my whole life, so there won't be any surprises." We stopped at an intersection, and the cacophony of horns and engines made it impossible to continue the conversation. We launched ourselves into the pedestrian crossing, making it safely to the other side.

"Do you think people feel more alive in Italy because they are always on the brink of death?" said Jenny. We all laughed.

"My answer about Ethan wasn't very romantic," said Tara.

"You don't have to sell me on Ethan," I said. "He's my brother."

"I know," said Tara, "but I didn't explain it well. When I'm with Ethan, I feel calm and sure and safe. He's a rock.

I know in my bones that he'll stand with me no matter what comes at us in life."

"He will," I said. My voice caught.

"The two of you!" said Jenny. "Honestly. Enough crying. Is this the restaurant, Avery?"

"Yes," I said.

"I can't help it," said Tara, wiping away tears. "I love you guys so much."

The waiter ushered us to a table on the patio. *"Acqua?"* he asked. *"Frizzante? Naturale?"*

"Naturale," I said. *"Grazie."*

"Prego," he said. Jenny and Tara looked disoriented.

"Do you want me to order for you?" I asked.

"Yes," said Tara.

"No," said Jenny.

We decided on pizza to share. I ordered a bottle of prosecco. We were here, in Rome, together. Tara was getting married. It was cause for celebration. We sat in the sun, savouring the food and the soft alcoholic buzz.

And then Tara said, "Jenny, there's something I have to tell you. Don and Peter are coming to the wedding." Wine had a confessional effect on her.

"Peter?" Jenny and I said in unison.

"My mother insisted on inviting Don," said Tara. "I thought that since we were having Greta, we should leave him off the list. But my mother had . . . strong views on the subject. She has a few divorced friends and she decided on a blanket policy of inviting everyone with a guest. And then Don replied that he was bringing Peter."

Jenny was silent for a moment. "It is what it is," she said.

"Are you mad?" asked Tara.

"Yes," said Jenny, swallowing the rest of her drink. "But not at you."

"Is it really so bad?" I said. "Peter's okay. I know he's not your favourite person, but isn't that sort of a holdover from childhood?"

"Avery," said Tara. "I'm not sure this is helpful."

"I think it is helpful," I said. "I'm trying to help our friend see that she doesn't have to spend the rest of her life feeling like a displaced child. I think that she and Peter could have a perfectly civil adult relationship."

"Do you?" said Jenny. "Do you really, Avery?"

"I do," I said. We were well into our second bottle, and the wine had made me incautious. "I like you, and I like Peter. In my opinion, you are both smart, interesting, nice people who could have a decent relationship with each other if you could let go of all the baggage."

"Is that what you've been doing over here for the last four years?" asked Jenny. "Letting go of your baggage?"

"Guys," said Tara.

"This isn't about me," I said. "I'm Switzerland."

"My mother was in litigation with Don for five years," said Jenny. "Don and Peter are not my friends. They will never be my friends. And the people who are my friends don't get to be Switzerland. You're with me or you aren't."

"It's more complicated than that," I said.

On the last weekend of May, we opened the cottage for the season.

"Nineteen eighty-nine," said my mother. "Can you believe it, Brian? Time flies."

"Not quickly enough," said my father. "That was a long winter. I, for one, am ready for summer. In fact, I'm putting on my bathing suit."

"You're nuts, honey," said my mother. "The water's too cold."

"It's been colder," said my father. "I've never missed a May dip."

"And I've never missed trying to talk you out of it," said my mother, kissing him. "I won't change your mind, but I feel duty-bound to try."

"And I love you for it," said my father. "Who's coming in with me?"

We all shook our heads. I wouldn't have dreamed of stripping off my fleece pants and sweatshirt, let alone diving into the lake.

"Avery, you disappoint me!" said Dad. "You, my most reliable swimming partner! You must be growing up and getting sensible like your mother."

"Sorry, Dad," I said. "You're on your own."

He headed to his room and soon reappeared in his bathing suit and towel. "I won't be long," he said.

"Peter!" I heard him calling as he headed down the path. "Be a man and join me."

"I'll go watch," I said.

I followed my dad down the path and saw Peter coming out of the Haines cottage. I waved, and he waved back. He jogged along the path and caught up to me. He was wearing a bathing suit and a sweatshirt.

"Are you swimming?" I asked.

"I'm conflicted," he said. "I'm wearing a bathing suit in solidarity. My solidarity may not stretch far enough to go in the water. I'll start with my feet and we'll go from there."

I giggled, and mentally kicked myself. I sounded like such a ditz around Peter. I wished he knew how smart I really was. I was a completely different person than I had been when he met me two years ago. I was fourteen now. I wasn't a little girl anymore. But he couldn't see that yet. He didn't know that I dreamed about him, grown-up dreams, not little-kid ones.

"Hurry up, you two," Dad called. "I'm going in without you."

We heard the splash as he dove in. "He's nuts," I said. "It's freezing."

"He likes traditions," said Peter. "And an audience. Come on. Let's go watch, at least."

We ran down the stairs and around the corner of the boathouse. I expected to see Dad climbing out of the lake, shivering, but he wasn't on the ladder or the dock. "Still in?" I called. "It must be warmer than we thought."

Dad didn't reply. Peter stepped ahead of me quickly, threw off his sweatshirt, and started climbing into the water, one rung at a time, wincing at the cold.

"What are you doing?" I said.

"Stay there!" said Peter. His teeth were chattering.

"Why?" I said, walking to the edge of the dock and looking down at Peter, who was putting an arm around my Dad's floating body and pulling him toward the ladder. "What is Dad doing?"

"Avery," said Peter. "Run and call nine-one-one, as fast as you can."

★ ★ ★

Jenny and I reached a truce in Rome that afternoon, bro-
kered by Tara. We agreed to "keep it light" and focus on
having fun. So we did. Jenny and I had discovered a bar-
rier in our friendship that we couldn't cross, but we could
avoid it. And there were distractions everywhere: beaches,
ruins, museums, markets, food, and wine. The trip ended
as it had begun, with a group hug at a train station.

Several months later, decked out in a strapless blue
satin dress, I sat at the head table after the food had been
cleared and the speeches had been given, and watched
Tara dance with her dad. When the music stopped, I
excused myself. I locked myself in a stall in the bathroom
and put my head in my hands. Time passed; I wasn't sure
how much. When I could breathe, I went and stood in
front of the mirror and fixed my makeup as best I could.

In the banquet hall, Tara and Ethan were tearing up
the dance floor along with most of the wedding guests.

I felt a hand on my shoulder. "Nice speech," said Peter.

"Thanks," I said.

"A hidden talent for public speaking," said Peter. "Just
one more reason why you should go to law school."

"Why is it that every time I see you, you tell me to go
to law school?" I said.

"So that I can hire you," said Peter. "I told you years
ago that we'd make a great team."

"You barely know me," I said. "Maybe I'm feckless
and irresponsible."

"Maybe I like feckless and irresponsible," said Peter.
"Your eyes are red, by the way."

"It's a wedding," I said. "Everyone is crying."

"You must miss your dad today," said Peter.

106

I nodded. I didn't trust myself to speak.

"Come on," he said. "There's a bar down the hall. They make decent cocktails. You've had enough pinot grigio for one night." He held out an elbow, and I let him escort me out of the room. I caught the corner of a tablecloth near the exit and wobbled precipitously on uncomfortably high heels. Peter steadied me.

"Add unbalanced to the list," I said.

"What list?" said Peter.

"Unattached, unemployed, unfocused," I said. "The sad bridesmaid."

Peter laughed. "I'm glad you're not feeling sorry for yourself," he said. "So what is it that you'd like to be?"

"Mysterious," I said.

Peter steered me into the bar. We perched on bar stools and ordered. "I've got news for you, Avery," he said. "First of all, mysterious is seriously overrated. Second, if you want a man to find you mysterious, you'll have to pick one who hasn't known you since you were twelve."

"Maybe I've picked up some secrets since then," I said.

"I'm sure you have," said Peter. "But people don't change that much. You're still the same girl who built that raft with me: determined, disciplined, dogged."

"Any more 'd' words?" I said. I hoped I sounded unruf-fled, and not like someone who had just been described as "dogged" by her childhood crush. Was "dogged" the least sexy adjective in the English language? "Earnest" could be worse, I supposed, but only marginally.

"Decent? Direct?"

I rolled my eyes.

"What?" said Peter. "You don't like my word selection?"

"It could be worse," I said. "You didn't choose 'decrepit' or 'deficient.'"

"Defensive?"

I sighed. "You win," I said.

"Good," said Peter. "So what's your plan, Avery?"

"Honestly?" I said. "I don't have one."

"Are you scared?"

"Yes," I said.

"Good," he said again. "Scared is fine, Avery. Scared means you're awake. Scared means you're alive."

"I've been alive all along," I said. "I've been travelling. I've had amazing experiences."

"You've been hiding," said Peter.

"I don't think you know me well enough to say that," I said.

"Like I said, people don't change that much," said Peter. "You are a doer. Doers need to do. Find something to do and you'll feel more like yourself."

"But I want to find the right thing to do," I said. "I don't want to waste my time."

"Don't make the mistake of waiting for the perfect choice to appear," said Peter. "Just move forward. Apply for a job. Apply for grad school. Strike out on a new path. It doesn't really matter which one. What matters is that you get some momentum behind you."

"That's easy for you to say," I told him. "You're doing exactly what you've always wanted."

"Who told you that?" said Peter. "I didn't want to be a lawyer."

"What did you want to be?"

"A rock star," said Peter, grinning. "And I don't want to be a lawyer five years from now."

"You have a garage band?" I said.

"I have a campaign team," said Peter. "It's like a garage band, but quieter."

"A campaign for what?" I said.

"That's the big question," said Peter. "Federal, provincial, or municipal? I haven't made up my mind yet."

"Politics?" I said. "You want to be a politician?"

"I *am* a politician," said Peter. "I just haven't been elected yet."

"You'd be fantastic," I said.

Peter smiled. "We'd be fantastic," he said. "Now go get some experience so that I can hire you."

CHAPTER 9

Friday, July 14, 2017

I walk into the office later than I would like. It's only 9:10 and I've already been outflanked by my boyfriend and my mother.

After a late night with the architects, brainstorming solutions to what we are calling the Artist Problem, I'd made welcome progress on the work front. Coming home, however, I recognized that I was sliding into a serious deficit position on the domestic side. Matt, channelling his hitherto unknown 1950s housewife, had left a congealed plate of lasagna on the breakfast bar and gone to bed.

Brooding on the meaning of the lasagna, I failed to double-check that Matt had set the alarm, his usual habit. Consequently, when Matt nudged me awake at eight, handed me a mug of coffee, and said, "Sweetie, I hate to wake you, but I think you're running late," I could do nothing but scream, gulp down the coffee, and run through the shower; all higher brain functions abandoned me, which is, perhaps, why it didn't strike me as odd that Matt was bringing me coffee in bed and calling me "sweetie."

From behind the shower curtain, Matt said, "I had a nice chat with your mom yesterday."

"That's good," I said, shampooing wildly. "I'm sorry I was so late last night. I meant to call. Something came up on the project."

Matt's voice was soothing. "That's okay. Did you eat the lasagna?"

"I . . ." Huh. Maybe the lasagna was a gesture of peace and not of war? I felt wary. What was going on here? I didn't have time to assess it, or to shave my armpits, which were on their way to becoming noticeably woolly. "I ate at the office, but I really appreciated it. Thanks," I said, stepping out of the shower.

"No problem." Matt handed me a towel. "Your mom is excited that we're coming up to the cottage tonight. What time do you want to leave? I can pick you up from the office if you like."

"That would be nice," I say. "But I'm doing a surgical strike. I was planning on leaving first thing Sunday so that I can get back to the city in good time. Are you sure you want to come?"

"The weather's supposed to be gorgeous," said Matt. "Why don't we play it by ear? Do you want to pack now?"

And so, at 9:10, I happen to be standing at Bonnie's desk as Melanie swans out of Peter's office, eyes bright. Peter emerges behind her.

"Ah, Avery," he says. "Melanie was reporting on your meeting with the artists yesterday."

"I checked to see if you were here first," says Melanie, looking nervous.

Peter puts a hand on Melanie's shoulder. "Melanie has a terrific idea about soundproofing," he says. Melanie blushes.

"Peter," I say, "could I have a word?"

"Of course!" he says. "Come on in. Melanie? Are you joining us?"

"Best not," I say. Melanie scurries off.

Peter closes the door. "How is Melanie going to learn if you don't include her in meetings?" says Peter.

"I might ask how she's going to learn if she doesn't include *me* in meetings," I say. "But let's stick to the update. I was here until midnight with the architects last night, going over options. Extra soundproofing is too expensive. Instead, we are proposing moving the women's shelter to Building Two. The daycare centre is already there, and we can redraw the plans without too much extra expense. We can put office and retail in Building One, below the artists."

"Sounds sensible," says Peter. "What's the downside?"

"Building One is on a park, so it's slightly more desirable, but otherwise it's not a dramatic difference. Do you want to see the plans? I can have the architects in this afternoon to show you."

"No," says Peter. "My schedule's a mess this week. You obviously have it in hand. By the way, I have the constituency picnic this afternoon. Are you coming?"

"I can't," I say. "The advocacy group for the women's shelter has asked to meet, and I have to leave early."

"You never leave early," says Peter. "What's up?"

"I have to go to Berry Point," I say. "Matt's picking me up at five."

"I forgot you were away this weekend," says Peter. "Never mind. Is the raft still up there?"

"It is," I say.

"How about that?" says Peter. We share a smile. "I can take Melanie to the picnic with me."

"Sure," I say. "And, Peter, I'll be accessible by email and phone if you need me."

"Relax, Avery," says Peter. "We can survive for a couple of days without you. Have fun. Say hi to the old place for me."

"Peter," I say. I hesitate, then forge on. "Be careful with Melanie. She's very . . . enthusiastic."

"Enthusiastic is good, Avery," he says. "You used to be enthusiastic, too, remember?"

I did, it's true. But it's hard to muster any enthusiasm for my meeting today with the Women's Alliance for Affordable Daycare and Safe Streets, otherwise known as WAFADASS. WAFADASS is coming to city hall to advise me. Officially, WAFADASS only ever advises; in fact, they more commonly reproach, upbraid, berate, and ream out. Their executive director, Doris Renaud, has been offended for decades. Her face is pinched with the effort of long endurance. Doris was in my office weekly during our first months at city hall, determined to hold us to our campaign promises. Happily, it's been a while.

But at four o'clock, having reviewed a proposal from the Pedestrians' Coalition to close three major roads every Friday afternoon so that citizens can share the public space and walk freely; and from the Parks Department to eliminate all play structures built prior to 1985 (representing 75 percent of the city playgrounds) to avoid liability for injury; and from the university, sharing an extensive peer-reviewed study on the subject of how every other city in the civilized world does everything better than we do, I close my computer and trudge down to meeting room 2.

Doris and her long-suffering sidekicks Glynis and Charis are waiting. When I enter, Doris's eyes are closed, and her arms are folded with her palms pressed together at the middle of her chest. I recognize this as prayer position, and I understand the sentiment, although I feel that it would be more appropriate coming from me. Doris's breathing is slow and heavy.

"Is Doris all right?" I ask.

Glynis nods. "She's centring."

Charis adds, "She is breathing in strength and breathing out anger."

"Take your time, Doris," I say, and I sit.

Doris takes one more inhale and opens her eyes on the exhale. "Avery," she says, "thank you for your patience."

"No problem," I say. "What can I do for you today?"

"We had hoped, of course, that the mayor would be here as a signal of his commitment to women's issues," says Doris. Her cheeks redden, and she breathes in and out, twice.

"He would have, certainly," I say, "but he is in the west end of the city at his annual constituency picnic. There were several hundred people counting on him being there."

"I see," says Doris, with suspicion.

"Why don't we four start the conversation, and if the mayor is required, we can schedule a follow-up with him in the next few days?"

Glynis pats Doris's arm. "That sounds reasonable, doesn't it, Doris?"

"I suppose," says Doris. The lines around her mouth deepen.

"So," I say, "we are tremendously excited about the plans for the waterfront development, and in particular

the safe housing for women. I can tell you that the drawings are coming along nicely, the funding is in place, and
everything is on schedule."

"We read the paper, Avery," says Doris. "The Wozniaks
are trying to kill the project. I've also heard, on very good
authority, that there is a specific threat to the shelter from
the other proposed tenants."

"This is all normal tinkering," I say. "There is no major
threat here. The project will go ahead and the shelter will
be built."

"Stop treating us like silly old women who don't know
what is really going on here," say Doris loudly. She pauses,
takes a breath, folds her hands in front of her, and says,
"Namaste."

Charis says, "What Doris means is that we've been
informed that the shelter is moving to less desirable space
because the artists hate children."

"Children," says Doris, "are the future. The way to
measure the health and sustainability of a society is to consider how that society treats its children—its weakest and
its most precious members. And to hear that the children
are being moved in order to cater to the narcissism and
egotism . . ." Doris closes her eyes and breathes in and out
while the rest of us wait.

Doris opens her eyes. "What I mean to say is that
WAFADASS stands in solidarity with the abused women
of this city, and in doing so, we stand with their children.
We will not allow them to be revictimized by a project that
is supposed to offer them security."

"Why don't we all take a breath here," I suggest. We
do. "Let's deal with the facts," I say. "The artists were

unaware that children would be living in the shelter. They are concerned about noise." Doris snorts loudly. I continue. "We are proposing that the women's shelter be moved to Building Two, which will put it in the same location as the daycare. Since most of the children will be using the daycare, it will be a convenient cluster of services. We think this is a solution that will satisfy everyone."

"Well, it will definitely satisfy that arrogant son of a bitch Jim Crawford," says Doris, pounding the table. "It's all about him, all the time. Now he and his cronies have the best location on the waterfront, on the taxpayer dollar, with no messy reality to disturb their precious creativity. Fuckers." She pauses. "Namaste."

"Surely you don't want to have a situation where the upstairs tenants are complaining constantly. That would be stressful for the shelter staff," I say.

"Obviously, we aren't suggesting *that*," says Doris. "What we are saying is that the artists should be the ones to move to Building Two. The daycare can come to Building One with the shelter. Give the children direct access to the park. Set an example. Let children be given pride of place on the new waterfront. Show the world that this city believes in its children."

"Namaste," say Glynis and Charis. *I do not think that word means what you think it means,* I say, in my private thought-bubble.

"I hear you," I say. "I'll sit down with the mayor and the architects and the developers and use all of this great information to refine the plan. As always, your feedback is extremely useful and we appreciate it."

My phone rings. It is exactly five o'clock. "I'm outside,"

says Matt. "You'd better hurry. The parking officer is looking hungry."

"I'm on my way," I say. I stand up from the meeting table. "I'm very sorry, everyone," I say. "I'd love to stay and chat further, but I'm late for another meeting. My door is always open. Let's all reflect on today's conversation and reconvene next week, shall we?"

"I'll hold you to that," says Doris.

I run to the elevator, jabbing the button with my thumb. I watch four elevators open and close, all jammed with city staff heading for the hills. Am I the only person in this building who doesn't leave at five? I head for the stairs, race down and out the door, past the Sad Smoker, and find Matt's SUV idling in the lane. I glance around to make sure that none of my friendly neighbourhood environmental activists are watching before I hop in.

"Hi," I say. "Sorry to keep you waiting."

"No problem," says Matt. "I'm so glad we're getting out of the city."

"How was your day?" I ask. "You seem a little wired. Everything okay?"

"Of course," says Matt. "Everything's great. How was *your* day?"

"The usual," I say. "A few steps forward, a few steps back. I had a lovely meeting with WAFADASS this afternoon."

"Let me guess," says Matt. "They're offended."

"You must be psychic," I say. This is one of my favourite things about Matt; he's always willing to listen to me go on about the nonsense that happens in my office. And he always takes my side. It is an excellent quality in a partner. "Did I tell you we have an intern?" I ask.

"No. Who is it?"

"Melanie. She's a law student. Peter met her at a constituency event and hired her. I wish he wouldn't do stuff like that without talking to me."

"Pretty, is she?"

"I guess," I say. "But that's not the issue."

"Isn't it?"

"I don't know what you mean by that," I say. "The issue is that I don't have time to babysit a law student, especially one who has a tendency to freelance to get Peter's attention."

"Because you should have all of Peter's attention?"

"Is this about this morning?"

"No," says Matt. "It's about a lot more than that."

I can't seem to get my bearings in this conversation, so I open the window and let the warm air crash in. I close my eyes and hear nothing but the sound of the wind, and feel nothing but my hair tugging and flapping.

And then the sensation is gone. I open my eyes. Matt has put the windows back up. Resentfully, I think of the old crank windows in our station wagon when I was a kid. Technology isn't always a boon, and it doesn't always offer individual freedom. This is one of those times.

"I've got the AC on," says Matt. "And anyway, I want to talk to you about something."

"Are you breaking up with me?" I say. The words are out of my mouth before I even realize I'm thinking them. I register the shock on Matt's face, and realize that it mirrors my own.

"What?" says Matt, and at the same time, I say, "I don't know where that came from."

"Jesus," says Matt. "No, Avery. What the fuck? Why would I break up with you? I love you."

"That's good," I say. "That's good." I'm trying to identify and catalogue the flurry of physical sensations and their corresponding emotions: hunched shoulders = anxiety; increased heart rate = annoyance; prickling in nose = impending tears = relief; and then clenched hands = anxiety again. I want to turn this car around and go back to the office.

"Let's start again here," says Matt, merging onto the highway. "I think we should get married."

"Married?" I say. "I'm not good at being married."

"You weren't good at being married to the wrong person in your twenties," says Matt. "I don't think we should be drawing any broader conclusions from that experience."

"But we're married in every way that matters," I say. "We share a life together. What difference would a piece of paper make?"

"If you thought it was only a piece of paper, you wouldn't be hyperventilating right now," says Matt.

I swallow hard, fighting panic. "Why now?" I say.

"Because I want a family," says Matt.

"A family?" I say. "As in children?"

"Yes, Avery, as in children," says Matt. "You act as if I've never raised this with you before."

"But we both love our jobs," I say. "Why would we have a child now?"

"Many people who love their jobs also manage to get married and have children," says Matt. "But as it happens, I don't love my job, and I'm ready to make some changes. I don't like being away all the time. I want to feel more settled. I want to build something lasting."

120

"I'm forty-two," I say.

"I'm forty-three," says Matt. "Which is why I'm not letting you derail this discussion the way I usually do."

"I thought you were doing relationship maintenance before," I say. "You know, covering the bases, taking the temperature, checking in. I thought you were on the fence about kids too." I hate the way I mix my metaphors when I'm flustered.

"You got the wrong read on that," says Matt.

"I don't know if I can have children at my age."

"That is a different question entirely, and one that we will deal with after we address the threshold question of commitment."

"Matt," I say. "This is a lot to take in."

"I know," he says. "So let's start with a hypothetical. If I proposed, what would you say?"

"I'd say that I need to think about it," I tell him.

Matt nods once, his jaw tight. But when he speaks, his voice is calm and even. "Fair enough," he says. "I'll sleep in the spare room while you do."

CHAPTER 10

September 2001

I married Hugh at city hall in September 2000 in New York City. It was a casual, and very small, ceremony—my mother, Ethan, Tara, and Tara's parents. I'd invited Jenny, but she sent her regrets. Tara was my bridesmaid. Tara's dad was Hugh's best man. I wore a vintage gown from the 1950s, made of pink tulle. We had dinner at an Italian restaurant near Hugh's apartment, Rosalia's, which had been one of the few places we'd felt comfortable dining in our secret phase; we had a genuine fondness for it, even if the food was unexciting. It was an anti-wedding, as simultaneously hip and low-key as you could imagine, which was the point. I was trying to convince myself that getting married was something young, cool people could do on a millennial Saturday afternoon, without altering the course of their lives.

I hadn't wanted to get married. Hugh had wanted to, desperately, and he'd had to persuade me. I'd wanted a few years to get my bearings as a young intellectual with a more established partner. I'd wanted to go to openings and meet sparkling, witty people, and make plans to see them again for dinner, in public. I'd wanted some time to be a normal couple.

And I didn't want to be a dependent wife. I'd run through all my insurance money, and I had a minuscule income from a writing fellowship I'd won at graduation. I wanted to find my feet financially. I'd grown up surrounded by stay-at-home wives, all with various creative hobbies and "outlets," and I had no wish to emulate them. I was worried that marriage would alleviate the pressure I felt to figure out my career. Hugh, on the other hand, was encouraging me to write full time. He continued to believe in my talent in a way that I never had, and suspected I never would.

Hugh was committed to his own narrative about our relationship. In his version of events, he'd been felled by a once-in-a-lifetime freak accident of love that had swept through his life with the force of a hurricane, bending his generally upstanding nature in uncharacteristic ways. He thought of himself as a decent, dependable, responsible man—and he was—but our relationship had stained his reputation. There were people in his department, former friends, who wouldn't sit with him at faculty meetings any longer.

"I want to make an honest woman of you," he'd say.

"What does that even mean?" I'd say. It was at moments like these that I felt the age gap most strongly.

"It means that I want to show the world how much I love you," he'd say. "I don't want to live in sin."

"Sin?" I'd say. "I remind you that neither of us is remotely religious. Let's keep it secular."

"Sorry," he'd say. But then he'd be back at it the following weekend. I hadn't realized how persistent he could be, how stubborn. Eventually, I gave in. My own arguments defeated me. If marriage was only a piece of paper, why was I denying him? I loved him, didn't I?

And for most of the first year of our marriage, not much changed. Hugh taught, and I wrote, and we continued to cohabit as we had before. But the summer after the wedding, once classes ended, Hugh was home most days. He was supposed to be researching his next book-length project, but he was restless. He'd written an article earlier in the year to test some of his ideas for the book, and the critical response from his peers had been mixed. Now he was rethinking the entire premise, which he couldn't do at the library, apparently. He was reorganizing the pantry shelves, dusting off his old cookbooks, testing recipes. He made me breakfast every morning before I left for the café to write, and told me what he had planned for dinner. I dreaded the weekends, with no easy escape from Hugh's oppressive domesticity.

"I think we should have a baby," said Hugh, one Sunday morning. We were sitting on the couch together. Hugh was reading the *New York Times*. I was reading a romance novel. I'd told Hugh that the novel I was writing was a conscious deconstruction of the romance form, and that I was doing research. I was doing no such thing, but Hugh approved of research, if not of experimental deconstructionism in fiction. In fact, I was fantasizing about Matt.

Matt and I had been spending time together. On Wednesdays we'd meet at a subway station and go on an adventure. It had begun the day I'd taken Matt to the bookstore. We hadn't gone far—the bookstore I'd selected was in the Village—but we'd gone for lunch afterwards and it was the most fun I'd had in weeks. He was so funny, and so familiar. He could quote long passages from *Wayne's World*. He'd stood in line for six hours to buy a new Tragically Hip album. He'd been to summer camp in Temagami and been sent home for sneaking onto the girls' island with his buddies. We knew enough people in common that we'd probably been at the same bars on the same nights.

So it seemed neighbourly to show him the sights of New York. We took turns planning the day. I took him to the Frick and the MOMA. He took me to the Statue of Liberty and the Central Park Zoo. We pursued the perfect cannoli in Little Italy. We dipped our toes in the ocean at Brighton Beach. We cheered for the Blue Jays at an afternoon game at Yankee Stadium. We couldn't believe we hadn't met before.

I didn't lead him on. I told him about Hugh on our second Wednesday excursion. We were on the subway platform, about to board. I said, "I'm married."

He stepped back from the subway car, and waited until it had left the station before he said, "I wondered. I didn't think you were married, but I wondered if you lived with someone."

"I don't want to give you the wrong idea," I said. "I really like spending time with you."

Matt didn't respond for a moment. Then he said, "I'm fine with this if you are."

And I was, until that Sunday.

"A baby?" I said. "I'm way too young to have a baby. I'm only twenty-six."

"Physically, darling, you're a perfect age to have a baby. And I'm turning forty soon. I don't want to be mistaken for the grandparent at parent-teacher interviews."

"Parent-teacher interviews?" I said. I felt wobbly and weak, and a little sick.

This was so far beyond what I'd signed up for that I didn't know what to say. I'd agreed to constancy and stability, yes, but regular-sexual-partner-with-fixed-address constancy, and access-to-laundry-machines-that-didn't-require-coins stability. Parent-teacher interviews had never been in the shared existence I envisaged for us. But what had I expected? I was realizing, far too late, that Hugh, while a fully formed adult when we met, hadn't been a finished product. He was evolving, to my dismay, into a family man. And I was evolving too, into a woman who recognized that she was in way over her head.

I leaned forward and kissed Hugh's cheek, carefully, a peck, so he didn't get the idea that I was angling for more. I'd started faking orgasms with him, something that I'd sworn I would never do, and worse, looked down on other women for doing.

"Listen to you," I said. "You're adorable. I've got to run down to the drugstore. Do you need anything?"

"I have everything I need," he said, meaningfully. "But Avery, I mean it. I want us to think about this seriously."

"Absolutely," I said.

I grabbed my jean jacket from the hook by the door and sprinted out of the apartment and down the stairs. Once I was on the street, I turned in the opposite direction from the drugstore and headed for Central Park.

I sat under a tree and took off my shoes; it was too warm for the jacket, but it made a passable cushion. How I loved this park, how I admired the stubborn vision required to rip so much land from the rapacious jaws of a growing metropolis. I plucked a blade of grass from the lawn and rubbed it between my thumb and finger, releasing the pale scent. I believed that the grass here, even freshly mown, wasn't as fragrant as the grass back home, but its very existence seemed to me a towering achievement. This park made me feel as though anything was possible.

The park was full of families that day. It was the second week of September, but it still felt like summer. Everywhere, parents were sitting, looking exhausted, drinking coffee that was probably cold by now, and pretending to watch their children play. Pretending that they wouldn't rather be at home, in a nicer, smaller apartment— the one they had before the baby and the nanny and all the gear that ate up their vacation money—reading the paper after a good night's sleep.

I pulled out my cellphone—a birthday gift from Hugh—and called Matt.

"Hey," I said. "What are you doing right now?"

"Studying," he said. "Sad, I know. Do you have a better offer for me?"

"It's a gorgeous day," I said. "Want to hang out for a bit?"

"On a Sunday?" he said. "That's . . . sure. Where are you?"

I told him, and thirty minutes later, he was handing me a latte and flopping down on the grass.

"You were fast," I said.

"I was motivated," he said. "And the subway cooperated."

My phone rang. It was Hugh. "What happened to you?" he said. "I thought you were going to the drugstore. I was getting worried."

"I ran into a friend," I said. "We're grabbing a coffee. Are you going into the office?"

"I will if you're not planning to be here," he said. He was put out, and there would be a discussion about my reliability later, not our first.

"It's one of my writer friends," I said. "She needs to talk through her outline."

"Which friend?" asked Hugh.

"Maddy. One of the writers from the café where I work," I said. "You haven't met her before."

This is how it begins, I thought. *It begins with a lie.* I'd told lies of omission, when he asked me about my progress on Wednesday afternoons, but those were easy, as easy as faking an orgasm. This lie sat in my stomach like a stone. *I'll make an honest woman of you.* How wrong Hugh was about me.

I could tell that he was softening. Hugh often talked about how important it was for writers to have a network. "I'll make dinner," I said.

Hugh snorted, and I knew I was forgiven.

"I'll pick it up, then," I said. "Do you want pasta? Rosalia's?"

I could almost hear him smile. "That would be lovely," he said. "I'll see you at dinner, beautiful girl. I love you."

"Bye," I said.

I disconnected. Matt was watching me closely. He hadn't pretended not to hear my conversation, but he didn't comment on it. He said, "So what are we doing?"

I said, "We're suspending reality for a few hours. Can you do that?"

"For you? Definitely."

"Let's move," I said. "I'm in a restless mood today."

We walked north. There was an area that had been designed to look like a wilderness, and it reminded me of the woods around Berry Point. I climbed onto a rock ledge near the tiny waterfall and sat.

"This is my favourite place in the whole city," I said.

"It's Northern Ontario without the mosquitoes," said Matt.

"I usually come by myself," I said, "when I'm feeling homesick."

"Does it help?" he asked.

"Sometimes," I said. "Sometimes it makes it worse."

We sat together and listened to the water and the sound of the wind in the leaves. "I wish I could make it better," he said.

"What?" I said.

"Whatever it is that's making you so sad," he said. "Because I don't think it's homesickness."

I reached for him, pulled him toward me. I closed my eyes, I felt his breath on my face, and then I felt his hands on my shoulders, holding me away from him.

He said, "I can't, Avery. I want to. You know I do. But I can't. You need to figure out what you want."

"That could be a lifelong project," I told him.

"Then start by figuring out which one of us you want," he said. "And when you do, I'll be here."

CHAPTER 11

Saturday, July 15, 2017

I wake up early, after a bad night's sleep. I'm used to sleeping alone these days; it isn't that. Guilt, though, makes a poor bedfellow. I'm rattled by Matt's proposal, but even more so by his hurt. I realize that I rely on him to be the one who keeps his shit together.

I slip into my bathing suit and wrap myself in a robe. The house is quiet when I creep downstairs. I make a pot of coffee in the portable carafe, choose the largest mug I can find, and head down to the water. I come around the side of the Gillespie cottage and find Kerry, Tara's mother, in her garden. She gives me a hug.

"Coffee's hot," I say.

"That gets you a spot on the dock," she says. "I'll go in and get a mug, and a towel to wipe the chairs off. Be right there."

I walk out onto the old boards. They've replaced a few of them this year, but others are showing their age. The mist rises off the water as Kerry pulls two chairs into the best spot and dries them off. I pour the coffee.

"How's Matt?" she says. "Martine said he was driving up with you last night."

"He's great," I say. "Still in bed. Jet lag."

"I don't know how you modern couples do it," says Kerry. "Such a hectic life you lead."

"It can get wild, for sure," I say. Personally, I can't imagine how Kerry and Greta and my mother did it, trapped up here all summer long, waiting for civilization to arrive in the form of their husbands every Friday night, herding squabbling children all day like sheepdogs in polo shirts. "Is Tara coming up today?"

"I hope so," says Kerry. "That's the plan. Anna promised to help me in my garden. She'll call when they're on the road." We don't mention Claire, out of deference to our own fourteen-year-old selves. We respect her right to be a complete pain in the ass, but we don't have to look forward to her company.

We sit without speaking for a while. Kerry is better at this than I am. She has taken more than one "vacation" to a monastery to meditate in silence.

"Avery, I have to tell you something you won't like," says Kerry.

"It's a popular week for that," I say. "Hit me."

"Hugh is driving up tomorrow with Bill," says Kerry. "It's his week."

"Of course it is," I say. "Why wouldn't it be?"

"I'm sorry, Avery," says Kerry. "You're never here, so it didn't occur to me to check with you."

"It's fine," I say, smarting a bit at the word "never." "I'm sure we'll be able to avoid each other."

"It's hard, isn't it, to feel kindness toward the people we've hurt?" says Kerry.

"Kerry," says Mom, coming out onto the dock in her

bathrobe, "we want to encourage Avery to visit, not send her screaming back to the city. Don't poke at her."

Kerry laughs. "I'm practising. Tara's due at lunchtime. All three of you girls need some mothering. Which reminds me, have you seen Jenny yet?"

Tara, I think. *Still telling her mother everything.* "Not yet," I say. "Tonight, maybe. It's been a long time. It will be nice to see her."

For the record, it won't be nice to see Jenny. Thinking about seeing Jenny makes me want to sedate myself. Or throw myself down on the floor and howl.

"How about a swim across the bay?" says my mother.

That'll do, I think. "Perfect," I say.

I peel off my robe and take a few steps that pick up speed until I'm flying off the end of the dock, just like when we were kids, a spectacular entry that would have won our regular diving competition—shallow, minimal splash, head locked between the arms, toes pointed. When I surface, Mom is in the lake, too, coming toward me with brisk, clean strokes.

"Gorgeous dive, honey," she says. "You still have it."

"In diving, at least," I say.

We set out at a gentle pace, but still one that prevents much talking, past the raft and then out into the middle of the bay. We use the Murphys' yellow boathouse as our beacon, because we know them well enough to know that they won't mind if we catch our breath at their dock for a few minutes before heading back. When we were kids, it was a rite of passage to be old enough and deemed to have sufficient endurance to swim to the opposite shore and back. Each of us made the first crossing with an adult, and everyone cheered us on from the dock; I swam the first time with my dad. As we got older, we'd make the swim in packs, and gradually the adults stopped worrying about us. They had bigger worries by then.

I think about Hugh and Jenny as I swim. I can't decide which one of them I would rather see. It's like that game we used to play on car trips up here, trips that seemed to last forever. I can still feel the anticipation as we turned off the highway at Mr. McKay's corner store, the car rattling and the suitcases shifting as we moved from pavement to gravel, and then to dirt and pine needles. Ethan and I would get our parents to stop the car and let us out at the last turn, and we'd run, screaming with pleasure at our arrival, into the field where we parked the cars. I still remember the questions from the game: Would you rather boil to death or freeze to death? Would you rather be blind or deaf? Would you rather be able to see into the future or change the past?

I'd change the past. God, how many things I'd change. Things I didn't control, and things I did. I realize, as I pump my arms in a steady crawl, that I hope Hugh is happy, and it both pleases and surprises me. When I was young, and desperate to leave New York, and him, I became cruel. I had to; my very survival seemed to depend on it. I catalogued Hugh's shortcomings, itemized them, and reviewed them regularly. It allowed me to dislike him enough to be utterly indifferent to his happiness.

Now I hope that he got over me quickly, after that initial shock; that he found love again; that he forgot all about me. I no longer want to be the sort of woman who leaves an indelible mark on her past lovers, to be the standard against which all others will be measured, as I did when I was young. I no longer want to be the one that got away, the one to whom thoughts drift in the dark, beside other, less enchanting women. Failed love is a ghost that haunts everyone associated with the disaster. What I want now is an exorcism.

Halfway across the lake, we switch from front crawl to breaststroke. I could probably do the whole swim without shifting to a more leisurely pace, but I don't want to push Mom too hard. It is, in fact, exactly what used to happen when we were kids; but then, the parents pretended that they needed to slow down so that the younger swimmers wouldn't overexert themselves.

"So," I say, "I hear you're dating an archaeologist."

"News travels," says Mom.

"It does when you tell Kerry," I say.

"Did she get under your skin?" asks my mother, puffing a little.

"She's become very . . . organic," I say.

"Politics agrees with you," says my mother. "Kerry is certainly into holistic living, as she calls it. But she'd still give you the shirt off her back."

"Hemp shirt," I say.

My mother laughs, takes in water, and coughs.

"Are you all right?" I ask.

"Yes," she says, wheezing and floating onto her back.

We are getting close to the Murphys' dock now, and we swim the last few strokes in silence. I grab onto the edge, kick my feet hard, and lift myself out of the water to the waist, heaving my torso onto the dock, leaving my legs still dangling in the water. This is the unspoken rule of etiquette on the lake. You can hold on to another person's dock, but you can't climb up their ladder and sit unless they are there. "Holding on" is an expansive term, though, and includes flopping on the surface of the dock like a hooked fish, as long as some part of your body is still in the water. My mother climbs up the ladder and sits, breathing heavily for a minute or so. "I'm an old woman," she says. "Mr. Murphy can deal with it."

I climb up as well. "I'm providing medical attention," I say.

"A solid defence," says my mother.

"Who is this archaeologist?" I ask.

"His name is Bernard, and he's retired professor. He's volunteering on a dig in Mexico at the moment. He's supervising students and labelling pottery shards. I talked to him last night. It was forty degrees yesterday, apparently."

"That sounds horrible," I say.

"I agree," says Mom. "But he's having a ball. And he's not really a cottage person, so he's better off there."

"Not a cottage person" is a loaded phrase in these parts. We mean many things by this: an unwillingness to swim in cold water; an impatience with disagreements about predicted weather systems that could be resolved immediately by consulting a computer; a dislike of lumpy mattresses and ancient pillows and musty furniture; an inability to sit on the dock for hours in the fog, pointing out patches of blue in the sky; a preference for personal space over community living; and a general distaste for rusticity. Come to think of it, Hugh was never a cottage person either, and I've always been puzzled as to why he insists on coming up here every summer.

"Is that why you're talking about selling?" I ask.

"Partly," she says. "But only partly."

"You can't sell," I say.

"Certainly I can," says my mother. "I own it. I can come up any time I want and stay with Kerry. Ethan rarely comes, and when he does, he stays with Tara and the kids at Kerry's. I'm rattling around in this old place. The only time you express any interest in the cottage is when I talk about selling it. I think you are being very selfish."

"Selfish?" I say. "I'm not the one being selfish. You act as though it only belongs to you! It belonged to all of us: you and Dad and Ethan and me. We were a family here."

"Yes, we were," says my mother. "But your dad is gone, and you've grown up, and all of our lives have changed. I accept that, which is why I can let the cottage go. But maybe you aren't ready to yet."

"I'm not," I say, wiping the lake water from my face.

"Why don't we leave this topic for now?" says Mom. "I want to think some more about it. Are you ready to swim back?"

"If you are," I say.

Mom climbs carefully down the ladder, rung by rung. My throat tightens at this evidence of aging. I launch past her with a showy dive and stay under for an extra few strokes. When I surface, Mom is treading water, her eyes on me.

"Do you want me to invite Jenny to the party?" she asks.

"Yes."

"Are you sure?"

"No," I say, "but I promised Tara I'd see her while I was up, and it'll be less awkward in a group."

"Whatever you like, sweetie," says Mom. "It's a treat to see Matt, by the way. It's been ages since he's been to the cottage."

"He loves it here," I say. "He's missed it."

"I gather he's travelling a lot."

"Most weeks, yes."

"How is that working for you?"

"Fine," I say. "We're used to it. We both love our work."

"That's nice," says Mom.

"We're very independent. We don't demand much from each other."

"I've always thought," says my mother, "that if you expect very little from a relationship, you tend to get exactly what you expect."

"Jesus, Mom," I say, "what's with all the life advice today? Do I look like I need it?"

"Actually, darling, yes," says my mother. "You do look like you need it."

We finish the swim in silence. Back at our place, Kerry is still in her chair.

"Good swim?" she asks.

"Excellent," I say. "I'm heading up."

"I'll be up in a minute," says Mom.

I jog up the stairs and pull open the screen door to the verandah. Matt is at the table with a newspaper, wearing his running clothes.

"Did you see us in the water?" I ask.

Matt looks at me. He raises his eyebrows in a false expression of puzzlement. "I slept badly, thanks."

"Matt," I say.

"Don't," he says. "Don't pretend that you didn't slink out of here this morning to avoid me. Don't pretend that what happened yesterday wasn't a big fucking deal."

"I'm not," I say. "I thought you were asleep! I didn't want to wake you up!"

"For future reference, Avery," says Matt, "when a man asks the woman he has been living with for fourteen years to marry him, and she says that she needs to think about it, you don't need to worry about waking him up in the morning, because he didn't fucking sleep."

"Lower your voice, Matt," I say. "Mr. Murphy can hear you across the lake."

"Forgive me if I don't give a shit," says Matt.

"My goodness," says my mother, coming onto the verandah, "that's quite the colourful language, Matt."

"My apologies, Martine," says Matt. "Avery and I are having a disagreement."

"Well, that's none of my business," says my mother. "Have you had breakfast yet?"

"I'm not hungry," says Matt. "I'm going for a run." He pushes his chair from the table and walks out. The screen door slams behind him.

"That's not like Matt," says Mom. "You never fight. He's usually so calm."

"He wants to get married," I say.

Mom beams. "Oh, how wonderful!" she says. "Don't worry, darling, every couple fights about their wedding. Your father and I had terrible arguments about the invitation list, I remember. And the flowers. He was furious that we spent so much money on flowers. We used to laugh about it. When are you getting married? Where? Oh, Avery! I couldn't be more pleased." She pauses, catches her breath. "I know I shouldn't ask, but are you pregnant? Is that why you're getting married now?"

"I . . ."

"Oh, Avery, how inappropriate of me. I'm so sorry. Of

course, you'll tell me when you and Matt are ready. Just so you know that I wouldn't disapprove."

"Mom," I say. "Mom, stop. Please. I didn't say yes."

"What do you mean, you didn't say yes?"

"I didn't say no, either. I said I needed to think about it."

"What's to think about? You love Matt, don't you?"

"Yes," I say.

"You don't believe in marriage?"

"Once was enough," I say.

"Ridiculous," says my mother. "That marriage doesn't even count. It wasn't in a church and it didn't last a year. And to a man twice your age. He had no business persuading you to marry him."

"He wasn't twice my age," I say. "And we're not talking about Hugh."

"Aren't we? Because for the life of me, Avery, I can't understand why you wouldn't want to marry Matt if it mattered to him. He's been by your side for how many years?"

"Fifteen."

"Fifteen! That's longer than most marriages. That's as close to a guarantee of success as you are likely to get."

"It's not that," I say.

"Than what is it? Are you waiting for something better to come along?"

"No!"

My mother sits down at the table, and takes my hand in hers. "Is it Peter?" she asks quietly.

"What are you talking about? This has nothing to do with Peter. Why would you even say that?"

My mother says nothing.

"I know all of you think I have a thing for Peter, some

ancient unrequited crush. But it's not like that. The work we do is incredibly important and the entire reason that we are able to do it is because we've known each other forever and we make an amazing team. We trust each other completely."

My mother says nothing.

"It's entirely professional. Why don't you believe that?" I say.

"I haven't said anything," says my mother.

"You don't have to," I say. "You have that look. I can tell what you're thinking."

"I'm thinking," says my mother, "that I miss your father, and that if he were here, he would know the right thing to say."

The tears start and I can't make them stop.

"Let it out, darling," says my mother. "The house won't mind. It's seen a lot of tears."

I cry even harder. My mother hands me napkins, which I use to blot my eyes and blow my nose, until eventually the fit passes and I'm left with a pyramid of damp, snotty paper.

"Better?" says my mother.

"No," I say.

My mother looks at me with unmistakable pity. "There's nothing broken that can't be mended," she says.

But she's wrong. This house is full of objects—plates and cups and toys—which have been mended. And we handle these relics with care, cracked and chipped and marred with crooked seams of glue; we know that they are weak in the broken places and will never be whole again.

CHAPTER 12

September 2001

In our bedroom, I pretended to sleep. I'd told Hugh that I might be coming down with a cold, a ploy to stay in bed and prevent a leisurely breakfast discussion about our future family. I could hear the murmur of NPR in the kitchen, then an exclamation that made me sit up, wondering if he'd burned himself. I was getting out of bed to investigate when the bedroom door opened.

"We have to turn on the TV, Avery," he said. "Something's happened. A plane flew into the World Trade Center."

"A plane?" I said. "What, like a Cessna?" I couldn't believe it. I imagined some poor novice pilot, working on his licence, out trying to accumulate some flying hours on his day off. It was peculiar to me how often people's hidden dreams involved getting off the ground—flying, skydiving, mountain climbing.

"I don't think so," Hugh said. He was sitting with one leg folded under him on the bed, fiddling with the remote, and then CNN was up on the screen.

"My God," said Hugh.

"Holy shit," I said, falling back against the pillows as we both caught our first glimpse of the iconic skyscraper topped with a cloud of black smoke.

"That's a huge fire," I said. "There's a giant hole in the tower. It couldn't have been a Cessna."

"Shhh," said Hugh, turning up the volume. CNN was interviewing someone from another office with a view of the World Trade Center, who was saying that he'd seen a jet hit the building.

"Why didn't it land in the river if it was having mechanical problems?" I said. "I thought they were supposed to land in the river."

"Avery, be quiet," said Hugh. "I'm trying to listen."

"Don't speak to me like I'm a child," I said.

"Then don't act like one," said Hugh, while a dot, a bird, a dart, a plane sailed in from the right side of the screen, getting larger with each fraction of a second, and then glided into the second tower, which was shrouded, instantly, in a ball of fire.

I cried out and Hugh moaned. He pulled me to his side. "I'm sorry, I'm so sorry, so sorry," he said.

"It's okay," I said. "It's fine." I let Hugh hold me while we watched the footage repeat over and over again: the impossibly blue sky, the building, the smoke, the plane, the fire. It wasn't, though. Nothing was okay. Nothing was fine.

"All those people," said Hugh. "My God. I know people who work there."

Matt, I thought. Matt's law firm was in the north tower. Or was it the south tower? Hadn't he told me he was going in today for a lunch meeting? I took my cellphone into the bathroom, but there wasn't any cell service. I went into the kitchen to try the landline, but realized that I only had a cell number for Matt.

Hugh called me back to the bedroom. There were tears running down his face. "People are jumping, Avery," he said. "They're jumping from the towers to get away from the fire. They're killing themselves."

The phone rang. I grabbed it. "Hello?" I said.

"Avery?" It was my mother. "Are you all right?"

"Mom," I said. *Not Matt. Where is Matt?* "I'm at the apartment. I'm fine."

She was crying. "Come home, Avery," she said. "Get the hell out of that godforsaken city and come home. I need you safe."

"Oh, Mom," I said. "I'm safe. Nothing's going to happen to me. I promise."

"I want you home where I can see you and touch you," said my mother, and in that moment, I wanted nothing more than to be home, away from this city and this apartment, and to be wrapped in my mother's arms.

"I'll come as soon as I can," I said. "I promise."

By the time I got off the phone, it was almost ten o'clock. It had already been one of the longest days of my life. "What can we do?" I asked Hugh. "What are they saying we should do? Can we help?"

"They're telling people to stay at home," he said. And that's when the first tower fell, elegantly, like a planned demolition, folding inward on itself all the way to the ground.

The hours crawled by. We watched the second tower fall, watched the end of the world on live TV. Eventually we crawled out of bed to shower and dress, to make the bed as if it were an ordinary day, and to move out to the living room and turn on the radio.

Hugh was restless. He wanted to go down into the street, speak to our neighbours, talk about what has happened. He wanted to line up for emergency provisions, bottled water, batteries. We made a list. Hugh was glad to have a purpose. I was relieved when the door closed behind him, and I could give myself over to my terror.

I tried Matt's cellphone over and over again, never finding a signal. I checked my email again—no word from Matt there either—and sent a note to Tara and Ethan. I paced. I lay on the floor. I crawled into bed. I crawled back out. I turned on the television, saw the eyewitness interviews from Tribeca residents, imagined Matt trapped under a pile of rubble, or under a pile of crumpled bodies. *If only*, I thought. *If only I had kissed him on Sunday.*

There was a knock on the door. I assumed that Hugh's hands were full, or that he had forgotten his key. It was the sort of day when people who never forget their keys might forget their keys. But it wasn't Hugh.

I don't remember now if I said anything. I don't think I did. I launched myself at him, sobbing, latched on and wouldn't let go. It was only once I had my arms around him that I could process how he looked, which was terrible: he was covered in dust and ash, his eyes were red, and he had an abrasion on his cheek. He was dragging a filthy suitcase behind him. He was the most beautiful sight.

"It's okay," he said, over and over again. "I'm okay."

"Thank God," I said, wiping my face with my sleeve, trying to pull myself together. "I was so worried about you." I reached for his hand. "Come inside," I said.

He stepped into the apartment. "Sit," I said.

"I can't, Avery," he said. "I'm covered in—" His voice caught. "I'm too dirty. I'll ruin your sofa."

"Sit here, then," I said, dragging him over to the kitchen table by the hand. I couldn't seem to let go of him. "Tell me what you need."

"A drink," he said.

"Water?"

"Yes, and something stronger, as well."

I filled a glass of water and handed it to him, then opened a bottle of wine while he gulped the water down. I poured two glasses of wine and sat down with him.

"Tell me," I said. "Tell me everything."

He put the glass down on the table and was quiet for a moment, looking at his folded hands.

"I was at home," he said. "I'd been for a run in Battery Park. It was such a gorgeous morning. I was going to a lunch at the office with my mentor, to check in on my bar prep, and I wanted to be sharp for it. I was showering when the first plane hit. I felt the building shake." I reached over and put my hand on his. He continued. "The windows were open in the apartment, and I could smell the smoke when I came out of the bathroom. I could hear people yelling in the street, so I got dressed and went down. Everyone was running toward the towers to see what was happening, and I went with them. Broadway was full of people, all looking up. No one knew what was happening, but everyone was talking about a plane."

He paused. "We started to be able to see flames, not just the smoke. And then someone said, 'What's that?' and we all watched the second plane hit. And then people were screaming and crying. There were things falling from the building. Paper mostly. But then someone yelled, 'They're jumping!' And when I looked more closely, I could see that they were right." There were tears running down Matt's cheeks. "They were jumping, Avery. I watched them fall."

"I know," I said. "I saw it, too."

"I've never seen anything so horrible," he said. "It was like I was frozen up to that moment, and then suddenly all I wanted to do was to get away. I ran back to the apartment, and started packing a suitcase. I threw in all my bar materials and a couple of changes of clothes. I thought I'd bunk with my buddy in Brooklyn for a couple of days. I was heading for the subway when the first tower came down."

I refilled his wineglass. He kept talking. "It was the most terrifying sound. I was screaming. Everyone was screaming and running for their lives, running up Broadway. And then I was inside this cloud of dust and ash and I couldn't see where I was going. My eyes were burning and I was coughing, and people were bumping into me and then disappearing into the cloud. And I found a wall to lean up against and I pulled my T-shirt over my face and tried to breathe through it."

I took Matt's hand and pulled him up from the table and over to the couch. He sat, and I sat next to him, curling my legs under me.

"The air seemed to get clearer after a while, and I could see around me a bit more. Someone handed me a bottle of water and I drank the whole thing down. And I suddenly knew where I needed to go, so I started walking."

"What about when the second tower came down?" I said.

"I was halfway to you by then," he said.

"To me?" I said.

"To you," he said. "The world was ending and I wanted to see you. So here I am. But I can leave. I didn't exactly think it through."

"You are not leaving," I said. "You're staying here."

"What about your husband?" he asked.

I unfolded my legs and moved away slightly so that I could look straight at him.

"You're my friend from home," I said. "It's non-negotiable. I'm not letting you out of my sight."

He said, "I don't know when I can get back to my place. It was like a disaster movie down there. God. All I was thinking about was packing my fucking bar materials, Avery. The people I was going to work with might all be dead right now, but thank God I've got my bar materials."

"You're going to stay here for as long as you need to stay," I told him. "We have a spare room, and everything will sort itself out. One thing at a time, okay?" He nodded. "Why don't you start with a shower?"

I got him organized with a towel and was beating the dust out of the sofa when Hugh burst in.

"Avery," he said. "It's like nothing you've ever seen before. No one has words to describe what is happening. No one has anything to compare it to except the movies. We are living through one of the most important moments in history. Strangers are embracing each other in the street. They've closed everything south of Fourteenth Street. We'll have friends with nowhere to go. We need to open our home. Someone will need a safe place to stay."

"Yes," I said as Matt came out of the bedroom, his hair damp from the shower. "And he's already here."

Matt's apartment was in the frozen zone, and as the days passed it become clear that he wouldn't be returning anytime soon. Meanwhile, my mother was melting down, which was unnerving to say the least. She'd been our rock for our entire lives, but now she called, weeping, several times a day. My brother, Ethan, called too. "There are trains running, right?" he said. "Take one. I'll pay for it. I can't take much more of this."

Matt was careful, almost professional, around me. I began to wonder if he'd changed his mind, if the spark between us, which had caught and flared in a moment of crisis, had been extinguished. We were in transition, Matt and I, and the citizens of New York, and the world more generally, and there was nothing to do but wait for the future to unfold.

Hugh, alone among us, was vigorous in the days following the attacks. He was fired up with civic duty, delighted to have taken in a stray, and eager to make Matt comfortable. He lent Matt clothes and toiletries, cooked him dinners, bought him an extra copy of the newspaper each day. Hugh's classes were cancelled, but he'd been pulled into several university committees dealing with the disaster. He'd come home in the evening with dispatches from the outside world, optimistic, defiant, and resolutely American. I would have loved him all the more for it, if I had loved him.

Matt, after a tense couple of days, had learned that everyone from his law firm was safe and accounted for. They had been evacuated early, from floors well below the crash. There were temporary offices being arranged, though not for soon-to-be associates without licences to practise law. The atmosphere crackled with things unsaid. The second morning after the disaster, Matt announced that he wanted to get back to work, packed a bag, and went off to find a library that was open. Four hours later, he was home.

I was on the phone with my mother. "I'll come soon, Mom," I said. "It feels disloyal to leave now."

"Disloyal to whom?" said my mother. Even in extremis, her grammar was excellent. "Your family deserves your loyalty. Come home. If Hugh won't come, you can bring that friend with you, the one who can't go back to his apartment. I'm sure he'd love to get out of there."

"I'll think about it," I said.

"Stop thinking," said my mother.

I hung up the phone, and Matt was watching me with an uncertain expression. "My mom is still freaking out," I said.

"Mine too," said Matt.

"I wasn't expecting you for a few hours," I said.

"I went to the library," he said. "And I couldn't sit. I couldn't concentrate."

"That's normal, after what you've been through," I said. "I told you I thought it was too early to try to get back into your study routine."

Matt continued as though I hadn't spoken. "I must have walked to the washroom six times. I packed up my things and went outside and started walking. I walked all the way to Penn Station. I need to get out of here, Avery."

"Where do you want to go?" I asked.

"Home," he said. "I want to go home."

"Of course," I said. "I totally understand. When are you leaving?"

"Tomorrow morning," he said. "Early."

My throat felt tight. "Oh," I said. I started to cry. "I'll miss you," I said, embarrassed by my tears, brushing them away with my hands.

"I bought two tickets," he said. "I want you to come with me."

"You want me to come with you?"

"Yes," he said.

"What about Hugh?" I said.

"I can't tell you what to do about Hugh," said Matt. "Only you can decide that."

I went into my bedroom and closed the door. I sat down on the bed and looked around. There was so little of me in this room, in the whole apartment, really. Hugh's duvet, Hugh's bed, Hugh's dresser, Hugh's plates and cups and knives and forks. Everything I had brought could fit in a small suitcase. I picked up the phone and called Hugh's office.

"Darling," he said. "Are you all right?"

"Yes," I said. I was weeping.

"What is it?" he said. "What's wrong?"

"It's all just so overwhelming," I said.

"I know," said Hugh. "It's terrible. You wouldn't believe the stories I've heard today."

"My mother wants me to come and visit," I said. "There's a train tomorrow morning."

"Do you want to go?" he asked.

"It would make her feel better," I said. "And I worry about the air quality." Everyone knew that there were chemicals in the debris cloud, and it wasn't only the hypo-chondriacs who were talking about cancer and infertil-ity. I stood on the precipice, hesitated, and leapt. "Given our . . . plans, it might not be a bad idea to get out of town until the air clears."

"Darling," said Hugh. Now he was the one who was choked up. "Of course you should go. I hate to be apart from you, but you're right. And, Avery, we have so much to look forward to when all of this is over."

"Yes," I said, hating myself, and hating him a little for the person I'd become, the person lying to him on the phone, planting heartbreak like a bomb timed to detonate once I'd cleared the area. "Yes, when all of this is over."

Hugh took us to the station in a taxi. "Take care of my girl," he told Matt. He'd been completely unfazed by the idea that Matt was coming with me. He was pleased that someone reliable, someone who owed him a favour, would be keeping an eye on me, the future mother of his child.

"I will," said Matt. They shook hands.

I let Hugh kiss me and load my suitcase on board. "Call me when you get there," he said. He stood on the platform as the train pulled out, waving.

I sat back in my seat. I was so tired. Had I really just left my marriage? I thought so, but thought, possibly, that I was simply hysterical, that I'd go home, sleep in my childhood bed, remember how much I liked adulthood, realize that I'd invented an entire relationship with Matt that didn't actually exist, and return to New York when the literal dust settled. And then Matt leaned over the armrest between us and reached for my hand. He raised it to his lips and kissed it, once, gently.

"Thank you," he said.

We held hands as the train picked up speed, carrying us toward something both old and new.

It was a long journey, and it felt old-fashioned, as though we had stepped out of time. Who travelled by train anymore except to commute? But here people were friendly, they weren't rushing, they soaked up the experience; they played cards with strangers to pass the time and told stories about where they'd been and where they were going. They looked out the windows and commented on the landscape. They put their phones away— cell service was still spotty, anyway—and they talked to each other.

One girl, an Australian, had been on the ferry looking at the World Trade Center when the first plane hit. She was on a year-long backpacking trip, and had planned to spend six months of it in America, where she'd always dreamed of living. Now she was forsaking America for Canada, the closest thing to home on this side of the planet, or so she'd been told. She had a Canadian guidebook and wandered the aisles asking for advice. "Has anyone been to Whitehorse?" she'd ask. "Has anyone been to Lake Louise?"

I raised the armrest and put my head on Matt's shoulder. I closed my eyes. I felt his lips touch my forehead and I slept.

Near Albany, I jolted awake. "There you are," said Matt. "How about some food?"

I was on the verge of saying that I wasn't hungry, but Matt handed me a bag of almonds and I devoured them. He handed me a bottle of water and I drank it down. I only wanted what was required for basic survival. That Matt appeared to be one of these requirements was unsettling.

"Let's get you some proper sustenance," said Matt. "They have a bar car here somewhere."

"Yes, please," I said.

We found a pair of window seats in the lounge.

"You'll get a nice view of Niagara Falls from here," said the waiter. "Can I get you anything?"

"Most definitely," said Matt. "You can't have your third drink until you've had your first."

"Do you know any jokes?" I asked, once the waiter had left.

"Only lawyer ones," said Matt. "What's the difference between a lawyer and God? God knows he isn't a lawyer."

"More," I said.

"A lawyer, a vegetarian, and a marathoner walk into a bar. How can you tell which is which? They all tell you in the first thirty seconds."

"Again," I said, giggling.

"What happens when you cross a blonde and a lawyer? I don't know. There are some things even a blonde won't do."

The laughter bubbled up and spilled over. I laughed until I could hardly breathe, until my ribs hurt. "Those are absolutely terrible jokes."

"I know," he said, smiling at me. Then his smile faded, and he said, "I need you to understand that I don't care about your husband. Don't get me wrong. I care that you're married. I care about that, and I don't like it. Your husband is on his own as far as I'm concerned. I'm a nice guy, Avery, or I used to think I was, but when it comes to you, I'm a selfish son of a bitch."

"I understand," I said.

And then he leaned over and kissed me, while the Honeymoon Capital of the World flashed by our window.

CHAPTER 13

Sunday, July 16, 2017

On Sunday morning, a persistent buzzing wakes me. I dive over the empty half of the bed for my cellphone, registering anew that Matt is not where he should be, and answer.

It's Peter. "Sorry to do this, Avery," he says, "but I need you to come back to town."

"What happened?" I say.

"It's not an emergency, exactly," says Peter, "but I need you to brief me on the waterfront dissidents."

"Is that what we're calling them?"

"That's what Adam Rothman was calling them, when I saw him at a party last night."

"Oh dear," I say. "Adam's concerned?"

"Adam would like to see less in the way of negative press. He asked me to see if I could get them settled down. Unofficially, of course."

"Of course," I say. "I met with Jim Crawford and the artists and with Doris Renaud and WAFADASS this week and they're both waiting to hear back from me on their proposals. They should be quiet until then. I'm not sure what could have stirred them up in the meantime."

"There's a new player," says Peter.

"Who?"

"Mel," says Peter.

"Who's Mel?" I ask.

"M-E-L," says Peter. "Mother Earth League."

"Oh God," I say. "Shit."

"My thoughts exactly," says Peter.

"Right. I'm on my way. I'll meet you at the office by noon."

"I know you haven't had a day off all summer. I'm sorry to ruin your weekend."

"No problem," I say, surprised that he's noticed. "I've had enough country air. I'm ready for some smog."

I slide out of bed and ease into the hallway. The house is silent. It's not quite seven o'clock. I knock on the door next to mine, and Matt opens it. He's already dressed.

"I heard you on the phone," he says. "Did you want a shower?"

"Yes," I say.

"I'll pack the car," he says. "And put on some coffee."

I reach for his cheek. "Thank you," I say.

"You're welcome," he says, a bit too formally for my comfort. Evidently, he can hold a grudge in extreme circumstances, one more thing I've learned about him in the last twenty-four hours.

Last night, we'd thrown a party for Tara, as promised. After Matt's abrupt exit in the morning, the dinner party had given the day a focus. Mom and I had dispatched Matt to the liquor and grocery stores, and we'd baked a chocolate layer cake and assembled a retro dinner, hearkening back to birthday parties of the past.

Waiting on the verandah, watching the guests arrive, I had a sense of time unwinding. Here were Ethan and Tara and their daughters, and Kerry, her mother, coming up the path from one side of the point, and Jenny walking up from the other side, but in my mind I could see the original families: mothers wearing dresses and oven mitts, carrying hot trays, dads in collared shirts with the top button undone, kids with clean hands and faces. Seeing Jenny approach the house, looking so much like her mother once did, lovely in a soft cotton dress, her blonde hair still thick and lustrous, I realized with a jolt that we were now the age our parents had been then. At our age, my father had only a couple of years left to live. At our age, he believed he had all the time in the world.

I met Jenny at the door. She smiled, but her eyes were wary. "You look wonderful," I said. "I've missed you."

She touched my arm, squeezed briefly, but made no move to close the distance between us. "It's good to see you, Avery," she said. "I follow all your successes in the papers. Congratulations on the waterfront redevelopment. What an achievement that is."

"Thank you," I said. "It's a team effort."

"Politics suits you," said Jenny.

We were both relieved to have Tara and Ethan and their entourage pour onto the verandah then. Jenny had never been a person who appreciated the purpose of small talk. She thought it lazy and inauthentic. But for us, there was nothing between small talk and bloodletting. Tara folded Jenny in an embrace, and they moved to the old swing sofa, chatting about Jenny's upcoming art exhibit and Tara's new campaign. "Basically, I'm using sex to sell beer," I heard Tara say, and Jenny replied, "A time-honoured tradition."

"Shall we take drink orders?" asked Matt, wrapping an arm around my waist.

"Yes," I said, grateful for an occupation.

"Shirley Temples, ladies?" I called out to the room and was rewarded with a chuckle from Tara and Jenny and a "Yes, please!" from Anna, Tara's youngest daughter. Claire, the oldest, rolled her eyes but asked politely for a Coke instead.

I went into the kitchen and helped Mom put the finishing touches on dinner. She patted my back. "Three is a difficult number," she said.

"Sorry?"

"Groups of three. Greta and Kerry and I used to talk about that with you three girls. Someone was always on the outs. Someone was always in tears. The dynamic was always shifting. But at the root, you all loved each other like sisters."

My eyes welled up with tears.

"It's still there," said my mother. "You can find it again, you and Jenny, if you both want to."

"She's the one who won't make up," I said.

"How old are you?" said my mother.

"Point taken," I said, mopping myself up with a tea towel.

"Then we're ready for dinner. Do you want to call everyone to the table?"

I seated everyone. Matt poured wine, and Mom put a plate of chicken Marbella from the Silver Palate cookbook down in front of each place. Jenny raised her glass. "To Tara," she said. "Happy birthday."

"To Tara," we echoed.

"This is the best birthday present you could have given me," said Tara. "Having all of us together again? It means so much to me."

"I'm so glad we could do this," said my mother, reaching across the table for Tara's hand. "You girls are like family. It's been too long."

"Ladies!" said Ethan. "It's a party. Stop crying. Game time. The person who tells the funniest story gets an extra slice of cake." It's an old tradition, one that we all remembered.

"Do you remember the stories your dad used to tell about law school?" said Jenny. "He had that great one about the time he lived with a med student."

"The one where they drilled a tiny hole in the door and squirted the neighbour with a syringe?" said Tara.

"I've never heard this story," said Matt.

"Brian loved that story," said Mom. "If it was worth telling once, it was worth telling a thousand times."

"They hated their neighbour across the hall," I explained. "He was always throwing these wild parties and keeping them up half the night during exams."

"So they'd wait for him to come home, and shoot water at his neck. He never knew what it was." Tara could barely get the words out, she was laughing so hard.

"And then, after a week or so, the neighbour snapped," said Jenny.

"And he tore the fire axe off the wall and slammed it into their door," I finished.

"The door still had the crack in it when I started dating Brian a year later," said Mom.

We all howled with laughter. Matt and my nieces looked at all of us as though we were crazy.

"It's possible that you had to be there," I said. "The way Dad told it was so funny."

Matt's smile was gentle. "I'm sure it was," he said. "Did I ever tell you about the time I met Johnny Depp?"

After dinner, after we'd put the dishes away and climbed up the stairs to bed, Matt and I paused in the hallway.

"That was fun," I said.

"It was," he said, moving to the door of the spare room. "Goodnight."

"Wait," I said. "You're sleeping in there again?"

"Yes," he said.

"Why?"

"Because I want to be just like family too, Avery," he said. "I want to join the club. Nothing's changed since yesterday. I can't figure out what I need to do to qualify."

"Matt," I said. "You qualify. God. This is so out of hand."

"I need some time alone, and so do you," he says. "Sleep well." And he left me standing alone in the hallway.

We set off for the city by eight, and there's no traffic on the road. We've been driving for almost an hour when Matt says, very calmly, "If you don't put that phone away, Avery, I am going to throw it out the window."

I look over at him, wondering if I've misheard. He glances away from the road for a second and meets my eye. "I am so completely not kidding, if that's what you were thinking," he says.

It was, in fact, but I don't say so. I put my phone away in my purse and fold my arms in my lap.

"Let's review," says Matt. "We have been together for fifteen years. We have lived together for fourteen of those years. You left your husband for me. You tell me that you love me."

"I do," I say. "I do love you. I love you more than anyone."

Matt softens. "That's the right reason to get married, Avery. If we have that, we can make it."

"It scares me, Matt," I say. "You don't understand. You haven't been married and had it fail. I never want to feel that way again."

"I'm not Hugh," says Matt.

"You don't even know how much you are not Hugh," I say. What I don't say is *But I'm still me. I'm still the person who did that to him.*

Hugh suffered for a long time after I left. I know this because of what my mother reported from Kerry, and from the letters that Hugh wrote to me for a couple of years afterwards—letters that I stopped opening—and from the phone calls I received from his friends in New York. But I would have known it anyway. You can't be married to someone, even someone completely incompatible, and not know what your leaving will do to him.

It might have been easier on him if I'd been honest about my confusion and my doubts, if I'd let the relationship unspool instead of snapping the thread. For the record, I never missed Hugh. I regretted his pain, but I never longed for his company. I never once thought, *Hugh would have loved this,* or *I wish I could share this with Hugh,* or *Hugh was so much fun at parties*. I take no pride or pleasure in this; I've always considered it a tax on my freedom. I chose myself over Hugh, and the cost to me is the knowledge that I am capable of deception and disloyalty and cruelty.

It's true that Matt isn't Hugh, but it's also true that Hugh has everything to do with the way my relationship with Matt has unfolded. I'd always thought that there was an unacknowledged impermanence to the life that Matt and I built together, and it comforted me. For the first few years, it was because I wasn't divorced, and after that, it was because it gave us (or perhaps only me) a sense of choice. We weren't together because of a legal obligation, or because of shared bank accounts, or because of dependants, but because of our ongoing desire to be with each other. I realize now that I had assumed something enormous: that our domestic arrangements reflected Matt's preferences, too. But today I see what I had never noticed before: that Matt has been staking out a homestead too sprawling and too generous to trigger my flight instincts, that he has been quietly and deliberately fencing me in.

"So what is it?" says Matt. "If you don't try, you can't fail? That doesn't sound like you. You try your guts out for Peter."

"Peter is my boss," I say. "I care about my professional reputation. Of course I go all out at work. That's what makes me good at my job. But Peter has nothing to do with my feelings about marriage."

"You are the only person in this car who believes that," says Matt. "Peter is your backup spouse. It's like you need two of us so that you don't have to commit to one."

"That is the craziest thing you've ever said to me," I say. "Why are you doing this? Why are you creating problems that don't exist?"

"I'm identifying problems that have existed for years, and that I have ignored in order to make you happy. But I spent several weeks where I barely spoke to you, let alone spent any time with you, and I want more. I want more from life and I want more from you."

"I feel like you're changing the deal," I say.

"If that's how you feel, then we have a serious problem," says Matt.

I can see Matt's point of view. I can see the merits of his argument, and I can also see how to take it apart. Matt chose me. He chose me at my most confused, my most unreliable. He chose me despite the fact that I was a proven liar, a betrayer, and a deserter. He loved me first. He took the leap, and I followed, but he must have wondered over the years how much of my motivation was escape. I know I have.

This is what Peter never told me about law school: how legal education is like a virus that infects, that burrows into your brain and rewires it, so that you can never think about problems in the same way again. Any position can be argued. Any position can be made reasonable. You can argue either side, and never be wrong.

We drive the rest of the way in silence. It is dangerous to say more, and we both know it. We are angry, certainly, but also tentative. We are at that moment when you realize you have handled something carelessly, not understanding that it was breakable.

Matt lets me out in front of city hall. "Will I see you tonight?" he asks.

I hesitate. "I hope so," I say. "But I'm not sure. I need to figure out what's going on. Can I call you once I know?"

"Sure," he says. He looks shaken. "I might go into the office as well."

"All right, then," I say. I stand at the open passenger door for a few moments, unwilling to walk away.

"You should go," says Matt.

"I know," I say. "I should." But I wait.

"We'll talk later."

"I love you," I say.

"I know you think you do."

"That's not fair."

"That doesn't mean it isn't true," he says, and he reaches over and pulls my door shut.

I watch him pull into traffic and drive away. And then I go and find Peter.

Bonnie is at her desk, which means that we are on high alert. Peter is never off the job, but he rarely asks Bonnie to work weekends. "He asked not to be disturbed," she says.

"Is he in a meeting?" I ask.

"No," she says.

"On the phone?"

"No."

"Is anyone else in the office?"

"No."

"He's waiting for me," I say. "He asked me to drive down to meet with him."

"I'll let you know when he's free," says Bonnie.

"Free from what?"

Bonnie exhales with frustration. "He's in the washroom," she says.

The mayor has his own bathroom attached to his office, so that he doesn't find himself in awkward situations with the public or the press. "So, five minutes?" I say.

"I'll let you know when he's free," Bonnie repeats.

"For the love of God," I say. "Do their colons work differently from ours? Is there a special reason why men need thirty minutes and a magazine?"

Bonnie presses her lips together. I hope she is trying not to laugh, but it's hard to tell with her. And then the door opens and Peter looks out.

"There you are," he says. "Come in."

"So," I say. "MEL? How did MEL get invited to this party?"

"Figuring that out is one of our jobs today," says Peter.

"It's so incongruous, their name," I say. The Mother Earth League has a history of green guerrilla tactics. More than one of their leaders has been sent to jail. MEL refers to them as "political prisoners."

"I know," says Peter. "They sound like a geriatric social club, not like a bunch of guys who set fire to aquariums for fun."

"They were never convicted of that," I say.

Peter smiles grimly. "I have no idea why they are paying the slightest attention to our little waterfront development, but we can assume it isn't because they love it."

"What's the issue?" I ask. "They should like the waterfront development. It's not as though it was green space before."

"They approve of the development in principle," says Peter. "But they feel, according to their draft press release,

that we've been 'inattentive to its environmental impact.'"
He hands me a piece of paper.

I scan it. "Parkland, green roof, community garden . . .
We consulted on all these issues, Peter. There is a park,
but we decided against a community garden in favour of a
playground. And the green roof was incredibly expensive.
We wanted it, but it was one of the first things to go when
we started cutting the budget."

"It may have to go back in," says Peter.

"I could use some research help," I say. "Can we call
the intern to come and help out?"

"Her name is Melanie," says Peter.

"I know," I say.

"I'll call her," he says.

"You don't have to do that," I say. "I can get Bonnie to
make the call."

"I'll do it," says Peter. "The personal touch is always
better, don't you think?"

CHAPTER 14

September 2002 and November 2001

The fall I went to law school felt simultaneously like a throwback to high school and a firm step into adulthood. It was an odd combination. I had a backpack again, full of textbooks. I had a locker. I had required classes, which I attended with the same group of people day in and day out. I got invited to an orientation week that involved a pub crawl. It was as though I had rewound the last few years of my life, been given a do-over. It felt like a gift.

We were studying law as it had been studied for decades. We read cases about cricket matches and broken windows, about explosions in train stations, about snails in bottles of ginger beer, about poachers and foxes and trespasses and easements. I read excerpts to Matt over the phone at night. He loved these old cases too, although he claimed to have forgotten everything he learned in law school. I was living with my mother, sleeping in my childhood bedroom, studying at my old desk. Matt was working late every night. On the weekends, I'd stay at his apartment with him, but during the week we rarely saw each other.

On September 11, there was a memorial service at the law school. The dean made a speech about law's essential role in protecting our security and freedom in a changing world. He said that we were the best and the brightest, and that we were part of living history. He said that we could change the world. My classmate Olivia turned to me with tears in her eyes. "I feel like it's our generation's chance to do something real, you know? Something that matters?"

I nodded. I didn't trust myself to speak. Olivia made me feel old before my time. I no longer dreamed about making a difference. I only wanted to be financially independent. I wanted an education that delivered earning power and mobility. I wanted to be safe.

Matt and I commemorated September 11 in our own way. We had dinner with Matt's friend Will Shannon, who still worked at Matt's old firm in New York.

"Avery," said Will, rising from the table. "It's great to finally meet you." He brushed both of my cheeks with a kiss, gripped Matt's hand hard, and pulled him in for a half-hug. He was the most handsome person I'd ever met in real life. I was old enough to wonder if that was difficult for him. "I'm thrilled to see you guys. You have no idea. I hope you're drinking."

"You bet," I said.

"I like you already," he said.

"It's been way too long," said Matt. "Where have you been?"

"I've been travelling a lot for work," said Will. "I'm one of the lucky ones." We all understood what he meant. A lot of lawyers were struggling that year. People were cautious, consolidating what they had, minding the store. There wasn't much appetite for change and expansion, and that meant less work for the lawyers who managed deals. The anxiety permeated every level of the profession, right down into the law school. Already, first-year students were fretting about their job prospects, angling for research jobs with professors, volunteering for clinics, checking footnotes for the *Law Review*. I didn't care about any of those things. I went to class, and I went home and studied.

"What are you doing in town?" I asked. "Are you here for work?"

"A wedding, actually," he said. "But I came a few days early to check on the kids in the Toronto office." He grinned at Matt.

Matt had ended up writing the New York bar exams. He passed on the first try. The firm was expanding into Canada, and Matt negotiated a one-year assignment in the Toronto office, citing family reasons. By then, I'd written the LSAT and applied to law schools—none of them in New York—and our relationship was still in its infancy. I understood that Matt was buying us some time, and time was what I needed. But we knew that New York could recall him at the end of the year. So far, we hadn't talked about what that would mean for us.

"The kids are doing fine," Matt said.

"I can see that," said Will.

"Will," said Matt. "I've wanted to thank you for advocating for me. I know the firm wouldn't have let me come to Toronto without your support. I really owe you."

"No worries," said Will.

"I'm not supposed to know," said Matt, "but Margaret told me, last time I was in New York, that you were supposed to be assigned to the Toronto office. They wanted someone with more experience than I had. They were only going to send one guy. You told them to give me the job."

"It didn't take much persuasion," said Will. "And look how well it turned out. Being in New York suits me, and being here suits you. But if you want to think I'm responsible for all this, you can buy dinner."

Matt laughed. "It's business development. The firm's buying dinner."

"You guys met at the firm?" I asked.

"When I was a summer student, the year before I met you in the café," said Matt. "Will was a very impressive, experienced associate."

Will laughed. "I knew marginally more than you did. That didn't stop them from making me a mentor, though. They're very keen on mentorship, at least in theory."

"Will was supervising this heinous document review," said Matt. "There were twenty of us in a boardroom going through boxes of files for weeks at a time."

"Soul-destroying labour," said Will. "So I took them out drinking every night. Most of the team gave up on the drinking portion of the file after a few days, but Matt stuck it out."

"Someone had to do it," said Matt.

"He impressed his mentor with his ability to drink late and function the next day," said Will. "It's a key life skill for lawyers."

"I've noticed," I said as Will topped up our glasses. "Matt won't ask, so I'm going to."

"Avery," said Matt.

"What are the chances that Matt will be able to stay in Toronto after the one-year trial period is up?"

"Does he want to stay?" asked Will.

"He might," said Matt.

"Under normal circumstances, the firm would want you to come back to the mother ship for at least two years before letting you settle in a regional office," said Will. "But we're still not operating under normal circumstances. People like the Canadian office. It's stable. There's an appetite to grow it. And we're still trying to find places for all of the people we offered jobs before 9/11. So I'd say there's a chance that you would be allowed to stay, particularly if your mentor recommends it."

"Will his mentor recommend it?" I asked.

"Absolutely, if that's what Matt wants," said Will.

"I'm trying to figure that out," said Matt. "What's the potential career damage if I stay?"

"It's hard to know for sure," said Will. "It's always better to have allies in the head office when discussions about partnership talks begin. That seems far away now, I know, but it comes up sooner than you might think. There's a risk of being out of sight, out of mind. Toronto is a small office."

"So you think I should go back?" said Matt.

"As your mentor, probably. But as your friend? There's more to life than making partner at a law firm, based on the general happiness levels of law partners I know. It's a cliché, but 9/11 changed my perspective. The internal politics of law firms are pretty much bullshit, and a waste of time. If being here makes you happy, that puts you way out ahead of most lawyers, and certainly the vast majority of the lawyers in the New York office."

"Thanks, man," said Matt.

Will nodded. Matt nodded. Information appeared to pass between them in the manly silence.

"Were you in New York on 9/11?" I asked, attempting a return to verbal communication.

"Yeah," said Will. "I was. I was at home, not far from Matt's old apartment. We'd been working late on a transaction, and we were supposed to reconvene at ten o'clock. I was drinking a second cup of coffee, reading the paper. I was taking my time. I was tired. And then I was more wide awake then I've ever been in my life."

"Yeah," I said. "I know exactly what you mean. Were you able to stay in your place?"

"No," said Will. "I moved uptown. My aunt Lil had a place on the Upper West Side that she wasn't using and she insisted that I stay there. I ended up staying for over a year."

"That's a nice kind of aunt to have," I said.

"She's my great-aunt, really, and yes, she's pretty incredible. I'm seeing her this weekend at the wedding."

"Is it a family thing?"

"No," said Will. "My old roommates are getting married to each other."

"That's nice," I said.

"It is nice," he said. "They are really nice people and they have a nice, happy future ahead of them."

"That's a lot of niceness," I said. "You must be looking forward to it."

His eyes met mine, and I saw approval in them. "Clever, I see," he said.

"I have the LSAT score to prove it," I said.

"It's one of those events that I should be thrilled about," said Will. "But because of something I did in my early twenties that was very, very stupid, I am instead dreading it. And I would have found a way to avoid going, except that it would have been obvious to everyone that I was doing exactly that, so I'm overcompensating and making a speech about what an ideal couple they are."

"Are they?" I asked.

"Is anyone?"

"You are so asking the wrong woman," I said. Matt's head whipped around. "Except for us," I said. I squeezed Matt's hand.

Will took a long drink. "The bride, Sophie, is terrific. You'd like her. The groom, A.J., is a solid guy, and he loves her, and he'll do his best."

"You liked her," I said.

"I had my chance," said Will. "See 'I did something stupid in my early twenties,' *supra*. I'm certainly not suggesting she'd be better off with me. Far from it."

"For what it's worth, I did something stupid in my early twenties, too," I said. "And I lived to tell about it."

"You callously broke someone's heart that you actually liked, and made it impossible to have a relationship with him in the future?"

"I took it a step further and married him," I said. "Let's just say that if he ever gets married again, I won't be invited to make a speech."

It was my mother, eventually, who broached the subject. "You aren't going back, are you?"

"No," I said. It was the first time I'd admitted it aloud. Matt hadn't pressed me, and I hadn't offered.

"It's been two months, Avery. It's time to face the music."

"I'll call him," I said.

"Avery Graham," said my mother, "I expect more of you than that. I do not judge your decision. It is your life and you have the right to choose your path. But I did not raise a coward. Put on your big-girl underpants, get on a plane, and deal with the life you've made."

So I did. I would like to think that I would have done the mature thing even if my mother hadn't intervened. I hope I would have. Because Hugh was most definitely not expecting the news I gave him.

I emailed to tell him I was coming, and he insisted on meeting me at the airport. Walking out of the airplane, through the plastic tunnel with the bright blue carpet, I felt a mounting sense of dread. Surely he knows that this isn't working, I thought. Surely he knows that we are over.

But when I saw the joy lighting his face, and the flowers in his hands, when he wrapped me in his arms and whispered, "You're home," I saw that I had been horribly, terribly mistaken. "Where's your suitcase?" he asked.

"I left some stuff at my mom's," I said. "I hate checking a bag, and there are more restrictions now."

"Yes," said Hugh, "flying will be a different experience for all of us now."

"We've turned a page in history," I said.

"The city is coming back to life," said Hugh. "It's inspiring. It's an amazing time to be a New Yorker, Avery. I'm excited to experience it with you."

"Hugh," I said. I felt as though I might vomit. "I need to sit for a moment."

We sat down in a row of vinyl chairs, one empty seat

between us so that we could face each other. "Darling," Hugh said, taking my hand. "Is there something you need to tell me?" He had a look of astonished wonder. "Are you . . . ?"

"No, I'm not pregnant. God. No."

"Oh," he said. "That's fine, that's good. We want to plan for that."

"No, Hugh. Listen to me. We don't want to plan for that. I don't want to plan for that."

"What are you saying?"

"I don't want a baby, Hugh," I said. I started sobbing. Other travellers gave us a wide berth. "I don't know how things got so out of control. I don't belong here. I don't want to be a writer. I want to go to law school."

"This is a lot to take in. You've been through a lot. We all have. We've all survived a trauma. It's going to take some time to feel normal again."

"You don't understand. I've felt more normal since I left than I've felt in years." I was gulping for air, making a scene.

"Let's go home, Avery," said Hugh.

"This isn't my home," I told him.

It is astonishing, really, the actions you can justify to yourself.

"You had a starter marriage?" said Will.

"I had the comprehensive package," I said. "A starter marriage and a starter divorce." Why was I telling him this? I rarely spoke about Hugh. I was mortified to be a statistic, to prove everyone right who had said that I shouldn't tie myself down, that I didn't know what I was getting into, that he was too old for me and I was too young for him.

The mere fact of the divorce said it all. *Res ipsa loquitur*, Matt would say: the thing speaks for itself.

"I'm sorry," said Will unexpectedly.

"Thank you," I said.

"He was completely wrong for her," said Matt.

"No doubt," said Will. He topped up my glass of wine. "How are you liking law school, Avery?"

"I love it," I said. "At least, so far." It was true. I loved the focus and discipline of law school, so at odds with any of my other efforts at higher education. I liked the linearity, the short-term objectives, the endless tide of reading, and the emphasis on logic instead of emotion.

"Keep me posted," said Will. "Maybe we'll lure both of you to New York when you're finished. Anything's possible."

Matt and I walked back to his apartment from the restaurant, holding hands.

"I like your friend," I said.

"I do too," said Matt. "He's done a lot for me."

"He doesn't see it that way," I said.

"I know," said Matt. "It's funny about Will. He has an idea of himself as a lightweight."

"He's a Wall Street lawyer," I said.

"Yeah," said Matt. "It doesn't add up. He's a brilliant guy, funny, good-looking . . ."

"I hadn't noticed," I said.

Matt laughed. "And he's decent. I saw him protect younger lawyers when we worked together. I saw him take undesirable assignments so other people didn't have to miss vacations. But that's not how he sees himself."

"Putting on my MFA hat, we all have origin stories," I said. "Narrative is powerful. Not even reality can shake it."

"Hmm," said Matt. "Deep thoughts. Speaking of which, I realized tonight that you never talk about Hugh."

"No," I said.

"I didn't know you felt so guilty about him."

"I'll always feel guilty about him," I said.

"Do you blame me for that?" he asked.

I was surprised. It was a good question; Matt was a fine lawyer and he knew how to ask them. I didn't immediately know the answer, and Matt didn't press me as we walked. The September days were still warm, but in the evening the heat didn't linger. There was no stickiness between our linked fingers. In a few weeks, there would be frost at night.

"No," I said, "I don't. I used to blame Hugh, but I don't anymore. Now I blame myself."

"He wasn't the right person for you," said Matt.

"I know," I said. "But still. I never want to disappoint someone like that again."

"You won't," said Matt.

But I knew that I might. Because I knew, now, that I was not entirely a good person. I had hard proof.

"Avery," said Matt. He sounded tentative. "They may insist that I go back to New York, no matter what I want. And if that happens, I'm planning to resign."

"Matt," I said. "You shouldn't do that. The job market's brutal. Please don't do that for me."

"It isn't all about you, Avery. There are lots of reasons to stay in Toronto. It's my hometown. I love it here." He squeezed my hand. "And I love you. And I want to make a commitment to you, and staying in Toronto will let me do that."

"Matt," I said. "I'm not ready for a commitment. That's too much pressure for me. I don't want to let you down."

"Let's talk this through," said Matt. "In six months, I'll find out one way or the other about staying in the Toronto office, which is my strong preference. My family is here, most of my friends are here, you're here, and I like living here better than I like living in New York."

"Okay," I said. I was trying to slow my breathing, without drawing Matt's attention to my efforts.

"Stop hyperventilating," said Matt. "Breathe."

I exhaled. "I'm scared."

"I understand."

"You think you do," I said. "But you can't, not really."

"Do you love me?"

"Yes. I do," I said. "I love you."

"That's all we need."

"Matt," I said. "Let me put this in law terms. Love is a necessary but insufficient condition."

"Do you think it's sufficient to make a plan to move in together, once I sort out my job? That's the only commitment I'm suggesting now."

"No other expectations?"

"None," he said. "Just a rental apartment. Can you handle that?"

I took a cautious breath in and out. My shoulders dropped. My belly unclenched. "I think so," I said. "I think I can handle that."

"Okay," said Matt. "Okay." He pulled me into a hug. "This is going to be great. We're going to do this at your speed, Avery. However long it takes."

My cellphone rings. It's Tara. "Is everything all right?" she asks.

"Yes," I say. "Why?" I've been at the office for hours now, and her call is disorienting.

"We all rolled out of bed late this morning and went looking for you. Martine said you and Matt had left at the crack of dawn."

"Not quite that early," I say.

"Are you guys okay?"

"We're fine," I say, wondering if it is true. "Peter called. There was a problem at the office, a political one. And it was my file so I had to come down and brief him. I'm at the office now."

"Oh, that's good," says Tara. "I thought you and Matt seemed off last night."

"We are," I say. "We are a bit off. Matt wants to get married."

"Ah," says Tara. I give her a lot of credit for not saying what most people would in these circumstances.

"And have babies," I say. "Or maybe just one baby. I haven't really pursued that line of inquiry yet."

"That's an interesting development."

"Do you have an opinion?"

"Many," says Tara. "But my opinion is irrelevant. It's your opinion that matters."

"You're no help."

"Do you want help?" She waits a beat, and says, "Let me know when and if you do. In the meantime, I have some bad news to report."

"Join the club," I say.

"I spoke to Hugh," Tara says, "in person, no less. He didn't buy the cover story. He said, and I quote, 'If Avery wants a favour, she will have to ask for it herself.'"

"Fabulous," I say.

"Are you surprised?"

I sigh. "Not really," I say. "Thanks for trying."

There is a knock on my door. "Come in," I call.

It's Gloria, my assistant. She's getting paid overtime to work this weekend and is therefore only mildly cranky. "Rick Wozniak is on the line for you," she says. "Do you want me to tell him you're in a meeting?"

"I'd better take it," I say to Gloria. "I'll be off in a second." To Tara, I say, "I have to go. I'll call you later tonight. I hope you had fun at your party."

"I loved it," she says. "And I love you. Bye."

"Put him through," I call to Gloria.

"Avery," says Rick, "How are you today?"

"I'm well, thank you," I say. "City hall never sleeps, as you know."

"Indeed I do," says Rick. "Which is the main reason for my call. My father, as you may know, is concerned about the environment."

It is fair to say I do not know this, Roger's enormous SUV being a fixture in the city. I've lost count of the number of times he's declared an end to the war on cars while voting against a bike lane, or questioned the return on investment of our recycling program, or tried to pave a paradise to put up a parking lot. But instead of mentioning any of these debates, I go with a noncommittal hum of support.

He continues. "My father has been contacted by a representative of the Mother Earth League. Are you familiar with them?"

"Yes," I say. I am extremely familiar with them. I have spent the past three hours researching and writing a memo on them. Melanie is in the office but is, apparently, unavailable to assist me with the memo, having been recruited by Peter for a special project.

"I must say that I was surprised to learn of their interest in our little waterfront development," says Rick.

"So was I," I tell him.

"It seems," says Rick, "that there is some connection between the local chapter of the Mother Earth League and the Artists' Cooperative Council."

"Oh?"

"Yes," says Rick. "It seems that there is a gentleman involved in both organizations."

"Let me guess."

"I doubt that will be necessary. Mr. Crawford is a very engaged citizen."

"Thank you for letting me know."

"You are most welcome," says Rick. "Oh, and Avery? How is that other project coming along? The literary project?"

"I haven't forgotten," I say. "In fact, it is on the top of my list for tomorrow morning to follow up."

"That is most appreciated," says Rick. "Most appreciated." He clears his throat. "May I ask your advice?"

"Yes, of course."

"I found yet another folder of poems in my dad's archive. They seem to be from a later period."

"Oh?"

"These ones are more . . . sensuous, I suppose is the word I'm looking for. I'm not sure the quality of the verse is higher, necessarily, not that I'm an appropriate judge of that. But I thought you should see an example of a later poem in case you thought it would make a more compelling submission to *The Beak*."

"Did you want to send me the whole folder?"

"No," says Rick. "Thank you for offering, but I don't think so. There's only one that seems suitable for our project. Could I read it to you, so that you could share your opinion?"

"Yes," I say. "Sure. Right now?"

"Yes," he says. "Why not? I have it right here."

"Okay, then," I say. "I'm listening."

He reads:

I didnt't want perfection.
I didn't want a doll,
Or a woman who could parallel park,
Or spend wisely at the mall.
I wanted a companion
Who knew me through and through,
And the first time that our eyes met,

I knew that it was you.
When did we stop trying
To turn each other on?
When did you pack up your lace?
Your fishnet stockings are long gone.
And so too are the midnight hours
We spent together in love play.
Now we just lie side by side
In silence 'til the break of day.

Could it be the case that while art moves us, terrible art moves us terribly? I grip the edge of my desk. I am aware that I might cry.

"Do you know what?" I say, after a few moments. "I think we should submit both of them. I think they are equally strong."

"I'm so glad that I called you," says Rick. "Thank you so much."

"I'm happy I could help," I say. "Writing is a rare gift." There is a pause. "Hello?" I say.

"I'm here," he says. "I was thinking about how to say something to you."

There is another pause, and this time I don't fill it.

"I'm not a politician, Avery," he says. "I admire directness. I admire hard work and loyalty and service. I see those qualities in you."

"Thank you," I say. *Surely he knows that I have a partner,* I think. *Please let him not be asking me out right now. Please let that not be happening.*

"But I've come to appreciate that these traits are not always rewarded in the political sphere," he continues, "and that, in fact, the people who represent these values—people like you, Avery—are vulnerable in times of crisis."

"I have to ask: What crisis?"

"I don't know yet. It isn't coming from us, from our campaign."

"Rick," I say, "you aren't giving me much to go on here."

"I know. And I hesitated to say anything at all. But forewarned is forearmed. Watch your back, Avery."

"I'll try," I say.

I hang up the phone. Where is our enemy, if not in the Wozniak camp? Jim Crawford seems the most likely candidate, but why now, when I'm literally writing a memo on how to bring him joy, or at least how to decrease his pathological level of malcontent?

The phone rings, and "Unknown Caller" flashes up. It's a sign. I pick up the phone, smothering a giggle. I must stop allowing myself to be drawn into paranoia. It is an occupational hazard of politics, but I know that it clouds judgment. Not everyone is an enemy.

"This is Avery Graham," I say.

"This is Jim Crawford," he says.

And on the other hand, some people *are* the enemy. "Hello, Jim," I say. "What can I do for you today?"

"I'm calling you in my capacity as the president of the local chapter of the Mother Earth League," says Jim. "And I would like a meeting with the mayor to discuss the waterfront redevelopment."

"I'm sure that can be arranged," I say. "But in the meantime, could you share with me some of your concerns?"

"Lack of consultation, obviously," says Jim.

"There were a number of environmental consultations done during the design planning process," I say. "But it seems that MEL was not involved in those meetings. Can you tell me about your group?"

"MEL is an organization with international standing," says Jim. "It has instigated some of the most influential environmental protests of our time. Have you heard of the Marigold Standoff? The Aquaworld Freedom Blitz? The Test Animal Uprising?"

"I've heard of all of them," I say. "But none of them happened in our city or even our country. And I wasn't aware that MEL was operating here, or we would have invited them to participate in our discussions about the waterfront, because, as I'm sure you'll appreciate, it is easier to incorporate feedback at the early stages of planning than it is after the plans have been approved."

"I must say I expected this kind of resistance from the mayor's office," says Jim.

"You shouldn't interpret my questions as resistance," I say. "I am merely asking for information, which will help me advise the mayor, among others."

Jim harrumphs. The harrumph, rarely experienced in real life, is a triumph of human communication: contempt, irritation, righteousness, indignation, and self-love all in one exhalation. Jim's version is impressive. "MEL moves into a jurisdiction when the need for their wisdom and activism becomes evident. Up until recently, other cities had greater need. But now one of the treasures of the Great Lakes is threatened by political whims. We will not sit idly by and let our birthright be polluted so that Mayor Haines can have his precious legacy."

I take a hit of coffee. It is revoltingly cold. "Jim, let's slow down here. It's just you and me on the phone. What I hear you saying is that the local chapter was set up recently."

"That is correct," says Jim.

"How many people are involved in the organization? Locally?"

"Twenty or so," says Jim.

"And how many of them are also members of ArtCo?"

"I resent the implication," says Jim.

"What implication?" I say.

"That our environmental concerns are not extremely serious. That our organization is some sort of shadow operation whose only purpose is to bolster ArtCo's agenda."

"I completely did not say that," I say, although it is a nice summary of my feelings.

"You didn't have to," says Jim. "I can see that we are going to have to take this to eleven to get a proper hearing."

"There is no reason whatsoever to take this to eleven," I say. What "eleven" might be in MEL terms, I can't fathom. It won't be a cause for celebration, this much I know.

"We'll see," says Jim. "You set a meeting, Avery, and you make sure the mayor is there. And then we'll consider our options." And he hangs up.

Absently, I take another slug of coffee, choke, and spit it back into the Styrofoam cup. I make a mental note not to have Styrofoam cups at the meeting with MEL. I make a mental note not to drink any more of the coffee, but I don't trust myself to remember, so I pick up the cup and walk out of my office to the kitchen and pour it down the drain. I reflect on the plight of indigent coffee workers whose labour I have disrespected. I reflect on my failures as a spouse, a daughter, a friend, an employee, and a human being, which seem in this moment to be manifold.

Bonnie appears in the doorway. There is no place to hide from this woman.

"Where's Gloria?" I ask.

"A good question," says Bonnie. "Not at her desk, to pick up an urgent call from Doris Renaud, that much I can tell you. I came to see if you were in. I see that you are, so I'll put her through."

"Thank you," I say, and return to my desk, where the phone flashes malevolently. I pick it up. "Hi, Doris."

"Avery," says Doris, "I would like, no, I demand an explanation."

"An explanation for what?" I ask.

"For the outrageous, underhanded collusion that is occurring between Jim Crawford and the mayor's office, which is a clear effort to undermine the rights of women in this city."

"Doris," I say, in what I believe to be a calm and even tone, "I would never be involved in a conspiracy to undermine the rights of women. I can assure you of that personally. As to the particulars of the accusation, you're going to have to enlighten me. I'm in the dark."

"Are you aware that Jim Crawford has brought in MEL to back his cause?"

"I was under the impression that his cause was adequate soundproofing in the studios," I say.

"Where have you been?" says Doris. "He wants to eliminate the playground for the women's shelter and erect some ghastly excuse for public art. He wants to plant a community garden where the family picnic area is supposed to be. He wants to move the daycare to Building Five, which has no access to green space. He wants to use the budget for the learning commons for a green roof. He wants—"

"Obviously, I've missed some developments here," I say. "This information is all extremely helpful."

"We are voters, Avery," says Doris. "You can't just ignore the women of this city and hope they'll go away. Women put Peter Haines in office and they can take him out."

"Doris," I say. "I'm sure there is a solution here that will satisfy everyone. Let's all sit down and figure this out."

"I want the mayor there," says Doris. "I want him there in person. Does he even know what's happening on his watch?"

"Of course he does," I say. "This project is his top priority."

"Then I'll expect to be sitting across from him by tomorrow afternoon," says Doris, "and not one minute later. This administration is asleep at the switch."

One thing we are not is asleep. Sleep feels like the most precious and most inaccessible of prizes. I could solve every conflict on the waterfront project, I could get Peter re-elected, be named WAFADASS's Woman of the Year, have my portrait commissioned and painted by members of ArtCo, have an essay published in the *New York Times* about how cities are transformed by visionary chiefs of staff. I could knit the threads of rent relationships back together. I could do all these things and still not know the peace of an untroubled sleep, which is why I find myself back in the kitchen for another cup of horrific coffee.

Bonnie appears in the doorway again. "For the love of God, Bonnie," I say. "There's a reason I don't bring my phone in here."

"The chief of staff doesn't get breaks," says Bonnie, in a rare demonstration of humour. Or possibly she is dead serious. "And might I suggest that you look at how often your assistant is taking them?"

"Thank you for the suggestion," I say. "Anything else?"

"Someone named Marshall Westwood is on the line," she says. "He says he's from the Mother Earth League."

I close my eyes. When I open them, I'm still in the kitchen, with a cup of coffee in my hand, and Bonnie looking at me with mild concern. "It was worth a try," I say.

In my office, I sit and wait for the call to ring through. It is, as promised, Marshall Westwood, who claims to be the "international greenkeeper" for the Great Lakes region of the Mother Earth League. "I've been speaking to Jim Crawford, our local representative," says Marshall, "and MEL is troubled by the dismissive treatment he has received so far from city officials."

"I spoke to him twenty minutes ago and promised him a meeting with the mayor," I say.

Marshall continues as if I haven't spoken. "MEL feels that an international presence is required at this meeting, and so I will be in attendance. Could you please ensure that all the meeting notes are forwarded to me with forty-eight hours' notice."

"Well, Marshall," I say, "since everyone involved seems to want to have the meeting tomorrow, and since I haven't drafted up any meeting notes, I can say with complete assurance that I won't be doing that. But you're welcome to come to the meeting, and if you email me your contacts, I'll make sure you're in the loop."

"I can see we have a lot of work to do," says Marshall. He takes my email address and hangs up.

It's time to talk to Peter. I head to Bonnie's desk and fill her in. We find a conference room to book, and I give her all of the contact details of the various players. "I'm going to brief Peter now," I say.

"Not a good time," she says.

"I can stand outside the bathroom door, if need be," I say. "But this is going to take a while and I need to go home for dinner if I want to have a home to go home to."

I feel Bonnie rising from her desk behind me, but I'm already opening the door. Which proves to be a mistake, because what I see as I step inside is Melanie sliding off Peter's lap, rebuttoning her shirt, and finger-combing her hair into a ponytail; and Peter pushing in closer to the desk as if there is something in his lap that he wants to hide.

I say, "Special project?"

But what I think is *You fucking asshole. How could you?*

And this, ultimately, is what makes me so blazingly angry. Not the knowledge that I've spent every day of the past three years putting my personal life in peril to be the unsung hero of this administration; not that I've selflessly accepted the slings and arrows of every bitter, crazy, disenfranchised taxpayer in order to deflect them from Peter; not that I've twinned my reputation to a man I think of as my mentor, my dear friend, and even my hero, only to find that he is capable of doing something as reckless and stupid as screwing an intern in the office; but that all of these appropriate, adult reactions are absent, swamped by the devastation of a rejected twelve-year-old in love for the first time.

I don't look at him. I can't.

But I can look at Melanie. And when I can speak, I say, "You're fired. Get out of here and don't come back."

{CHAPTER 16}

July 2009

After law school, I went to work for Peter.

Matt tried to talk me out of it. "Peter's a good lawyer, Avery," he said. "It's nothing against Peter. But you could get a wider range of experience at a large firm. You don't know what kind of practice you'll enjoy until you do it yourself. Being a lawyer isn't like law school."

"I'm betting on it," I said. The novelty of law school had been thrilling in the beginning, but three years later my life seemed, yet again, to be in a state of suspended animation. I longed to graduate into active and independent personhood.

"But what if you don't like being in a small firm?" said Matt.

"Matt," I said, "I don't have it in me to compete with a bunch of kids for daddy's attention, trying to jump higher than everyone else for a chance at being hired back."

"They're, at most, five years younger than you are," said Matt.

"Five big years," I said. "I want to catch up. I did my research. Peter has a good reputation. His firm is growing. He trusts me. He'll put me on the fast track to partnership."

"You shouldn't be thinking about partnership now," said Matt. "Avery, a law career is a long haul. You need to find the work you enjoy. You'll be exposed to only a few types of litigation at Peter's shop. What if you decide you don't like acting for individuals?"

"And decide that I'd rather be defending the rights of companies?" I said. "Matt, the only thing that got me through law school were the stories. I don't give a shit about the law. I want to do something useful with my life. I want to engage with the world, with real people."

"I respect that," said Matt. "But understand that when you're acting for real people, you aren't usually seeing them at their best."

"I know what it's like not to be at your best," I said. Helping people extract themselves from their own bad decisions seemed like something I might be qualified to do at this stage in my life.

Peter's firm, Haines & Associates, was wildly busy and chronically understaffed. His detractors called it Peter's "revolving door" problem. His friends said that exceptional courtroom lawyers, like Peter, didn't always make good managers, and that Peter was the victim of his own success. Peter wasn't remotely interested in these assessments, either positive or negative. He prided himself on his independence.

His career was the stuff of legend, at least to young lawyers trapped in soulless towers. All of them wished they could be like him; all of them knew he was one of a kind. He had started at a large, prestigious firm, the best one, the one that every student applied to and secretly wanted an offer from more than anything in the world.

And the firm had adored him, too; he'd been a "fit." But he'd been restless, and confident, and he'd left after a few short years to start his own practice. Everyone had warned him against it, but his faith in himself had never wavered. He loved being on his feet in court, and hated being trapped behind a desk on a conference call or in a meeting room sixty floors above street level. He'd rented a funky loft space in an old Victorian warehouse and set to work. Before long, he'd taken over two entire floors of the building, and was turning away medal-winning applicants from the best law schools in the country. He told this story over and over again at the conferences and law school panels where he was invited to speak on career choice and diversity.

In truth, Peter was a talented lawyer, but his real gift was business development. He barely slept in the early years, out at industry events every night, in the office at six in morning, and in court at ten. He golfed and sat on boards, and the entire legal community waited breathlessly for the arrival of his annual holiday card, which was invariably hilarious and creative and just a step away from inappropriate. When he went to a funeral, he arrived after the church had filled with mourners, walked up the centre aisle, and sat at the front, whether or not he was a close friend. "Never sit at the back," he told me. "If people don't know you were there, there's no point in going at all."

He made me a partner in my third year of practice.

I had my own routine in those early years. Matt and I would rise early and have a coffee together. In the summer we'd often go for a run, and in the winter we'd huddle on the sofa and share the paper, easing into wakefulness.

We'd drive downtown while the streets were quiet; Matt would drop me off and continue on to his office. I treasured those groggy, peaceful hours. Once the day started, we could never be sure that we'd find each other again, but we could begin together, and we did, as often as we possibly could.

I'd spend the first two hours of my day working on my own files. I had mostly matrimonial clients then. When he wasn't planning his political future, Peter was building up a personal injury and class action practice, and I often pitched in, mostly by managing the young lawyers who were confused by his instructions and in over their heads. I specialized in "leavers," those who had left their marriages. Most of my clients were men who thought it would make them more sympathetic if they had a female lawyer. They tended to be angry and defensive, but they weren't criers like the personal injury clients. I didn't feel responsible for them except in a purely professional sense. My job was to get them to the point where they understood that they would have to pay, because the leaver invariably does; the lucky ones only pay with money.

Once Peter arrived in the office, I'd lose control of my day, unless I had enough gravitational force of my own (a court appearance, a client meeting, an urgent deadline) to resist the pull of his orbit. There were people to be interviewed for positions that desperately needed to be filled. There were staff to manage and young lawyers to mentor, although I was barely a real lawyer myself. There were holiday card designs to approve and performance evaluations to give. There were accounts receivable to chase and clients to soothe, because Peter was smart and talented, but he didn't always win, and he didn't like cleaning up the mess afterwards.

Peter would start his day by wandering into my office. "I was at the art gallery opening last night," he'd say, "and I saw Howard. His son is getting divorced and he needs to protect the family business. I told him you'd call him this morning." Or "Sylvia Garner's neighbour might be willing to start a class action on that airbag defect we were talking about last week. Let's check it out."

So I'd call Howard, or Sylvia. I'd open a file, staff it, and supervise it. I'd meet with the clients, assign research, review it, write correspondence, and generally move it along until it required Peter's presence. And then he'd get on the phone with opposing counsel and work his magic. He settled a lot of cases, but only because everyone knew that he wasn't afraid to take it all the way up. He loved going to court, and when he was prepared, there was no one better. I made sure he was prepared.

I'd eat takeaway at my desk every night. Stress kept me thin and alert. Late at night, I'd collapse into bed beside Matt, who usually arrived home around the same time I did. We'd huddle together like survivors of a shipwreck, trying only to stay afloat to see another sunrise. I was pushed to my limits in a way I had never been before, and although it wasn't much of a life, I was electrified by the singularity of my focus. Peter had done for me what nothing and no one had ever done: he had made me useful.

At court one morning, I ran into my friend Olivia from law school. She was at the firm that Peter had left, and was considered a rising star there.

"Avery!" she said, dropping her litigation bag and giving

me a hug. "I'm mortified. You emailed me about a coffee ages ago and I never got back to you."

"I never followed up," I said. "Don't worry about it."

"It's been way too long," she said. "I kept thinking I'd run into you."

"They weren't kidding about these first years of practice," I said. "The last three years have been a complete blur."

"I heard that you made partner," she said. "I should have called. I was so happy for you."

"Thanks," I said. "But honestly, it isn't that different from being an associate except that I do more housekeeping around the office." Making partner had turned out to be a much bigger deal for other people than it had been for me. It had accorded me more respect among my cohort, but less affection. At cocktail parties now, I received more business cards and fewer confidences. It was isolating, and I was glad to be having a real conversation for once. "What about you?" I asked. "How are you liking life as a lawyer?"

"God, Avery," she said. "I'm practically dead."

"Sure," I said. "As we all are. But also strangely alive, no?"

"Like vampires," she said.

"Exactly like vampires," I said. "I can't remember the last time I saw the sun."

"You were smart to go and work for Peter Haines," she said. "I owe you an apology. I thought you were crazy at the time."

"I know," I said. "So did everyone. Don't feel bad."

"I'm looking over my shoulder all the time," she said. "Watching the competition. Waiting to see if someone slips up. Hoping it won't be me. It's been one long episode of *Survivor* and it lasts until you make partner."

"Being a partner has its own issues," I said. "Trust me."

"I was going to be a crusader for victims of sexual violence," she said. "I was going to work at The Hague. Do you know what I'm arguing a motion about today? Condominium law." She made a face. "I hate myself."

"You aren't trapped," I said. "You can leave your firm."

"Aaron and I bought a house," Olivia said. "So I really can't. I've put myself in golden handcuffs. This is who I am now."

I knew about golden handcuffs. I rubbed the bare ring finger on my left hand. "You can change," I told her, and I wasn't thinking only of her job.

"Maybe in five years," she said. "I've got to run. Let's do coffee! Email me!"

I knew I wouldn't email her, and it made me wistful. Aside from Matt, my social life consisted of Friday drinks with Tara and Jenny at the hotel bar near my office, but even that was fraught. Jenny and I had rekindled a friendship under Tara's supervision when I'd moved back from New York, tacitly agreeing not to mention the Apartment Incident. But relations had cooled considerably when I'd joined Peter's firm. At Friday drinks, also known as the Outrage of the Week Club, the losers would foot the bill for the winner, whoever told the most shocking tale of professional abuse or injustice. But my stories inevitably infuriated Jenny, who thought I'd made my own bed and that I should lie in it without complaint or free alcohol.

That evening, I slipped out of the office at twenty minutes past five to meet Tara and Jenny. I ran into Peter at the elevator.

"Drinks night?" he asked.

"I'll be back afterwards if you need me," I said.

"Avery, it's Friday night. Your hours are through the roof. Take a night off. Go see your boyfriend."

"Are you sure?" I said. "The Coulter file is a mess."

"Then we'll deal with it on Monday," said Peter.

"We'll deal with it tomorrow," I said. "I'll see you at ten thirty. You're in court on Monday and you aren't ready yet."

"Ten thirty it is," said Peter. "What would I do without you, Avery? Bringing you on board was the best decision I've ever made."

My eyes welled up. I was so exhausted. "Thank you," I said.

Peter smiled. "Oh, Avery," he said. "Look at you." He put a hand up to my cheek and brushed a tear away with his thumb. "I should tell you much more often how much I appreciate you. You keep this place going."

Then his smile stretched into a wide grin and he went down on one knee, arms outstretched. "Did I ever tell you you're my hero," he sang, badly and loudly. "And I don't remember the next line. And I could do something with an eagle. You are the wind beneath my wings." He drew out the last line with some impressive vibrato. By this time a couple of lawyers and the receptionist had come out to the elevator bank and were standing in a semicircle around us. They burst into applause.

Peter stood up and dusted off his pants. "Thank you very much," he said, Elvis-like. "But it is Avery who deserves our applause. To Avery!" Everyone turned to me and clapped politely, having no idea why they were doing so. Peter pressed the button for the elevator, and it arrived immediately. He shooed me inside. "Go have fun," he said. "Tell the girls I said hello."

Tara and Jenny were already at the bar when I arrived. Peter's serenade had made me late. "Peter says hi," I told them.

"Tell him hi back," said Tara. Jenny said nothing, but I didn't expect her to. I'd been wondering if it was time to bow out of the Outrage of the Week Club, maybe by missing the odd one and gradually ramping up my absenteeism. But Tara would have had a fit, and I didn't want to have another infraction on my record.

"Happy Friday!" said Tara. "Are you ready to rage?"

"Is that a serious question?" said Jenny.

"You go first, then," said Tara.

"Anton is a complete dickhead," said Jenny.

Tara, our adjudicator, shook her head. "You know the rules, Jenny. Specifics, please."

"Also, this is not new information," I said. "You can't win on the same outrage more than once." I was growing weary of Anton stories. I knew too much about Jenny's boss at Brand Awareness, the marketing and communications firm where she worked as a graphic designer: how he tormented his employees by vacillating between excessive praise and unwarranted criticism; how he dangled promotions while taking credit for their work; how he promised them salary increases and holiday bonuses that never materialized; how he brought his dog to the office and made the most junior designers take him for walks.

"This time it's different," said Jenny. "I'm quitting."

Tara and I exchanged a look. Jenny talked about quitting constantly.

"I'm serious, you guys," said Jenny. "Remember my financial services client? The one who kept rejecting my concepts because they didn't 'pop' enough?"

We nodded.

"Anton wrote off all my time so management wouldn't see that he'd overinvested. And now it looks like I've been slacking on my hours, even though I've been living at the office. I fucking hate him."

We drank in solidarity.

"Good one," said Tara. "But I wouldn't count on your free drink just yet."

"Big talk," said Jenny, smiling, and in that moment, I missed her intensely.

"Perhaps you heard about it on the news," said Tara. "The company that gave out wooden spoons to everyone at the baseball game, so fans could 'stir up some excitement'?"

"Oh yeah," I said. "Didn't security confiscate the spoons?"

"They sure did," said Tara. "Which is exactly what I told them the stadium would do. And then they did a press release, without consulting me, about their plan to donate the confiscated spoons to a 'wooden-spoon-needing charity.'"

"Is there such a thing?" said Jenny.

"No," said Tara. "There isn't. Also, it sounds stupid. Which I would have told them, if they hadn't fired me for their epic PR fail that I had nothing to do with."

"It's going to be close this week," I said.

"What about you?" said Tara. "You can't win if you don't play."

"I don't have an outrage this week," I said. I didn't have the energy to deal with Jenny's disapproval just then.

"Really?" said Tara. "Earlier this week, you said you were going to dominate."

"I did?" The beginning of the week seemed like an age ago. And Peter had sung me into the elevator.

"Peter turned on the charm just in time, did he?" said Jenny.

I didn't want to rise to her bait, but I felt blood heat my cheeks. "I don't know what you mean," I said.

"He's good at that," said Jenny. And we were off again.

"I know you don't like him—" I said.

"Understatement," said Jenny.

"—but you need to respect my relationship with him."

"Well," said Jenny, "that's not going to happen any-time soon. My own quote 'issues' aside, Peter has turned you into an obsessive workaholic with no outside interests. When did you last read a book, Avery? Or see a play? Or do any of the things you used to enjoy before Peter got his hands on you?"

"Jenny," said Tara.

"He's a user," said Jenny. "He uses people for his own ends. And now he's using you. And the day you figure it out will be a bad day for you."

Every time, I thought. *Every damn time. Was it too much to ask for a night off?* "You don't understand how lucky I am for a lawyer at my stage," I said. "My classmates would kill to be in my position."

"Don't they call that Stockholm syndrome?" said Jenny.

"Two can play this game, Jenny," I said.

"Guys," said Tara. "Please."

"No, Tara," I said. "I sit here every week and Jenny judges me. Fuck that. I have a successful career that I enjoy. The person at this table who's throwing away her talent is Jenny."

"Avery," said Tara. "Don't."

"It's true," I said. "You're an artist. And you're sitting in a cubicle, making shitty graphic designs for companies you don't care about, and taking orders from people who you don't respect. Why do you get the moral high ground here? You don't like my boss. So what? I doubt I'd like Anton."

"Anton didn't steal the only father you ever knew and bankrupt your mother," said Jenny. "And if he had, I wouldn't be working for him, because he would be my sworn enemy. I am not Switzerland."

I shook my head and stood up. "Enough," I said. "Jenny, I'm sorry I'm a disappointment to you. I feel sad about that, but I can't keep living this drama over and over again. It's exhausting."

"Avery," said Tara. "Please don't do this. Stay. Don't walk away."

I gathered my coat. "I'm sorry," I said. Jenny said nothing.

"You can fix this," said Tara to Jenny.

"No," said Jenny. "Not this time."

I thought about going home, but Matt wouldn't be there yet, and I didn't want to be alone. I wanted to feel purposeful, competent. I walked back to the office.

Peter was in his office, reviewing my notes. He said, "You were right. The Coulter case is a mess."

I took off my coat. "I'm here."

CHAPTER 17

Tuesday, July 18, 2017

It's Tuesday morning, 8:30 a.m., officially forty hours since I've received any communication from Peter. My fury is starting to fade, or at least be overshadowed by my panic. He's never gone underground like this, not in all of the years we've worked together. People are looking for him. Specifically, people are looking for him for the waterfront development meeting at nine, which I scheduled and cancelled twice yesterday, and which I must hold this morning at nine in order to prevent a revolution among our left-wing base.

I circle the outer office again, cruising past Bonnie's desk. She barely raises her head.

"No," she says. "I haven't heard from him." She is unsympathetic to my plight. Her position requires no explanation: she told me not to open Peter's door. I have both disrespected her authority and triggered consequences that are raining down on the entire office. I am not entitled to her pity.

"What should I do about the meeting?" I ask her. I have my merry band of Jim, Marla, Doris, Glynis, Charis, and Marshall on their way, along with a team of architects.

I have agendas. I have briefing notes. I have copies of the newest version of the plans, which have the daycare centre and the women's shelter in a completely separate building from the artists' studios. I have a conference room booked. I have coffee and paper (not Styrofoam) cups. I have muffins from a local organic bakery that provides jobs to women transitioning back into the community after serving prison terms. I've even managed (thanks to Peter) to provide Marshall Westwood with forty-eight hours' notice of the meeting. But I don't have a mayor, and that is a big problem.

Bonnie shrugs. "That's why you're the chief of staff," she says. Her phone flashes and she holds up a hand to stop me from answering. "Good morning, Mr. Mayor," she says into the receiver. "Yes, sir. Everything is organized. We'll see you shortly, then." She disconnects and says, "He's on his way."

"Thank God," I say. "When will he be here? I'd like him to talk with the architects to go over the plan before he goes into the meeting."

"That's unlikely," says Bonnie as the door opens and Doris Renaud enters the office with one of Glynis or Charis. Twenty minutes early. Of course they are.

"I would like it noted that we are offended by the multiple changes in the meeting time," says Doris. "It underscores the mayor's contempt for women's issues. He could not have made it more obvious that we are not his top priority. This meeting should have been held yesterday morning. As it is, Charis was unable to be here today, having moved an appointment to accommodate the original meeting time."

"Please give her my apologies," I say. "We were attempting to work with eight busy schedules on short notice. It simply wasn't possible to get everyone in one room yesterday, even with Bonnie's scheduling wizardry." This offering fails to elicit even a hint of a smile from Bonnie.

Doris scowls. I smile harder. "Why don't I put you in the conference room now, and you can have some coffee?" I say. "I'll give you a copy of the agenda as well."

"Fine," says Doris. "I would appreciate a few minutes alone with the mayor when he arrives."

"So would we all," I say. "Let's play that by ear."

I lead Doris and Glynis to the conference room. "Make yourselves comfortable," I say.

Doris studies my admittedly sparse breakfast buffet. "Are these muffins gluten-free?" she asks.

"Uh, no," I say. "They're organic and socially responsible."

"Any herbal tea?"

"Let me check in the kitchen," I say.

"Doris is extremely sensitive to caffeine," says Glynis.

"On it," I say, and return to the reception area as Jim Crawford and Marla Kraft reach the heavy glass doors. Marlene struggles to pull one open while Jim watches. She holds it for him and he glides through.

"I understand you heard from the international green-keeper," says Jim.

"Marshall Westwood, yes," I say. "He was able to clear his schedule and be here this morning. I'm expecting him any minute."

"I'd like a private word with the mayor before the meeting," says Jim.

"That may not be possible," I say. "The mayor has had back-to-back meetings this morning. He's on his way now but may not arrive with time to spare."

"I'm sure afterwards would be fine," says Marla.

"Let's go down to the conference room," I say, ushering them back through the doors and down the hallway.

"Did you find any herbal tea?" says Glynis as I enter. She casts a worried glance at Doris, who is filling a paper cup with coffee.

"Still looking," I say.

"What the hell kind of muffins are these?" says Jim.

"Banana bran chocolate, pumpkin sunflower, and raisin cardamom," I say.

"Ridiculous," says Jim. "What happened to blueberry? What happened to chocolate chip? Who wants to eat stuff like this?"

"It's local and organic," I say.

"That's nice," says Marla.

"I'm going to look for that tea," I say to Glynis.

"There you are," says Bonnie as I enter the reception area. Logan Kim, my lead architect, and two of his juniors are waiting in a cluster off to one side of Bonnie's desk.

"I'm going to try to get us a few minutes with Peter," I tell them.

"Good," says Logan. "We can't keep moving units around, Avery. We can't make structural changes without escalating costs at this stage. If we're adding a green roof, we need to reinforce the structure. If we're moving the childcare centre, or the studios, or the shelter, or any other element of the design from one building to another, it involves structure."

"I get it, Logan," I say. "We need to give Peter a primer, that's all. There's no cause for alarm."

"Avery," says Bonnie. "This is Mr. Westwood." I turn to greet a middle-aged man in shorts, a Mother Earth League T-shirt, and sandals.

"Pleather," he says.

"I'm sorry?" I say.

He points to his sandals. "Pleather, not leather, in case you were wondering."

I wasn't. I shake his hand. "Thanks for joining us," I say.

"I wouldn't have missed it," he says. "I'm only sorry that MEL wasn't kept abreast of this project from the earliest stages of planning. It's always so much more expensive when we get involved this late." He smiles with only the slightest trace of humour. Behind me, Logan sighs. It is the sigh of a person who understands that his day is only getting worse.

"Do we have any herbal tea in the kitchen?" I ask Bonnie.

"No," she says. "Aidan Clarke has left five messages for you."

"Not today," I say. "I can't talk to any reporters today. Do we have any herbal tea anywhere else?"

She purses her lips and opens a drawer in her desk, pulls out a box, and hands me a single, wrapped tea bag. "Chamomile peppermint," she says.

"Thanks," I say. She nods, curtly, all business.

I deliver Marshall to the conference room. "Would you like a muffin?" I ask.

"God no," says Marshall. "Those things will kill you."

"I've gone gluten-free," says Doris. "It's added years to my life."

"Gluten is only one of the poisons in these muffins," says Marshall. "Lectins and phytates are every bit as toxic. Modern wheat causes all kinds of autoimmune disorders—multiple sclerosis, chronic fatigue, asthma, irritable bowel syndrome—all preventable!" He pats his ample midsection. "No wheat belly here!"

Glynis and Marla drop their muffins.

"They're made by women reintegrating into society after prison terms," I say, to no one in particular. "I'll be right back."

Glynis intercepts me as I head for the door. "The tea?" she asks.

"Right, sorry," I say. "Here. I found one. It's chamomile peppermint."

I hope it's not too late," says Glynis.

"Me too," I say. I don't have time to worry about what she means. It's after nine. I need to find Peter.

"He's here," says Bonnie as I enter the office. "He's in there." She points to his door.

"Mood?" I ask.

She raises an eyebrow, which I take to mean *You're on your own, kid.* I can hear cursing from behind the door. I knock tentatively.

"Peter?" I call. "They're waiting for you."

The door opens and Peter glowers at me. "Where's my fucking briefing note?" he says. "I've been looking everywhere for it."

"I emailed it to you last night," I say. "I have a hard copy here."

"I don't have time to read it now," he says. "I guess I'll have to wing it."

"I wouldn't recommend that, Peter," I say. "Let's take a couple of minutes now and I'll sketch it out for you. Logan Kim is here and he can take you through the drawings." *Wing it?* I think. *It's not enough for you to look unprepared? You have to make us all look incompetent as well?*

"You'll have to tell me while we walk," he says. "It's nine fifteen. These folks have been waiting too long already." The use of the word "folks" is a positive sign that Peter is putting on his game face. We can do this.

"Fine," I say. Logan falls into step with us. "The players this morning are the artists who live and work in the co-op, the women's organization that supports the shelter and childcare centre, and the environmentalists."

"MEL?" asks Peter.

"Yes," I say. "Jim Crawford is connected with them, but I haven't yet figured out how or why."

"Bottom line?"

"Everyone wants us to spend more money, which we can't do. Everyone wants something that, if we agree, will disadvantage one of the other groups at the table. Promise nothing. The project is over budget."

"We can't make structural changes to the plan, sir," says Logan, who has done a remarkable job of restraining himself thus far. "We are trying to cut all the frills and stay inside the boundaries of the structural drawings so that we don't have to open them up."

"I hear what you're saying, but we can't send them away empty-handed," says Peter. "First rule of politics."

"I thought that was 'Don't fuck the intern,'" I say under my breath.

"What?" says Peter.

213

"I said, 'I think with luck, they'll turn,'" I say.

"It's not about luck," says Peter and turns his back on us.

Logan and I exchange a glance. I hold up my hand and cross my fingers. Logan presses his palms together, yoga-style, in the centre of his chest. One of his juniors pulls a crucifix from underneath the collar of her shirt and kisses it. The second junior looks astonished, then awkward, and then gives us all a thumbs-up sign. It may not be about luck, but we'll take all the help we can get, and our little group is hedging its bets and covering its collective ass. It may not be the first rule of politics, but it's an important one.

To give him his due, Peter starts strong. He opens his arms to his activist brothers and sisters, and beams as if they are old friends, long separated, now reunited by common cause and felicitous circumstance. "I'm so pleased to have you all here at city hall," he says. "The waterfront development means so much to all of us. Let's roll up our sleeves and get it right."

Everyone nods, and I can see the body language softening around the table. "I've provided everyone with an agenda and a plan of the site," I say. "You have those documents in front of you."

"Thanks, Avery," says Peter. "Now, the first thing I'm going to do is depart from the agenda."

I fight the urge to put my head down on the table.

Peter continues, "I'm going to dispense with opening remarks. You all know how central this project is to my administration and to our city. For the first time in history, we have the political will and the funding to make this long-standing dream come true. I consider all of you to be partners in this great enterprise."

Doris fidgets in her seat. "I thought you were going to dispense with opening remarks," she says, with a nasty edge to her voice.

Glynis puts a hand on her arm. "Would you like some tea?" she stage-whispers.

"No," says Doris. "I would not like tea. I would like to understand why this mayor courts the women's vote with idle promises. I would like to know why our work of the past decade is now under threat. I would like to hear from the mayor why women aren't as special a special-interest group as the environmentalists and the artists. Women are not a minority. We put him in and we can take him out."

There is a brief silence, during which Marshall Westwood leans over to Jim Crawford and says something that sounds like "Where is the aquarium?"

"Well," says Peter, "I want to assure you that women are not a special-interest group in my eyes."

"Exactly," says Doris.

"What I meant to say," says Peter, "is that women's interests are an absolute priority. My administration understands that when women coalesce around a single issue, that issue must be core to our political mandate."

"Do you mean to suggest that women are not coalescing around the waterfront shelter?" says Doris.

"He's not suggesting anything of the kind," I say. "The mayor's office is well aware that the waterfront shelter and childcare centre enjoy widespread support among women." *Those of us in the mayor's office who read the briefing note,* I think.

"But that isn't at issue," says Jim Crawford. "The issue is coexistence. The issue is location, and accommodation of other uses. You can have as many screaming children on the property as you want. But I shouldn't be expected to create art over top of them."

"You are such an arrogant shit," says Doris.

"Let's take the temperature down," says Peter. "There are five buildings in the proposed development. I'm sure we can find a solution."

I pick up the agenda. "Why don't we move to the second item on the agenda, and ask Logan Kim, our lead architect, to walk us through the current plan, so that we are all operating from a common understanding."

"Good idea," says Peter.

Logan fires up his PowerPoint and, with clear and accessible language, a laser pointer, and just the right amount of detail, explains the purpose and design of each of the buildings on the site. He has itemized and colour-coded every space by use: green spaces, public spaces, retail, housing, offices, and institutions. I'm struck again by the ambition of the project, the generosity of the vision, the goodwill that has brought so many diverse interests together to create a public treasure that will serve every citizen in multiple ways. I don't need luck, I remind myself. I *am* lucky. I'm blessed, actually, to be able to do this work, to know that my labour will result in a tangible, permanent benefit to the city.

"Does anyone have any questions?" asks Logan.

"Why am I seeing the artists' studios in Building Two?" asks Jim Crawford. "It was bad enough to be sharing space with children, but now you've cut us off from

216

the light! Your contempt for the artistic community knows no bounds."

"As I said," says Logan, who has, in fact, explained the rationale for this decision several times in the past ten minutes, "all of the buildings get considerable natural light. It is true that Building One is slightly, but only slightly, brighter, since it sits further away from the other buildings. But we feel it is the appropriate location for the family-oriented activities onsite. It has the largest adjacent green space and can absorb multiple uses, in this case a fenced-in playground for the daycare and a community green space for shelter residents."

"Where is the community garden?" says Marshall Westwood. "MEL is recommending that all residential developments include community gardens so that people can be encouraged to engage in sustainable micro-farming."

"The community was consulted," I say. "The consensus was that residents would prefer communal green space in the form of a park, rather than gardening allotments."

"You can have both if you build a green roof," says Marshall.

"A green roof is not in the budget, I'm afraid," I say.

"Outrageous!" says Marshall. "You are ignoring one of the most important environmental technologies of our time!"

"Not ignoring," I say. "Considering at length, and rejecting in the circumstances."

"Why are you even here?" says Doris to Marshall. "This meeting is not about green roofs. It is about the rights of children."

"It is about protecting the precious resources of our planet," says Marshall. "How can you allow temporal budgets to threaten long-term environmental health?"

217

"It is about supporting the work of the creative class," says Jim Crawford. "The key driver of the new economy. Where are the great works of public art in this plan?"

"Several have been commissioned," says Logan. "There are designated spots for additional works as budget becomes available over time."

"Let me understand this," says Marshall. "There is a budget for public art, and not for a green roof?"

"It's not an either-or," says Jim. "Public art is an enhancement to the natural environment. We should be looking at the other publicly funded spaces to see where the budget can be cut. This shelter looks like a five-star hotel."

"Abused women should live in squalor so that you can commune with some pretentious hunk of metal? Are you completely disconnected from reality?" says Doris. "I refuse to treat women's rights like trading cards. This entire meeting is obscene." She points to Peter. "You'll be receiving a formal communication from WAFADASS." She and Glynis march out of the room.

"Well," I say, "obviously, there is more work to be done here. Why don't we all commit to putting our objections on paper, so that the mayor's office can respond to each and every point?"

"Typical," says Jim. "Bury us in bureaucratic process to make us go away." He points his finger at Peter. "You've underestimated us. You can read all about it in our press release." He follows Doris out the door, and Marla follows him, with an apologetic glance in my direction.

"How unfortunate," says Marshall. "However, I would like to take this opportunity to tell you that MEL will bring the full force of its influence to prevent this aquarium from being built. The kidnapping of wildlife is no different from human trafficking."

"What aquarium?" says Peter. "Is there an aquarium?"

"No," I say. "There is not, nor has there ever been, an aquarium in this plan."

"Oh," says Marshall. "Well, that's good, then. Thank you for a helpful meeting. I'll be in touch about the green roof." He rises and leaves the room.

The door swishes shut and those of us still at the table sit in silence for a moment.

"In the event that you didn't capture the full picture in your notes," says Peter, "that was a gong show."

"No argument here," I say.

He shakes his head. "I expect better, Avery. That was not your finest hour."

"No," I say. "It wasn't."

CHAPTER 18

July 2015

I woke to the tickle of Matt's stubble on my cheek.

I rolled toward him and gave him a sleepy kiss. "What time is it?"

"Six," he said. "You made me promise to wake you up."

"I take it back," I said. I opened my eyes. "This campaign is going to kill me. Is it still summer?"

"It is," said Matt. "See?" He raised the blind over our bed so that I could see the sunlight. "Still lots of time."

"I don't know if that's a good thing or a bad thing anymore," I said. We needed every minute of the remaining three months until the October election to work against Roger Wozniak. We had underestimated his tenacity and, frankly, his appeal. He had funding, and a strong team led by his son, and an uncanny knack for bonding with the lowest common denominator. It turned out that there were more voters in the lowest common denominator than you would expect, mathematically. They liked big cars and sprawling properties in the suburbs and all-you-can-eat buffets. They liked everything to be supersized except for government. And consequently, summer had been nothing more than a period of time with more daylight. It was otherwise an irrelevancy, punctuated not at all by patios, cottage weekends, or holidays.

"I don't know either," said Matt.

"I feel terrible about the weekend," I said.

"I know," he said.

"I'm sorry," I said.

He sighed. "I know."

"Are you mad?"

"What would be the point of that?" he asked.

Matt and I were supposed to be spending the weekend at the Inn on the Bay, to make up for the fact that I'd worked every single day for months. We had planned to leave first thing tomorrow, Friday, but Peter had slotted some campaign events into the schedule, and he wanted me there. He hadn't asked me not to go away, but he didn't have to.

"Can I make it up to you?" I asked, sliding a hand under the waistband of his pajama pants and over the curve of his ass.

"I'm not that easy," said Matt.

"You kind of are," I said.

"I kind of am," he agreed.

Our friends who were married talked about "married sex" with affectionate resignation, as if its irregularity and predictability were signifiers of success. And perhaps they were. So many marriages we knew had faltered at the ten-year mark, leaving heartbroken children, financial catastrophe, and permanent disillusionment in the wake of their destruction. I considered myself lucky, in a way, to have escaped marriage with only disillusionment.

"Let me taste you," said Matt, moving down my body.

Sex had never been routine with us. Somehow, we'd

held on to the urgency, the desperation that fell by the wayside in most long-term unions. Maybe it was because our schedules kept us apart, but I liked to think it had to do with our origin story, which was, for me, one of flight and of rescue. "Don't stop," I told him, and after a time I let go with a cry, a different kind of flight.

"Thank you," I whispered, once I could form words again.

"My pleasure," he said, kissing me deeply. I took him inside me and held his gaze as he began to move.

"So beautiful," he said. "You are so beautiful like this."

Afterwards, we lay together, our bodies cooling. One of the things I loved best about Matt was that he genuinely liked to talk after sex. I had told him this was unusual, which he found puzzling. "I'm lying here naked and relaxed with my favourite person," he said once. "Why would I want to sleep?"

"I love this house," I said.

"What brought that on?" said Matt.

"I don't know," I said. "It's an oasis here. It's a shelter from the storm." We'd bought a Victorian row house five years ago, in what our real estate agent told us was an up and coming neighbourhood. We'd only half-believed him then, but sure enough, a couple of years later, a Starbucks had moved in onto our retail strip, along with a few excellent restaurants and a home furnishings store. I loved our patchy lawn and raccoon-tortured garden, I loved our sunny kitchen with inadequate counter space, I loved our stained bathtub with the ornamental feet, and I even loved our gigantic Restoration Hardware bed with matching bedside tables that Matt had insisted we buy.

"I'm glad you feel that way," said Matt, and kissed the top of my head. It was astonishing to me that twelve years had passed since we'd first rented an apartment together. It was strange to remember how much we'd worried about Matt's job then, and whether it would keep us apart; he was still at the same firm all these years later, and a partner. We'd grown into responsible adults together.

But we weren't married, because I didn't want to be.

The truth was that I'd given myself a real scare with Hugh. I had relied on him to provide me with an adult identity, and then resented him for choosing one that didn't suit me. I wouldn't be so irresponsible again. "Adulthood is about taking responsibility for yourself," my therapist had told me in the aftermath, and I had. When I moved in with Matt, it was as an equal partner, with separate bank accounts and every bill split down the middle. Our first apartment wasn't fancy, but I had at least a one-half entitlement to everything in it. This time, I was starting as I intended to finish.

"What do you have on today?" asked Matt.

"I have a lunch with Jenny," I said.

"How long has it been since you last saw her?" he asked.

"Almost a year," I said.

"Are you taking her out to make up for missing her show?"

"Yes," I said. "As a matter of fact, I am." There was another reason for the lunch, too, but I wasn't telling Matt that.

"Be sure to tell her I think her new work is spectacular," said Matt. "I'm saving my pennies. I'd love to own a Jenny Beck."

Jenny had changed her name from Haines to Beck—her mother's birth name—a number of years earlier, but I wasn't used to it. Jenny Beck, establishment artist, was a person I didn't know.

"You went to the opening and I didn't," I said. "You don't need to remind me. I feel guilty enough as it is."

"Occasionally you need reminding," said Matt.

"What's that supposed to mean?" I said.

"It means that saying you feel guilty isn't worth much if you don't change your behaviour," said Matt.

"I'm trying to win an election here," I said.

"Yeah," said Matt. "I'm aware."

"Do you think I want to have no personal life?" I said. "Do you think it gives me pleasure to disappoint people all the time?"

"No," he said. "I don't think that about you. But you need to get some perspective. You won't be any use to Peter if you fall over from exhaustion."

"The Wozniaks are gaining too much ground," I said. "Every day, every event. We can't afford to take a night off. And if Jenny had agreed to invite Peter to the opening, like I asked her to, I could have done both. It was an opportunity for Peter to score some points with the women's community and the artistic community, and she said no."

"I expect that she wanted her first major exhibition in her hometown to be about her and not about her estranged ex-stepbrother," said Matt. "Which, for the record, is fair."

"I'm saying she could have made it easier for me," I said.

"And I'm saying that it's not every day that an artist gets three works featured in a major show at the Art

Gallery of Ontario," said Matt. "So you might want to cut her some slack. Not everything is about you."

"I don't want to talk about it anymore," I said. "I have to get to the office."

Down in the kitchen, I went to open the fridge and saw the invitation to Jenny's opening still stuck to the door with a magnet.

The exhibition was called *The Glass Ceiling*, and it showcased the country's best female artists. There was a strong feminist bent to the selection and organization of the works. The painting on the invitation was one of Jenny's, called *Thanksgiving*.

Like her other recent works, it was an oil portrait, highly realistic, of a woman—Greta, although few would know it. Greta was in a kitchen, her back pressing against a partially opened door. Her anxious face was framed with huge round earrings of bright plastic gemstones. One of the earrings was real—it had been Greta's once—and the other was painted. Jenny's art was famous for its use of found objects or, as the description on the invitation card called them, "artifacts recording women's social history."

Greta's hands, encased in red quilted oven mitts, held a platter upon which sat a turkey. The meat and Greta's face both glistened with moisture. Through the opening behind her, you could see a man seated at the head of the dining room table. He looked dour and impatient. I'd seen that expression many times on Don's face when he felt he'd waited too long for his evening meal. And here it was, recorded for posterity. According to the curator's notes online, the painting exposed the false promise of holidays and celebrations in women's lives.

I took the card off the fridge and threw it in the garbage. I didn't want to look at it anymore.

At the door to the campaign office, I almost collided with an elegant lady in a black linen suit and a silk scarf, her silver hair in a pixie cut.

"Good morning," she said. "I have a meeting with Avery Graham."

"Mrs. Parker?" I said.

"You can call me Lillian," she said. "My nephew, Will Shannon, is very fond of you and your friend Matt." Lillian was obviously not the sort of person who thought the word "partner" should be applied to romantic relationships.

"Will is your nephew?" I said.

"My great-nephew," she said.

"He's a terrific guy," I said.

"He's a rascal," she said, "but a most adorable one. Are you ready to see me?"

"Absolutely," I said. "Follow me."

I led her to the conference room and offered her coffee, which she refused. "I have a few commitments today," she said. "Let's get down to business, if you don't mind. I'm not a delicate flower." Even on five minutes' acquaintance, this seemed an understatement. "What is Peter hoping for from me?"

"We're hoping you might make a donation to the campaign," I said.

"What did you have in mind?" she asked.

I said a number. She didn't flinch. I would have wagered there wasn't much that made Lillian Parker flinch. "I'll consider it," she said.

"Thank you," I said. "We'd also like to be able to rely on you for a public endorsement."

"Oh," said Lillian Parker. "I'm afraid that won't be possible. I never give endorsements."

"You should make an exception for Peter," I said. "I've known him since childhood. He is a superb candidate. He's qualified for the job in every way. He is worthy of your trust."

"My dear," she said, "very few people have that, and none of them are politicians."

"I would trust him with my life," I said.

"Without knowing either of you," she said, "that strikes me as unwise. But I'm not inclined to give anyone that kind of power, and certainly not a man. I'll give the same amount to every candidate with a shot at winning."

"You'll give money to Roger Wozniak?" I said. I was so stunned that I tripped over my words.

"Yes," she said.

"But he's—" I stopped myself. "He doesn't seem like your sort of person."

She laughed. "Oh, you might be surprised, Avery. By me, and by Roger Wozniak. He can be quite charming, in his own way."

"I'll take your word for it," I said.

"You never know, my dear," she said. "About people, or about what the future holds. Life is full of surprises, and it produces enough enemies naturally. I've always taken the view that there is no need to create them on purpose. And that is why I support everyone in an election who asks for my help. So you may tell Mr. Haines that I'll write him a cheque. You may also tell him that whether or not

Roger Wozniak is my sort of person, he asked me for the donation himself."

"I'm sorry," I said. "I didn't think. It won't happen again."

"Don't fret," she said, patting my arm. "I'm not offended. That takes far too much energy at my age. Good luck with all this."

And with that, she was gone.

I spent the rest of the morning preparing for my lunch meeting with Jenny. It wasn't entirely a social call. It was damage control. A junior reporter covering our campaign had uncovered the family connection between Peter and Jenny, and had called her for an interview. She'd declined to comment on Peter's candidacy, she'd said, since she wasn't planning on voting.

The reporter had called the office, and I'd been able to avoid a negative story by explaining that Jenny was planning to be out of the country during the election, which was why she wasn't voting. Then I'd pulled in a few favours to give him access to some high-profile political supporters who didn't usually agree to interviews. But still, with the Wozniaks vacuuming up the right-wing vote, we needed to lock in endorsements from every identifiable group on the left: women, environmentalists, visible minorities, urban activists, writers, food security advocates, and artists of all kinds. Jenny could hurt us if she wanted to. I needed to know if she did.

At the restaurant, Jenny rose from the table and brushed a cool kiss on each of my cheeks. She was, as she had been since childhood, beautiful. "It's been a long time."

"Since last summer, I think," I said. "I don't know where the time goes. The campaign has been nuts, but that's no excuse. I am so sorry, again, for missing the opening. Matt's been raving about it."

"That's fine," she said. "Matt explained that you had an emergency at work. It was nice to see him."

"He's a fan," I said.

She smiled. "It's mutual," she said.

"I popped in to see *The Glass Ceiling* last week," I said. "Congratulations. Your work is the highlight of the show." I knew I was on safe territory here. All of the reviews agreed on this point.

"The art gallery did a nice job, I thought," said Jenny.

"It did," I said.

"I was pleased with the decision to hang all of my paintings together in one room," said Jenny.

"Yes," I said. "It was really powerful. The paintings spoke to each other."

"Which one did you like best?" she asked.

"I'd say it's a toss-up between *Charm* and *Stamp*," I said. The images were available on the art gallery's website, and I'd done my research.

Charm was a portrait of three women having lunch in the 1960s, in Chanel-style suits with tiny hats perched on the stiff waves of their hair. A glittering charm, a real one, dangled from the sleeve of one of the women, a gold Eiffel Tower. The curator's notes explained the work as a commentary on the hidden lives of women, forced to perform according to social norms but simultaneously dreaming of escape. My mother had posed for *Charm*, and it was her favourite. *Stamp*, on the other hand, was a portrait of Jenny's stepfather, Don, sitting at his desk, holding a stamp with a pair of tweezers and examining it with a magnifying glass. A blonde girl sat in a chair against the wall, wearing a bathing suit and holding a rolled towel in her lap. The notes for the painting observed that the girl's agency, depicted as her ability to to go swimming, is constrained by the male figure's attention, or "stamp of approval"; until she receives it, she, like others of her sex, is confined to the margins.

"My mother thinks *Charm* is the best painting anyone has ever done."

Jenny laughed. "It did turn out well," she says. "You can tell Martine that she's a terrific model. She gave me the charm, too."

"She told me," I said. "How's *your* mom doing?"

"She's well," said Jenny. "She's finally talking about retirement."

"That's good," I said. After Greta and Don's drawn-out divorce, Greta had gone back to school and completed a degree in education. Eventually, she'd become a kindergarten teacher. "She deserves a rest."

"She certainly does," said Jenny. "But she worries about money. It's hard to convince her to stop earning."

"Will she sell the cottage?" This had been a burning question on Berry Point for years.

"She did," said Jenny. "At the end of last season, to me. I'm going to build my studio up there."

"Oh," I said. "That's fantastic." I meant it. However tortured our relationship, Jenny belonged at Berry Point.

"So, Avery," said Jenny. "What can I do for you?"

"What do you mean?"

"Why are we here?"

"I wanted to congratulate you."

"And?" said Jenny. "Nothing else?"

"That was the main thing," I said. "Although I thought I'd ask you about the interview you gave about Peter, if it came up."

"And, miraculously, it has," said Jenny. "But I didn't give an interview. I specifically declined to do so, when asked."

"You said you weren't going to vote," I said. The waiter hovered near our table. I waved him off.

Jenny shrugged. "That was true. I'm not going to vote."

"You should!" I said. "It's irresponsible not to vote. Are you saying that you think Roger Wozniak would be a better mayor than Peter would?"

"I'm saying that I'm comfortable letting my fellow citizens decide," she said.

"You can't believe that," I said. "And you certainly shouldn't say it to a reporter!"

"Avery," she said, "I know this will be hard, perhaps even impossible, for you to grasp, but I don't care about this election. At. All."

I took a breath. It had never been a wise strategy to tell Jenny what she could and couldn't do. "Of course, you can do whatever you like," I said. "But Jenny, it's beneath you to be vindictive."

Jenny sighed. "You seem to think that I spend all my time obsessing over Peter," she said. "Nothing could be further from the truth. I'm over Peter. I'm over Don. I'm over the sadness and the disappointment and the regret.

I've done a lot of therapy to get to that point. I've made the choice to put my energy into my art and my mother and my friends. I've let go of the rest."

"Can you promise not to say anything negative about Peter in the press?" I said.

"Yes," said Jenny. "Is that what you came for?"

"No," I said. "I came to tell you how much I liked the exhibit."

"You didn't see it," said Jenny.

"Of course I did," I said.

"No," said Jenny. "You didn't. And I know that because my pictures were all hanging in different rooms."

"Oh God," I said. Shame washed through me. "I'm sorry. I'm so sorry, Jenny. I was going to see the show. I was. I swear."

"I'm not angry," said Jenny. "But I do have another appointment." She rose.

"Jenny, sit down," I said. "We haven't even ordered! Please. Let's talk this through."

Jenny shook her head. "It's time to let this go, too," she said.

It's early when all the phones in the house start ringing. The landline, both of my cellphones (personal and work), and even more ominously, Matt's cellphone as well.

"Jesus Christ," says Matt. "You need a new job."

He picks up his phone and leaves the room while I answer the landline. It's Bonnie. "Have you seen the news?" she says.

"It's five o'clock in the morning, Bonnie," I say. "No, I haven't."

"Turn on the television and meet Peter at the office as soon as you can get there," she says. I look at my phone and see two missed calls, both from Aidan Clarke, everyone's favourite city beat reporter.

Matt's returned to the bedroom and is fiddling with the remotes. "That was Will. There's a problem at your office."

"Mayor Peter Haines was questioned by police last night in connection with an alleged prostitution ring," says the voice of the news anchor.

"What the *fuck*!" I shout, kicking off the covers and half-falling out of bed.

"We go now to Aidan Clarke, our city hall reporter, for details on the incident," says the news anchor. "Aidan?"

"Thank you, Pam," says Aidan. "We don't have many details on this story as yet, but I can confirm that the mayor, Peter Haines, spent several hours at police head-quarters in the early hours of this morning. We are told that he is not under arrest and has been cooperating fully with police inquiries relating to an alleged prostitution ring. The mayor exited the building several minutes ago, and made no comment to reporters. We will be following up on this story throughout the day and will provide you with updates as soon as they are available."

The footage shows Peter, tousled and furious, leaving police headquarters, where only last week he stood at a podium and announced a new project to redirect at-risk youth away from gang activity, and getting into a car with tinted windows.

"Will said that it has something to do with one of your developers," says Matt. "Adam Rothstein?"

"Rothman," I say. "What about him? And why would Will know anything about this? Why would he know about it before I did? Why didn't Peter call me hours ago?"

"I don't know anything more than I just told you," says Matt. "As for Will, he's crazy connected and knows everything, and his family owns some piece of a news outlet, and he doesn't sleep much. And as for Peter, you can probably guess why he didn't call you better than I can."

"I'm his chief of staff," I say, throwing on clothes. "He tells me everything. He trusts me."

"Avery," says Matt. He puts a hand on each of my

shoulders, halting my frantic activity for a moment. "Listen to me. This is important. Whatever Peter has done—"

"Which may be nothing," I say.

"—it isn't your fault. You aren't Peter's keeper."

"I am his keeper," I say. "That's exactly what I am. That's my job."

"You might want to rethink that," says Matt. "But for now, I'm telling you that Peter is going to be in damage-control mode. You need to have your wits about you. You don't want to get caught in the crossfire."

"I don't even know what you're saying right now," I say. "I need to get to the office and figure out what's going on."

"I'll drive you," he says.

We head out into the semi-darkness. It's surprisingly warm already, and the sun is coming up. The streets are empty. But not at city hall. At city hall there are media trucks setting up tents and spotlights.

"My God," I say.

"Call Bonnie and tell her to have security let you in the door in the laneway," says Matt.

I do. We pull into the lane and wait until a crack of light appears as the security door opens. Matt flashes his headlights as if we are in a spy movie. "Wait," he says as I unbuckle my seat belt.

I turn to him, distracted, already inside the building in my mind.

"When this is over, I'll still be here," he says. "Remember that. I'm the one who's going to be here."

"Hopefully, we'll all still be here," I say.

Matt pats my hand. "Good luck in there," he says.

I slip into the darkened lobby and follow the security guard up to the mayor's office.

"You're here," says Bonnie.

"Why didn't you call me earlier?"

"It was Peter's decision not to," says Bonnie. She doesn't meet my eye.

"What is going on, exactly?"

"There was a misunderstanding. We are hopeful that it will all be resolved quickly."

"What sort of misunderstanding?"

"Peter had dinner last night with Mr. Rothman at his private club, at Mr. Rothman's request. It was a business dinner. Over the course of the meal, police arrived at the club and began arresting some of the patrons."

"What sort of club are we talking about here?"

"A gentleman's club," says Bonnie.

"Are we talking about a sex club?" I say.

"No," says Peter from behind me. I jump.

"Let's go into your office," I say.

I sit down on the couch and wait for Peter to close the door. It feels wrong to have this conversation across the mayor's desk, as if this were official business. Peter sits down in an armchair and waits for me to speak.

"Tell me what I need to know," I say.

"Adam invited me for dinner to discuss the water-front. He suggested that we meet at his club. We met in the dining room. We had a private booth. The prime rib was excellent."

"Peter," I say. "Spare me the menu, please."

"Around ten o'clock, there was a commotion at the entrance. We were in the back of the restaurant, so it was hard to see exactly what was happening. Adam got up to investigate and he didn't come back. I stayed in the booth. A few minutes later, an officer approached my table and advised me that a number of guests were being arrested in connection with criminal activities occurring in the building. I was asked to come to headquarters voluntarily and assist with police inquiries. I did."

"What were the other activities?"

"It now appears that the club offered other amenities."

"Sexual amenities?"

"Apparently," says Peter. "I have no direct knowledge about that."

"You were in the wrong place at the wrong time?"

"Yes," says Peter.

"Is that what happened with Melanie, too?"

"Sarcasm doesn't suit you, Avery," says Peter.

"Are you kidding me, Peter?" I say. "I am killing myself trying to help you create your legacy, and you, as it turns out, are fucking interns and having dinner at sex clubs. Sorry, I mean *accidentally* having dinner at sex clubs. I'm in the office at the crack of dawn trying to figure out how a man as smart as you are has managed to wade into so much shit. I'm entitled to a little sarcasm."

Peter moves over to sit beside me on the couch. "I'm sorry, Avery. This is an incredibly unpleasant situation, and I hate that you've been dragged into it."

"Peter," I say. I sound tired, and wary. "This could hurt us."

"I know," he says. "And I know you're angry. But I need your help."

There's a sharp knock at the door. Bonnie steps in

without waiting for Peter to answer. This is a day full of dark portents, it seems.

"There's a lawsuit coming," she says.

"From the club?" I say. "That's ridiculous."

"Not from the club," says Bonnie. "From Melanie Christie. We got a courtesy call just now. The lawyer is making a statement at nine o'clock. I got the sense, though, that we weren't the only people who received advance notice."

"Wrongful dismissal?" says Peter.

"Sexual harassment," says Bonnie. "And wrongful dismissal, although that seems like a minor point in the scheme of things." She looks at me. "You're named in the lawsuit too, by the way."

I can't sit here any longer. "I'm going to my office," I say. "Tell me immediately if anyone calls from the press, or serves us with documents, or if the police show up here, or anything else remotely dramatic happens. Otherwise, please leave me alone for half an hour. In the meantime, Peter, figure out what lawyer we need and call him. I'm working on the PR strategy."

Bonnie gives me exactly fifteen minutes, and then my phone starts ringing.

"A friend to women?" says Doris Renaud, her voice crackling with rage over the phone. I hold it away from my ear. "I'm holding you responsible for what happened to this innocent young intern. Not to mention that the mayor was found in a *sex club* last night. You said women could trust Peter Haines. You must have known that he was a wolf in sheep's clothing. It's disgusting."

"The mayor will be addressing the allegations this

afternoon," I say. "Please wait to hear from him before you pass judgment."

"That ship has sailed," says Doris. "The man is a sexual predator. The idea, the *idea*, that WAFADASS put its support behind him makes me sick to my stomach. Our women's shelter was nothing more than a convenient disguise for him. Feminism is a sword, not a shield. Peter Haines used us, and he'll pay the price."

"Doris, please," I say. "Peter has a strong record on women's issues. No one is perfect, but he has been a genuine supporter of the shelter project from day one."

"He is a betrayer," she says. "He has betrayed his wife, and a young woman in your office who was in a position of great vulnerability. His so-called record is irrelevant."

"With respect, Doris, I disagree," I say.

"I can see that you have had the wool pulled over your eyes as well, and I am sorry for it," says Doris. "But WAFADASS is done with this administration. I recognize the soul within you. Namaste."

"Okay, bye," I say.

Five minutes later, Marshall Westwood calls.

"We were pleased to learn that, unlike so many other waterfront projects, your city has wisely rejected the proposal for an aquarium."

An aquarium was never proposed at all, but Marshall doesn't need to know this. I'm thrilled to be talking about something other than Peter's sex life. What a difference a day makes. "We felt that it wouldn't send the right message," I say.

"Exactly," says Marshall. "I wish more city officials

understood that an aquarium is a prison, not an entertainment. Someday, in a more enlightened age, we will judge people who visit aquariums the way we now judge people who toured lunatic asylums for fun back in the eighteenth century."

"Could be," I say. "In any event, Mayor Haines stands with MEL on the aquarium issue."

"We have photographic evidence of Mr. Wozniak visiting aquariums in both Baltimore and Chicago," says Marshall. "Confidentially, when asked by an undercover MEL operative, Mr. Wozniak said that he thought an aquarium would be 'a great idea' for the city."

"I can't say I'm surprised," I say.

"I'm calling to let you know that MEL will not be taking a position on the current scandal in the mayor's office," says Marshall.

"Thank you for letting me know," I say.

"Good luck," he says.

When the phone rings a few minutes later, it's exactly the person I'm expecting.

"I want the mayor to know that he has the full support of ArtCo," says Jim Crawford.

"I'm delighted to hear that," I say.

"Naturally, there are conditions," says Jim.

"There usually are," I say.

"We will need to see the studios moved back to Building One, and the daycare centre and the shelter moved to Building Two. Also, we would like to see an increase in the number of rent-controlled spaces for artists."

"What kind of increase?" I ask.

"At least thirty percent," says Jim.

"Thirty percent," I repeat. "Anything else?"

242

"We would like to see members of the ArtCo receive special consideration in the selection process for the public sculpture competition."

"We've announced that it will be an international competition," I say.

"We are aware of that," says Jim. "But we are taking the position that our members produce work of international quality and they should have pride of place on the city's waterfront."

"That may be a bridge too far, Jim," I say, in what I hope is a mild tone of voice.

"That's the bridge I'll be taking over to the Wozniak camp if I don't see some good faith from the mayor," says Jim, and hangs up the phone.

"Who does that?" I say out loud in my office. "Who issues a threat and hangs up the phone?"

"People do that all the time," says Bonnie from the doorway. "You'd be surprised." She hands me a faxed press release. "Another quarter heard from," she says.

"Judy Mendelson?" I say, scanning the document. "I thought she was in and out of consciousness."

"Well," says Bonnie, "she woke up long enough to throw Peter to the wolves."

"Peter and the wolves," I say. "Funny." Although it really isn't. "According to Doris Renaud, he *is* the wolf."

Bonnie shakes her head. "Beware of fair-weather friends," she says. "I thought the law business was bad. It was nothing compared to politics."

"This must be hard on you," I say.

"No," says Bonnie. "It's stressful, and it's busy. It isn't hard."

"I mean emotionally," I say. "Because you and Peter have worked together for so long."

"Avery," she says, "unlike you, I don't invest emotionally in my work. I have relationships outside the office. Peter treats me with respect and he pays me more than anyone else will pay me to do the same job. I have no other expectations of him. Peter and I aren't friends. We're colleagues." She looks at the press release from Judy Mendelson and shakes her head. "I told Peter those flowers we sent were too expensive," she says.

CHAPTER 20

Thursday, July 20, 2017, and September 2001

"You need some sleep," says Matt. It's seven o'clock in the morning. I can hear in his voice that he's just woken up. I feel a wave of love and relief to know, however annoyed he might be with me right now, his first coherent thought this morning is for me.

"I know," I say into the phone. I arch back in my chair and stretch my lower back. "I'm too stressed and there's too much to do."

I've never been the kind of person to pull all-nighters. For all my artistic proclivities, I'm an advance planner at heart. I remember each and every time I watched the sun come up: the overnight with Tara and Jenny when we were ten that resulted in a year-long sleepover ban; the first and only attempt to write a university essay in one day; the day before the mayoral election; and today. I have a healthy respect for the power of sleep, both to heal and to completely undo me in its absence. On the street last week, I heard a woman say to her friend, "Your skin looks amazing. Have you had Botox?" And the second woman laughed and said, "No, I'm taking a lot of naps." I believed it.

"What's happening?" asks Matt. "Do you need me to come and bring you some food?"

"I don't even know what's happening," I say. "I've been in meetings all night with the PR people. Now they're in with Peter and I'm responding to email from half the city and trying to figure out what we tell the staff when they come in at nine. We're waiting for polling data following yesterday's statement."

"Ah," says Matt.

"You thought he did well, right?" I say. We've already had this conversation, twice, since Peter took the podium outside city hall late yesterday afternoon. He was perfectly on message. The PR people are pleased.

"I thought it was extremely smooth," says Matt.

"I thought it was brilliant," I say. "He explained in detail how he ended up at Adam's club, he was generous to Melanie without getting drawn into the specifics of the lawsuit, he talked about his family and how much he loves them, and he still managed to convey his vision for the city!"

"Yes, he did," said Matt. "He was incredibly prepared. You did a fantastic job."

I try again. "I thought he displayed real gravitas," I say. "He looked like a person of substance and power. He looked trustworthy."

"Avery," says Matt. "I'm only prepared to go so far with this for you. He didn't take many questions, and I don't think we've heard the whole story here."

"But you believed him, right?" I say.

"Why is that so important to you?" says Matt.

"Because you're smart and affluent and left-wing and fall squarely into our voter demographic," I say.

"Any other reason?"

"Because I trust you," I say. "And I'm scared."

I hear Matt take a long breath, in and out. "Avery," he says, "I'm waiting for the other shoe to drop."

"I don't know how to help him."

"Maybe that's the wrong question."

"It's the right question for today." Bonnie appears in the doorway. "I have to go," I say. "I'll call you later."

"Peter needs to see you," says Bonnie. I start to collect up all my documents and binders. "Leave them," says Bonnie. "There's a new development."

The outer office is quieter than it has been in the past twenty-four hours. It should be reassuring, this sudden absence of PR people with serious faces milling about, but the unexplained change has a menacing quality. Is it a sign of something? We are in a world now where every small detail is pregnant with meaning, because our powerlessness has made us superstitious. I hope that the PR people are merely locked in a conference room to work on yet another draft, but the silence feels larger than that.

Bonnie says, "He's waiting."

I enter Peter's office and find him alone. "Close the door," he says. I do.

"How are you?" I say.

"I've been better," he says.

I brace myself. "What is it?"

"I just had a call from Aidan Clarke," says Peter. "He's working on a story about Adam Rothman and he wanted my comments. He wondered if I knew that Adam owns the numbered company that owns the sex club attached to the restaurant."

"Oh my God," I say. I feel weak. "Adam is part of the prostitution ring."

"According to Aidan Clarke, Adam is at the centre of the prostitution ring."

"Shit," I say. "Shit, shit, shit."

"The fact is, Avery, there aren't many people in life who you can trust," says Peter.

"That's true," I say. We sit in rare silence. Peter is a talker, ordinarily. Sometimes I have to tell him to stop talking so that I can catch up. But we're in the trenches now, anticipating the next rocket, and being so close to the edge of disaster has made him pensive.

Perhaps it is the lack of sleep, but I find my mind drifting. What constitutes trust, anyway? Is it the willingness to let someone see you for who you really are? And if so, have I ever trusted anyone? Peter? Matt? Not Hugh, certainly.

And who is that person, the one I really am? I've been so many different selves. Is your true self the one you are born into, or the one you cultivate and mould? Is it the self in which you invest the most belief? Is it the self you most want to be? I was once Avery the backpack-toting citizen of the world, Avery the aspiring novelist, and Avery the young professor's wife. And then I was Avery the law student, who celebrated the beauty of a well-reasoned argument and who preferred numbered paragraphs to emotionally charged prose. And then Avery the young law partner, faking it until she made it, willing herself to become the competent professional that Peter told her she was. And Avery the chief of staff, always prepared, never flustered, the woman behind the great man. And finally, Avery the modern not-wife, thriving in a partnership of true equals, neither needing nor wanting the assurance of marriage, secure in the solidity of a life built on shared objectives and desires. Were any of these selves true, really? Were any of them more than wishful thinking on my part, or evidence of the adaptive genius of humans more generally?

"I thought you were one of those people," says Peter, jarring me into the present.

"Did you say you *thought* I was one of those people?" I say. "I *am* one of those people."

"Apparently not," says Peter. "I am neck-deep in shit here, Avery, and you're the one who put me here."

"Are you crazy?" I say.

Peter waves a sheaf of paper at me. "Have you read Melanie's claim? We wouldn't be in this situation but for you. There are pages here outlining the toxic work environment in this office. There are full paragraphs about how you belittled her, shunted her aside, rejected her ideas, screamed at her."

"I never screamed at her," I say.

"I heard you fire her," says Peter. "My ears are still ringing."

"This is insane," I say. "Melanie is suing us because you fucked her, Peter, not because I wasn't the big sister she wanted."

"Your expression is telling," says Peter.

"Yes, Peter, I dislike the idea of you having sex with an intern in the office," I say. "It's gross. It's beneath you. It makes me sick."

"The PR people told me that you were jealous. I shut them down. I said, 'I've known Avery since childhood.' I said, 'She doesn't have a petty bone in her body. She puts the collective ahead of her own needs. She's all about the larger vision.' But I can see now that they were right. You've never really supported me in the way I thought you did."

"What are you saying?" I say. "My whole life is about supporting you. I changed careers for you, twice. I've put you first, ahead of any of the demands of my personal life, more times than I can count. I'm all in. We built this together!"

"And what have we built, Avery? We haven't built anything. We have a plan, that's all, a brilliant plan that could have transformed the city and now may never be realized because of your incompetence."

"My incompetence?" I'm whispering.

"Who handled the waterfront file for me? Who reviewed the bids? Who sat on all the committees? Who attended the meetings? Who wrote the briefing notes? Who sat here and assured me that we had the best possible team? That was you, Avery."

"Are you saying I should have known about Adam's secret business interests?"

"I'm saying that I've been blinded by my family feelings for you. You lacked the experience to be chief of staff, and my error was in giving you a level of responsibility that you clearly couldn't handle. The waterfront file is a mess. The major developer is an alleged criminal, and, despite your assurances to the contrary, none of our stakeholders support the plan. That meeting I attended yesterday was a joke."

"Peter, you have told me explicitly that you have no interest whatsoever in speaking to the stakeholders on the waterfront file. I've asked you repeatedly to engage, and you've always had a meeting with a developer or a street fair or, I gather, a rendezvous with an intern that was more important. That is not my fault."

"The more I hear, the more inclined I am to agree with the advice of our PR firm. You're a major liability."

"How could you say that to me?" I say. The air is thin in the room. "You can't believe that. You *know* me."

"I thought I knew you," says Peter. "But it turns out I don't know you at all. You're fired. You have ten minutes to get your personal belongings. Security will escort you to your desk and out of the building."

I hadn't expected to live in Toronto again after moving to New York. Certainly, I'd never imagined arriving in town with the urge to fall on my knees and kiss the stained concrete platform in Union Station. But here we were, displaced and disoriented, with our parents crying and holding us close.

"I'll call you tomorrow," I said to Matt as our parents pulled us toward the exits.

When I did, I said, "How do you feel about going to the cottage with me?"

"What's at the cottage?"

"Absolutely nothing."

"Perfect."

My mother, having had twenty-four hours to examine me, had been concerned. "You're peaky," she'd said.

"That's hardly surprising in the circumstances, Mom."

"You need fresh air," she'd said.

"I'll go for a walk later."

"Not city air," my mother had declared. "Cottage air." My mother believed that most psychological ills could be cured with a trip north for a dose of pine and lake water.

I doubted, frankly, that northern air, however fresh, could cure what ailed me. But I was keen to escape my mother's scrutiny. She hadn't asked me about Hugh yet, but it was only a matter of time, and I didn't want to talk about him.

Matt picked me up early the next morning. It was a strange, mostly silent, drive. We were exhausted and agitated. There was an intimacy to our wordlessness; we were long past small talk. But the conversations that lay ahead of us needed to wait until we could touch each other again.

Three long hours later, we arrived. I bolted out of the car and unlocked the door to the cottage while Matt unloaded the bags.

"We're here!" I said, walking into the kitchen. "What would you like to do first? We could go out in the canoe if you want. Or maybe we should run out to the store for some groceries? Are you hungry? Let me give you a tour of the—"

Suddenly Matt's mouth was on mine and his hands were everywhere, and he spun me around and up against the refrigerator. His lips moved down the side of my neck and up again, his thumbs teasing my nipples. I gasped and he answered with a deep, wet kiss that curled my toes, sliding his hands down my back and cupping my ass.

"Matt," I said. The kiss softened then, and Matt pulled away.

"Jesus Christ, Avery," he said, resting his head on my shoulder.

"Don't stop," I said. I tucked my fingers into the waistband of his jeans and flicked the top button open.

"I wasn't going to," he said. We kissed again. He said, "Were you going to give me a tour?"

"Let's start upstairs," I said.

"Let's," he said.

I held out my hand and he took it. I led him upstairs to my childhood bedroom. The Grandma Moses print was still on the wall, and the rag rug was still on the floor, and *Anne of Green Gables* was still on the bookshelf. And my body still knew how to find pleasure in the body of another, and to give it, and I was grateful.

Matt loved me. He told me so in bed, inside me. He told me as I fell asleep, curled against him. He told me while he fed me marshmallows that he'd roasted over the fire he'd made. He told me while we sat in the dark and looked at the stars, and I pointed out the constellations, just like my dad taught me to do. I kissed him when he said it, and asked him to be patient with me. I didn't want to break any more promises. I didn't want to pretend to be sure if I wasn't. He said he could live with that for now.

So we didn't talk about our future, but we talked about Matt's. He'd had a call from his mentor, Will, who was safe but shattered. The firm was in chaos, he told Matt. There was talk of a hiring freeze, and of layoff packages for associates who hadn't even started yet. Office space was suddenly scarce, and expensive. Will thought he could protect Matt, if that was what Matt wanted him to do. Matt asked for a few days to think about his options.

He had his bar materials with him, but a week into our stay, Matt hadn't cracked a book.

"Are you going to study?" I asked him.

"Are you going to call Hugh?"

I put up my hands. "It wasn't a suggestion," I said. "Just a question."

"Sorry," he said. "Sorry." He pulled me into a hug.

"It's okay," I said. "It's stressful. I know. You don't have to make any decisions today."

"We can't hide out forever, Avery," he said. "We need to make some kind of move soon. The temperature's dropping, for starters. In a couple of weeks, it'll be too cold to stay here."

"Did you hear something?" I said.

He laughed. "That was so transparent, it was sad."

"No, really," I said. "I think someone's here."

I heard a car door slam then, and a familiar voice calling. "Avery? You decent?"

"Who the hell is that?" said Matt.

I smiled. "An old friend," I said.

I went to the door, and there was Peter, coming down the path. I threw open the door and ran to meet him. "Peter!" I said. "What are you doing here?"

Peter scooped me up and swung me around. "Not so big now, are you, New York?" he said.

"I'm so happy to see you," I said. "But why are you here?"

"I have a client in Bracebridge," he said. "He's been bugging me to come up all summer and tour his manufacturing plant. And so I called your mom to see if she wanted me to check on the place while I was in the neighbourhood, and she told me that you were holed up here doing some sort of survivalist thing. So I came to see for myself. And this must be your law student friend?" His eyes tracked over my shoulder.

"Matt Nathanson," said Matt, coming around my side and holding out his hand. "And you are?" It would have been hard to miss the protective tone in his voice.

"This is Peter Haines," I said. "That's his family's place down there." I pointed vaguely in the direction of the Haines's cottage. "Sorry," I said to Peter. "It *was* your place, I mean."

"*C'est la vie*," said Peter. He looked at Matt. "Nice to meet you," he said. "Thanks for taking care of Avery for us."

"I can take care of myself, as you know perfectly well," I said, while Matt said, at the same time, "It's my pleasure."

"Hmm," said Peter. "Interesting. Do you have a drink for a thirsty traveller?"

"Come in," I said. "You still a G and T man?"

"Yes," said Peter. "Are you still a rum and Diet Coke girl?"

"No," I said.

"Interesting," said Matt.

"Peter's a lawyer," I told Matt as we settled in the living room with drinks.

"Guilty as charged," said Peter. "Martine mentioned that you're studying for the New York bar, Matt."

"I'm supposed to be studying," said Matt. "Candidly, I'm having some second thoughts about going back to New York."

I was stunned that Matt was confiding in Peter; it was as if "lawyer" were a secret password. But I thought it would be good for Matt to open up to a professional colleague, so I made a conscious effort not to be hurt.

"That's hardly surprising in the circumstances," said Peter. "And it's going to take more than a few weeks for the WTC firms to bounce back. No one will blame you if you decide that you want to change course. You may find that your firm is even relieved to have one less person to deal with."

"Do you think so?" asked Matt. "It won't hurt my reputation?"

"I'm positive," said Peter. "I was on the phone with three top-tier firms last week. They're all reeling, no matter what they say publicly."

"I was thinking that I might look for a job in Toronto," said Matt.

"What?" I said. "That is a huge decision, Matt. You need to take some serious time with that one."

"Say the word and I'll make some calls for you," said Peter.

"Really?" said Matt.

"Really," said Peter. "Avery and I go back a long way. And anyway, you're obviously a good influence on her. I've been telling her to go to law school for years."

"I'm not going to law school, Peter," I said.

"And I'm not going to say I told you so when you do," said Peter. "So, what are we having for dinner?"

"Matt," I say into the phone. "Matt, he fired me."

"That son of a bitch," says Matt. "That fucker. I knew he would find a way to turn this on you. Where are you?"

"I'm in a bathroom in the lobby at city hall," I say. "Security tried to escort me out of the building, but there are reporters outside. I said it was a public building and I wouldn't go outside."

"You did the right thing," he says. "I'm coming to get you. Go and stand by the door to the laneway. I'm fifteen minutes away."

"He fired me," I say. "He said—" I stop. I find I can't breathe.

"Breathe," says Matt. "Just breathe, Avery. You can tell me all about it in the car. All you need to do now is get yourself to the door and wait for me. Can you do that?"

"Yes," I say. I'm cold suddenly. My teeth are chattering. I wonder if the air conditioning is jacked up too high in the building, and if I should call someone in Facilities about that, and then I remember that it's none of my business anymore. My chest hurts, too, as though I've strained a muscle. I couldn't have, though. My cardboard box is light. In the end, there wasn't much to put inside it: three framed photos, one of me with Tara and Jenny, one of me with Matt, and one of me with Peter on election night; a coffee mug from the campaign; a small vase from my mother; an extra cardigan; and a pair of inoffensive black heels.

I sit for a while longer in the safety of my bathroom stall with my box on my lap. I'd rather be here than out in the foyer. I hear the door open and close, see shoes come and go from the neighbouring stalls, hear the private sounds of various bodies doing what bodies do in bathrooms. I watch the minutes tick by.

A voice says, "Can you believe it? I met her once at a town hall. She seemed normal, not like some incompetent psycho-bitch."

"You never know," says another woman. "Still waters and all that. They're saying she took bribes in return for recommending bids to the mayor."

"Who can't keep his pants on, apparently," says the first woman.

"Which makes him different from every other male politician how?" says the second woman.

The first woman laughs. "I feel kind of sorry for her. Her career is over. Chief of staff one day, punch line the next. Brutal."

"That's politics," says the second woman. "That's why I stay out of it. I take my holidays and accumulate my pension and keep my head down. And I bet you any money that Avery Graham is wishing she'd done the same thing."

The door swishes and it's quiet again. I'm frozen. I know Matt must be waiting but I can't seem to stand up. I curl over my box.

"Avery," says Matt. "Are you in here?"

"You can't be in here," I say. "It's the women's washroom."

His voice is gentle. "Don't worry about that," he says.

"How did you find me?" I say.

"You told me where you were when you called. I waited outside and then came looking for you."

I open the stall door cautiously. "Is anyone else here?"

"No," he says. "I put a pylon in front of the door."

"Where did you find a pylon?"

"I'm resourceful," he says, taking the box from me and putting it down on the floor. "Avery," he says. "I'm going to get you out of here and into the car, but you need to know that there are reporters in the lobby looking for you."

"Oh my God," I say.

"I'm going to take the box, and you're going to hold on to my arm and not talk to anyone. Got it?"

"Yes."

"Ready?"

"Yes."

"Here we go," he says and we walk out.

"There she is," I hear, and there are bright lights everywhere that hurt my eyes, and bodies pushing in on me, and everyone yelling horrible, horrible things.

"What do you know about Adam Rothman's sex club, Avery?"

"What do you have to say about Melanie Christie's allegation that you're the worst boss of all time?"

"Were you involved with Adam Rothman?"

"Is it true that you called Melanie Christie a slut in front of the entire staff?"

"Did you take bribes from Adam Rothman, Avery?"

And I hold on to Matt's arm as if the world is ending and let him lead me away from the life I knew.

CHAPTER 21

Thursday, July 20, 2017, and July 1989

We are on the highway, driving north again. Having made a brief stop at the house to pack some bags, we've left town for the cottage. Matt has taken care of everything. I am overwhelmingly tired. In the car, I close my eyes, drift off to sleep, and wake up with a jolt an hour later, Matt's hand on my knee.

"It was a dream," he says.

"No," I say. "It wasn't."

He glances over. "You called out in your sleep," he says.

"Oh," I say. "Right."

"We'll be there in another half hour or so," he says. "Close your eyes again if that's what you want to do. I don't mind."

I adjust myself in my seat. "No," I say. "I want to be awake."

We are off the main highway, well into the country, and sailing past fields with rolls of hay, and small, isolated houses where I imagine people living smaller, simpler lives. But perhaps they don't. Perhaps no one does.

"I don't know who I'm supposed to be," I say.

"You're in shock," says Matt. "You're exactly who you were yesterday."

"No," I say. "I'm not."

We pass the general store and turn. "Do they still rent movies there?" I ask.

"I don't know," says Matt. "It's been a long time since we did that."

"Are you getting sick of rescuing me from my own stupidity?" I ask.

"You didn't do this, Avery," says Matt. "Peter did this. And I'm not rescuing you. I'm helping you. That's what people do when they love each other. Okay?"

"Okay," I say.

We drive onto the property and park on the field. My mother appears first, wrapping me in her arms as soon as I step out of the car. "Oh my darling," she says. "My poor baby."

When I step back from my mother's embrace, Tara pulls me into a fierce hug. "Asshole," she says. "Not you."

I laugh, a weak effort, but a laugh nonetheless.

I feel a hand on my arm. Jenny says, "I'm so sorry this happened to you."

I shrug. "You saw it coming," I say.

"I wish I'd been wrong," she says.

"I'm declaring cocktail hour," says Matt.

"You are such a useful man to have around," says my mother.

"I'll take the bags up," says Matt. "And then I'll make the drinks. You guys relax."

Matt and my mother head into the cottage, and the three of us are left standing in the clearing.

"Shall we go and sit on the verandah?" asks Tara.

I'm restless from the drive. I want to walk. I want a distraction. "You know what?" I say. "I want to see Jenny's studio."

"I . . . okay," says Jenny. "Of course. Come on. I'll show you."

"I'll see if Martine needs help," says Tara. "See you in a few minutes."

Jenny leads me down the path to her cottage. Where the tool shed once stood, there's now a cabin, with large windows and a skylight. Jenny punches in a security code and opens the door. She looks apologetic. "Insurance," she says.

We enter.

On wall is a painting I recognize from the news coverage. But *Stamp* is larger than I realized, and more potent. There is a photographic realism to the figures, at once startlingly contemporary and hearkening back to the Dutch portrait masters. It's the complexity of the emotional states that is most arresting, though: the man's total reverence, even love, for the object of his attention, the stamp, and the girl's boredom, disappointment, and hope, are all somehow present in the picture.

"It's unbelievable," I say. "It's extraordinary. Why is it here? It should be in a museum."

"It will be," says Jenny. "There are a few institutions interested in it. But it's been on tour for a couple of years, and I wanted some time with it before it found a permanent home. My agent wants to do an auction in September."

"It's Don's Penny Black," I say, stepping closer to the painting. "He's holding his Penny Black."

Jenny looks pleased. "You remember," she says.

"It was the jewel of his collection," I say. "I must have heard him say that a thousand times. You stuck the real thing in your painting?"

"It was mine," says Jenny. "And that was what I wanted to do with it."

"I'd call it a heroic end," I say.

"Let me show you one other thing," says Jenny. She leads me over to the far wall, where a small painting is hanging. "This one wasn't in the show," she says. "It was the first of the series, but it isn't for sale. This one is mine."

The painting shows two girls in the water, near a dock where a third girl sunbathes in a yellow bikini. Their hair is slicked away from their faces, and droplets of water shimmer on their faces and arms, which are the only parts of them that are visible above the surface of the lake. The girls are looking intently at an object clutched in the fingertips of one.

"No way," I say. "Is it the piece we found that day?"

"The very one," says Jenny.

I move closer. "What is it called?"

"It's called *Shard*," she says.

And with that, fragments of memory appear, like found objects on the lakebed, watery and indistinct until they are raised up into the light.

I don't want to be at the cottage. I don't want to be anywhere. I stay in my room and read books, mostly. I won't go near the dock. I hate the sound of bodies hitting the water.

We haven't been here this summer, not since the accident. We've been home, in the city. I'm spending time with a therapist named Kaye, who wants me to talk about my feelings. I want to be left alone.

My mother's grief is raw and terrifying. I hear her sobbing at night and I bury my head under the covers to block the sound. Ethan is mercifully silent. I've barely heard him speak since the funeral.

But Kerry has persuaded Mom that we need to get some country air. She is worried about us, and wants to have us here so she can make a fuss over us. I think she is being selfish. If she's so worried, why doesn't she come and see us at home? Mom says that Kerry is right, that we need a change of scenery, so we've come up for a week.

Jenny and Tara are here every morning to see if I want to leave the house. I don't. Their efforts are flagging day by day. I can wait them out.

One afternoon, Greta bursts into the kitchen. Her eyes are red and streaming. "Where is your mother?" she asks.

"In the garden," I say. "Around the side of the house."

She goes back out the way she came in, and I hear my mother's voice. In a few minutes, they both return, my mother looking more purposeful than I've seen her in weeks.

"Avery, honey," says my mother. "The grown-ups need some private time. Could you go out for a little while?"

I want to argue, but I don't. I've never seen Greta so upset. I step out onto the lawn and linger for a minute, listening.

My mother says, "Are you sure he's made up his mind? It's a huge transition for him, having Peter in his life again. Trust me, Greta, it's not a time to make these kinds of decisions."

Greta sobs. "He promised me he would adopt her. How could he do this to me? How could he do it to her? How can I stay with him after this?"

"Does she know?" says my mother. "Does Jenny know that he won't adopt her now?"

"I think she heard us fighting," says Greta. "I don't know what she knows. I can't find her. God, Martine. I wish Peter had—"

"Shhh," says my mother. "I think we have an audience." She appears at the door. "Avery," she says, "Were you listening to our conversation?"

"No," I say.

"I'm glad," says my mother. "Because it is Greta's private business and none of yours. Do you understand?"

"Yes," I say.

"Good," says my mother. "Now go for a walk, please."

I head into the woods, following one of the trails that lead up to the ridge where the berry bushes are dense with fruit. I climb higher, my breath noisy in my ears. I'm surprised to find myself winded. I'm out of shape, and I'm relieved no one is here to notice.

There is a flat rock ahead, and I sit down. As my breath quiets, I become aware of other sounds around me: chipmunks darting through the undergrowth, a woodpecker somewhere nearby, and a propeller plane in the distant sky. And another, more human sound: someone is crying.

It is easy to lose your way in the woods if you count on your ears to tell you where to go. But there is a clearing nearby, with a rotten log where Ethan used to store beer and a dirty magazine, until Jenny and Tara and I found it and I told Dad. I remember the way: left of the flat rock, past the witch tree with its long branchy fingers, and behind the juniper thicket. And there I find Jenny.

"What's wrong?" I say.

266

"What are you doing here?" she says at the same time.

"I got kicked out," I say. "The moms are having a private chat. They wanted some alone time."

"So did I," she says.

"What's wrong?" I say again.

"Nothing," she says. "Nothing."

"But you're crying," I say.

"You think you're the only one allowed to cry?" she says. "You think you're the only one who wants to be alone?"

"I . . . no," I say. Although I do, sort of.

"I have to go," she says, and she walks into the woods and disappears.

I watch her go. I'm disoriented. I've been out of my own life so long that it is no longer familiar to me.

I take her place on the rotten log. It's as good a place to cry as any.

"Don was supposed to adopt you," I say.

"Yes," says Jenny.

"But he decided not to."

"That's right."

"When Peter came."

"Yes."

"Is that why your parents got divorced?"

"Yes," says Jenny. "My mother considered it an irreparable betrayal. He had been promising to adopt me since their marriage, and kept putting it off. When Peter came back, he told her he wouldn't do it."

"When did she tell you that?" I ask.

"In bits and pieces over the years," says Jenny. "But

I didn't get the whole story until he died. He consulted Peter, as it turns out, about the adoption. He asked how Peter would feel about having a legal sibling. Peter asked him not to do it."

"Jesus," I say.

"He left everything to Peter, as you can probably guess. Everything except his stamp collection. He left that to me."

There's a knock at the door.

"Guys?" It's Tara. "Are you ready to come up?"

I open the studio door and let her in. She pulls me into a hug. "You okay?" she asks.

"I'm ready for a drink," I say. "More than one."

"It's going to be fine," says Tara. "You'll see, Avery."

"How will it be fine?" I say. "I'm in disgrace. My career is over. Our major developer runs a prostitution ring, and we should have known. I should have known. A competent chief of staff would have known. Peter's right. I got in over my head."

"Wow," says Jenny. "Did he ever do a number on you."

"He's right, though," I say. "What experience did I have? I should have been able to protect Peter from someone like Adam Rothman. I didn't do enough research."

"Did his firm submit the best bid?" asks Tara.

"Yes," I say.

"Was there a committee that reviewed the bids?"

"Yes."

"Were there people on the committee that review bids more or less all the time?"

"Yes."

"Were you one of those people?"

"No."

"So," says Tara, "to recap, you participated on Peter's behalf in a committee process that determined that Adam Rothman's firm was an appropriate choice for the waterfront development, and you agreed with the decision of the committee."

"Right," I say.

"And that decision having been made, you worked with Adam and his employees, as you were required to do, and briefed Peter on those meetings."

"Right."

"So let's remember all of that," says Tara.

"Right," I say.

We troop up to the main cottage. Matt meets us with a tray of cocktails. "The news is coming on," he says. "Do you want to watch it? You can say no."

"Will you hold my hand at the scary parts?" I ask.

"Always," he says.

We gather as one tribe around the television. Peter is the top story. Aidan Clarke stands outside city hall, with a thin gloss of seriousness plastered over his obvious excitement at the scoop of his career.

"City residents are reeling from the news that their mayor, Peter Haines, is being investigated for influence peddling related to city contracts, and for his alleged participation in a prostitution ring," says Aidan Clarke.

"What?" I say.

"Shhh," says Matt.

"This story continues to unfold as we speak," Aidan continues. "Mayor Haines spent last night at police headquarters, speaking to investigators about his relationship with a local developer, Adam Rothman. Mr. Rothman was arrested yesterday on a variety of prostitution-related offences. The police statement issued earlier today states that Mr. Rothman is the owner of the Buckingham Club, an exclusive sex club that caters to the wealthy and powerful. According to police, yesterday's arrests were the result of a year-long investigation into a prostitution ring, allegedly operated by Mr. Rothman."

"Oh my God," I moan. "I think I'm going to be sick."

"Yesterday, city hall was shocked by the firing of the mayor's long-time chief of staff, Avery Graham, for 'errors in judgment' relating to the waterfront development file, Mr. Rothman's involvement in that development, and a wrongful dismissal lawsuit against the mayor's office." Footage appears on the screen of Matt leading me out of city hall.

"I look terrible," I say. "I look guilty." I hear myself moan. "My career is over."

Matt holds my hand. "Nothing's over," he says.

"Tonight, however, new revelations are emerging about the mayor's own involvement with Mr. Rothman and the Buckingham Club. Police have confirmed that the mayor has been a regular visitor at the Buckingham Club during the period of police surveillance. And several women employed by the Buckingham Club have come forward with their stories."

A beautiful blonde with more than a passing resemblance to Peter's wife, Hannah, appears on the screen. "Mr. Peter was a popular member at the Buckingham Club," she says. "Very handsome, polite. He liked to be with different girls each time. We were not allowed to take any money from him. Mr. Adam said that he was our honoured guest and everything for him was on the house."

"I need to stand up," I say. Matt lets go of my hand and I pace. I can't watch, but I can't stop listening.

"Aidan," says the news anchor, "this is extraordinary. What is the reaction from other members of city council?"

"Obviously, the news has rocked city hall at all levels," says Aidan. "We had the opportunity to speak to Roger Wozniak earlier, and here's what he had to say."

I glance back at the screen. Roger Wozniak appears, with Rick in the background. "The mayor and I disagree about many things," says Roger. "And today, it's clear that we disagree about even more than I thought. A real man doesn't have to pay for sex." Rick leans forward and whispers something in Roger's ear. "Of course, these are only allegations for now. We hope that this mess will be resolved quickly so that we can get back to the business of running our great city. That is all."

"I need another drink," I say. I go into the kitchen and fill a wineglass to the brim. I sit down on the floor with my back against the bottom cabinets and close my eyes.

A few minutes later, I hear footsteps. "Avery," says Matt quietly. "I know this is a lot to take in, but you need to see this. Peter is making a statement."

The screen shows the podium in the city council chamber. Peter strides to the microphone. "Good evening," he says. "I will not be answering any questions about specific allegations today, other than to say that I am absolutely innocent. However, it is clear to me that the current investigation will interfere with my ability to serve this city as mayor. The city needs, and deserves, a mayor who can lead with singular focus and attention. I cannot be that

mayor while devoting myself to disproving these outrageous accusations. These events have been traumatic for
my beloved family, and I want to apologize to my wife,
Hannah, for the distress this has caused her. I need to take
the time to heal my personal relationships and to cooperate
with the ongoing investigation. I have, therefore, come to
the very difficult decision that I must step down as mayor
until these matters are resolved."

"Karma's patient," says Jenny. "But she's a real bitch."
Tears are running down her face. And Tara's. And my
mother's. Matt's expression is one of deep satisfaction, but
not surprise.

"My God," I say. I look at Matt. "You knew."

"Will called an hour or so ago," says Matt. "The story
broke online this afternoon. I didn't want to say anything
until I was sure."

"I don't know what to say."

"You don't have to say anything. It will take some time
to absorb. We'll hang out here for a few days and avoid the
circus."

"But what then?" I say. "What happens after that?"

"That's up to you," says Matt. "You're the writer. You
get to decide what happens next."

"But I don't know," I say.

"You'll figure it out," he says. "I have faith in you."

CHAPTER 22

Friday, July 21, 2017, and July 1988

On Friday morning, we act as though it is a long-weekend Saturday, except that no one goes to get thc newspapers. I suggest that we do, and Matt says, "Let's take a little break from the news."

Mom bustles around the kitchen, making waffles and bacon and freshly squeezed orange juice. We chat about the neighbours, and Matt's job, and some of our friends that Mom knows, and then we are out of ideas. I make a mental note to develop interests unrelated to my employment, if indeed I have employment again someday.

I think of going for a swim, but I hear Tara's kids down on the dock. I'm not ready to see them. I'm not ready for them to see me. I find the idea that anyone feels sorry for me unbearable. "I'm going to go for a walk," I say.

"Do you want me to come?" says Matt.

"No," I say, smiling to take the sting out of the words. "I want to process a bit."

Matt reaches across the table and covers my hand with his. "I'll help your mom clean up," he says.

I walk down the driveway and out along the dirt road that leads to the paved road that leads to the highway. The way is lined with tall pines, whose slender trunks crack and sway in the wind. Pine needles in various stages of decay collect in the tire grooves and give a comfortable spring to the surface of the road as I lose myself in the steady rhythm of my body. I'm looking down, hands in my pockets, so I don't see him approaching until I hear the crackling of twigs under his feet.

He's dressed in shorts and a T-shirt designed for people who run on a regular basis, with a high-tech gadget strapped to his wrist and white buds protruding from his ears. He looks nothing like I remember him, but also exactly the same.

He stops, far enough away so that one of us could still make a break for it. I hold my ground. It is his turn to run, if that is what he chooses. And anyway, seeing him is strangely satisfying. Here is the one person on this earth who cannot possibly feel sorry for me.

But instead of retreating, he takes the buds out of his ears and turns off whatever it is he is listening to. I imagine it is an audiobook, but given the other transformations in evidence, it could be anything. It could be some band that only people on university campuses know about yet.

"Hi, Hugh," I say.

"Hi, Avery," he says. He comes closer, not close enough to hug, but close enough to talk without projecting. "It's been a long time."

I brace myself. "Hit me with your best shot, Hugh," I say. "Say whatever you want to say to me. I deserve it."

He smiles, but there isn't any malice in it. "You look older," he says.

★ ★ ★

Dad takes me out in the rowboat for a talk. I'd prefer the sailboat, so we can sit side by side, or the canoe, so I can sit with my back to him, but he isn't having any of it.

He's proud of his even strokes. He used to row at school, and he likes to exercise on a rowing machine in the basement at home. He can make the boat fly across the lake. But now we are drifting down the shoreline, because Dad gets winded when he pulls the oars too hard, and he wants to save his breath for me.

Jenny and I had a fight this morning, a bad one. She's been edgy this summer, quick to take offence. I complain about this to my mother and she says Jenny isn't the only one. She says that Berry Point is awash in hormones, and it is getting tiresome. She says Peter should stay in the city for a few weekends and let everyone settle down. I say it has nothing to do with Peter.

We were out on the raft, Tara and Jenny and I. I said, "I can't believe Peter figured out how to build this. He's amazing."

"Do you have any idea how ridiculous you look, chasing after him?" says Jenny.

"Jenny!" said Tara. "Don't be mean."

"I don't!" I said, standing up. "Take it back, Jenny."

"I'm the one who has to watch it all the time," she said, rising to face me. "He's not interested in you. He thinks you're a cute little kid. Everyone is laughing at you."

I flushed, humiliation warm in my gut. I wanted nothing more than to make Jenny feel the same way I did. I said, "You're just jealous because your dad loves Peter more than you."

Jenny froze, then raised her palm and slapped me across the face. She turned, dove into the water, and swam to the dock. Tara and I could hear her sobbing as she climbed up the ladder and ran off.

My mother appeared on the dock a few minutes later. "Avery Graham!" she called. "You get over here, young lady."

Jenny and I had been forced to apologize to each other, but we couldn't meet each other's eyes. And now I was in the rowboat with Dad.

"So," he says. "Jenny embarrassed you."

"She told you?" I am aghast.

"No," says Dad. "But I know you, and I know that nothing bothers you more than being embarrassed. You're a perfectionist. You get it from me, I'm afraid."

"Jenny was being mean."

"I'm not talking about Jenny right now. I'm talking about you. I'm not wading into whatever you girls are fighting about. I'll let your mother do that."

"So why are we out here?"

"Because your mother asked me to get you out of the house so that she could have a break from the drama." I fold my arms over my chest and glare at him. He laughs. "I love that expression," he says. "You've been working on it since you were two."

"Stop making fun of me," I say as the tears start.

"Sorry, sorry," says Dad. He hands me a towel. "No need for that."

I wipe my eyes. "I hate it here sometimes."

Dad nods. "It's a lot of togetherness," he says. "It's hard to hide from your mistakes."

"Jenny was just as wrong as I was!"

"Again," says Dad, "I'm not talking about Jenny. However much you may hate it, Avery, you're going to make mistakes in life, bigger ones than having an argument with

276

Jenny. And when you do, you have to figure out how to admit it, to yourself most of all. And then you have to apologize."

"I did apologize!" I say.

"I'm not done," says Dad. "After you apologize to the person you've hurt, you have to do one more thing. You have to forgive yourself. You won't feel better until you do. No one is perfect, Avery, not even us perfectionists. The sooner you figure that out, the happier you'll be."

"I am older," I say. "I'm considerably older, even, than I was yesterday morning."

"I heard," he says. "I'm sorry, truly."

"Thank you," I say. "It is . . . upsetting."

Suddenly, I'm back in Peter's office, seeing his cold eyes and the firm set of his mouth, hearing him say that he no longer wants me in his life. I bend over at the waist. I'm out of breath. There is a frightening pain in my chest. "I need to sit down," I say.

"Here," says Hugh. He leads me over to a fallen log covered in moss and we sit.

"I think I might be having a heart attack," I say.

"I doubt it," says Hugh.

"It's not out of the question," I say. "My dad died young of a heart attack."

"Your dad was in his fifties, had an undiagnosed heart condition, and dove into a freezing lake," says Hugh. "Also, you are breathing and arguing. But let's take a look anyway." He puts two fingers on my neck and consults his wrist gadget. We sit in silence for a minute. "Nope," he says. "You're fine."

"I haven't felt like this since my dad died," I say. "At the time I thought I was having sympathetic heart pain."

"Well, that answers one outstanding question," says Hugh.

"What are you talking about?" I say.

"Did it break your heart to leave me?" says Hugh. "Answer: no."

"You're saying I have a broken heart?"

"That's what I'm saying."

"Will I feel better soon?"

"Not soon," says Hugh. "But eventually, yes."

"Why are you being nice to me?" I say.

"Oh, Avery," says Hugh. "Because I'm even older than you are. And I recognize my role in our little disaster. You were so sexy and young and such a breath of fresh air, and I was your professor and I had no business starting anything with you, let alone trying to pin you down in a marriage that you obviously didn't want and weren't ready for. I kept ratcheting up the commitment, thinking I could keep you, and that if I did it would justify everything that had come before. But the closer I held you, the further you ran. I even knew it at the time, but I couldn't seem to stop myself."

"That is so completely enlightened," I say.

"I had a lot of time to think about it. And I have another relationship now that is a much better fit, with someone my own age."

"Hugh," I say, "I am so, so sorry. The way I treated you, the way I left . . . I have no excuse. I ran away. It was the height of immaturity. You did nothing to deserve it, nothing at all."

"I accept your apology," says Hugh, formally. "How are you feeling now?"

"Calmer," I say. I rub a hand over my chest. "I'm okay now. Thank you."

"You're welcome," says Hugh. He stands up. "Oh, and Avery? Next time you want to ask me for a favour? Call me yourself."

"I wasn't sure if you were speaking to me," I say.

"I am," he says.

I stand also and we pause, wary, not sure whether to shake hands or hug. "How is *The Beak* doing?" I say.

He smiles. "It's limping along," he says. "Reports of its imminent death are unfounded."

"How do you feel about private sponsorship?" I ask.

"I feel highly enthusiastic about it," he says. "Do you have an idea?"

"I was wondering about funding for a community poetry page," I say. "Funding that would, of course, cover much more than one page of the magazine."

"I'd be delighted to hear more about it," says Hugh.

"I'll look into it and give you a call," I say. I hold out my hand, and Hugh takes it, squeezes, and lets me go.

"Take care of yourself, Avery," he says. "Take it from one who knows: this too shall pass."

And he puts his earbuds back in and jogs off down the road.

I watch him go, and when he disappears around the bend, the tears come. I cry for my dad, whose loss is woven into the fabric of every choice I've made in love. I cry for my mom, who found a perfect love and then had to learn to live without it. I cry for all the ways in which we think we know each other and don't. I cry for Jenny and her screwed-up childhood. I cry for Matt and the pain I've inflicted on him. And I cry for myself. I cry the hot, noisy tears of a child who has been stripped of her illusions. I cry tears of rage and regret. I cry for all the ways that I've failed and all the ways I've been disappointed. And when I run out of tears, I walk home.

"Rick Wozniak called for you," says my mom. "I told him that you weren't up for a chat, but he said it wouldn't be long. Here's the number."

"Thanks," I say.

"Are you ready for lunch?" asks Mom.

I look at the clock. "We ate breakfast an hour ago," I say.

My mother looks stricken. "I don't know how to help you," she says.

I give her a hug. "I know," I say. "You're doing everything right. I'll be fine. I promise."

"Matt's down on the dock," she says.

"I'll call Rick, and then I'll go down," I say. "A swim might be what the doctor ordered."

I go up to my bedroom and dial Rick's number. He picks up after the first ring.

"Avery!" he says. "Thank you for returning my call so quickly. I was concerned. I appreciate that this is an awful time for you."

"Yes," I say. "It is. Awful."

"I want you to know that I'm horrified at how you have been treated," he says. "I consider the mayor's conduct generally, but most particularly with respect to you, to be outrageous."

"Thank you," I say. "I'm touched." And I am.

"I won't keep you long," he says. "But I'm sure you are considering your options today, and I wanted to be sure I caught you before you made any major decisions."

"I haven't made any decisions at all," I say. "Major or otherwise."

"Good," he says. "Good. You shouldn't. But I hope you'll consider this when you're ready. With the mayor's resignation, there is a vacuum at city hall. Judy Mendelson, as you know, was the deputy mayor, but she is unable to serve due to her medical condition. Consequently, council met this morning and voted to have my father serve as deputy mayor until the election."

"That's a lot to absorb," I say. *So Eden sank to grief*, I think, and then smile to myself. Proof of life: I can still summon up lines of poetry in the midst of a disaster. How odd to realize that I may share this propensity with Roger Wozniak, the quality of the verse notwithstanding.

"Can you absorb more?"

"Sure," I say.

"There is substantial support on council for an early election to replace Peter Haines. I've discussed the issue at length with my father and others, and I've decided to run for mayor."

"You know what?" I say. "I'd vote for you."

"I'm delighted to hear it," says Rick, "and I hope you'll consider doing more than that. I respect what you've done during your time at city hall. We have been on opposite sides, but you have always been prepared, and courteous, and constructive. You are the only reason that the water-front file has progressed as far as it has. I'm committed to getting the project back on track. We'll need to run a new bid process immediately. But I'm getting ahead of myself. My point is, I'd like you to come and work for me."

"Why would you want to have anything to do with me?" I say, tears welling up. "The whole city thinks I'm incompetent and possibly corrupt."

"Are you?"

"No," I say. "Not even a little bit."

"Well then, Avery, I'd be proud to have you on the team."

I'm having trouble speaking. I say, "I'll consider it very seriously, Rick."

"That's all I was hoping for today," he says.

I clear my throat. "One other thing," I say. "I met with Hugh Crane this morning. He's open to creating a community poetry page if he can find a funder. Would you be interested in supporting *The Beak*, philanthropically speaking?"

"I'd like to hear more," says Rick. "Why don't we talk again in a few days?"

"Rick," I say. "If I agree to work for you, can I have the recipe for those cookies?"

He laughs. "We all need a few secrets," he says.

I change into my bathing suit, pull a towel from the linen closet, and wrap it around me. I slip out of the house, pausing at the top of the staircase down to the water. There is a light breeze today, ripples chasing across the surface of the lake. It's a nice day for a swim, but I have other plans.

Matt is sitting with a mug of coffee and the newspapers. Peter's picture is on the cover.

"Hi," I say.

He starts, spilling his coffee and gathering up the papers. "Shit," he says. "Sorry, Avery. I didn't want you to see these today. You've been through enough."

"You're allowed to read the paper," I say. "Is there anything about me? Wait. Don't tell me. I don't want to know."

Matt puts the papers down and throws his towel over top of them. "There," he says. "Gone." He sits. "Do you want to swim?"

"No," I say, sitting down next to him. "I want to talk."

"I'm here," he says.

"Rick Wozniak called," I say. "He wants me to go and work for him."

"Does that surprise you?"

"I thought I would be radioactive now," I say.

"Peter is radioactive. You arc the loyal soldier who got thrown under the bus."

"That was a healthy serving of metaphors," I say.

"You get the point," says Matt. "Little Miss MFA."

"I'm not that person anymore," I say.

"Sure you are," says Matt.

"Is that what you see? The same person you met all those years ago?"

"Of course not," says Matt. "You've grown. You've evolved. That's what people do. But all the qualities I fell in love with are still there. And some others that I merely tolerate out of affection, like the metaphor policing."

"Matt," I say, my stomach tight with nerves, "will you ask me again? Have I screwed up too badly? Is it too late?"

His gaze is soft. "Of course it's not too late," he says. "But it's been an emotional week for you. Are you sure you want to make a big decision right now?"

"I'm sure," I say. "I think it's the perfect time to make a big decision."

Matt stands up in his swim trunks and gets down on

one knee in front of my Muskoka chair. "Avery," he says. "I love you. I love all of you. I love the person you were then, and the person you are now, and I want to spend the rest of my life getting to know the person you will be in the future. Will you marry me?"

"Yes," I say. "Yes."

I'm upstairs in my bedroom when there is a tap at the door.

"Come in," I say.

Matt steps into the room. He's wearing a navy linen suit, crisp and unruffled. "I was sent to tell you that it's time."

"You aren't supposed to see the bride before the wedding," I tell him.

"You aren't supposed to sleep with the bride before the wedding, either," says Matt. "Obviously, I'm willing to tempt fate."

"Always the risk taker," I say.

"Only calculated ones," he says. "And they've tended to work out."

"Let's hope your luck holds," I say.

"We don't need luck, Avery," he says. "Marriage isn't about that."

I'm not sure he's right. Personally, I don't know what I did to deserve Matt's unwavering love. But maybe luck isn't the right word. Maybe the right word is faith.

He says, "I wanted to have you to myself for a minute."

"Hands off," I say. "Tara and Jenny will kill me if I mess up my hair and makeup. They were in here for hours." I do a slow turn, my white dress flaring out at the bottom. "What do you think?"

"You look perfect," he says. "You look like everything I've ever wanted in my life."

I clear my throat. "I told you not to ruin my makeup," I say.

Matt hands over a box of tissues. "Sorry," he says, looking not at all sorry, and then he sneaks a kiss. I kiss him back, gently, and rest my forehead against his.

"Everyone's here?" I ask.

"Everyone's here," he says. "The mayor is in full regalia. It's a major statement on the dock, I can tell you that. There's some boat traffic."

It is a small wedding, only our closest friends and family. We're doing the service on the dock at the cottage, which my mother no longer talks about selling.

Mayor Rick Wozniak, my boss, is performing the ceremony. This is one of his first official duties, and Rick is taking it seriously. He is a man of extraordinary self-discipline. I'm not sure when he sleeps.

I'll admit to a sense of déjà vu when Rick's landslide victory put me back in the mayor's office. But this time, it's different. This time, I know what I'm doing. The hours are still long, but being Rick's chief of staff is a job, not an identity. I'm setting healthy boundaries, as my therapist would say. My relationship with Rick is one of shared professional objectives and mutual respect. It is utterly uncomplicated, which is both a relief and, truthfully, a loss.

Peter has been charged with multiple counts of solicitation of prostitution. He was, as it turns out, a quite active member of the Buckingham Club. His former friend, Adam Rothman, is facing more charges than I can count. The press's new theory is that Peter received free services at the Buckingham Club in return for his influence behind the scenes, influence that included the awarding of city contracts. I don't know what I think. I keep my head down, and I don't speculate. Peter's lawyer says that he will defend the charges vigorously.

Melanie Christie has started a group called LASH (Lawyers against Sexual Harassment), and was honoured as an Influencer of the Year at the WAFADASS fundraiser this spring. She settled her lawsuit against the mayor's office. We nod politely when we see each other at industry events.

Marla Kraft took over as the president of ArtCo when the mayor's office refused to deal further with Jim Crawford. With Marla's help, the waterfront design issues were resolved fairly quickly, and the project broke ground six months ago. I visit the site every week. Even though there isn't much to it yet—only metal skeletons rising from the mud—I can see it, fully formed, in my mind. I know it like I know my own home. It's going to be beautiful.

The Community Poetry page of *The Beak* has been a popular addition to the publication. Roger is a regular contributor.

And today, Matt and I stand at the top of the long wooden staircase that leads down to the water. It's sunny and brisk: a good morning to set out on an adventure. I take a moment to remember my dad and wish that he were here, and to remember Peter, as I once believed him to be, and wish that he were here too. And I think of all of the people I've been, at all the stages of my life, and I accept and forgive them, and I gather them all to me, so that I am here, entirely, in this place with Matt.

"Are you really ready to join this family?" I ask.

"Completely," says Matt, holding out a hand.

And we walk down together.

THE END

{ACKNOWLEDGEMENTS}

I wrote this book during a two-year period which was, I sincerely hope, the worst time of my life. Believe me when I say that these acknowledgements are as heartfelt as any acknowledgements could ever be.

Thank you to the unflappable Beverley Slopen, my agent, who is also a dear friend and an excellent person to have around in a crisis. She is my first reader, and she knows a good thing when she sees it. She knows an imperfect thing too, and she knows how to say so without generating a crisis of the kind mentioned above.

Thank you to Jennifer Lambert, my editor at HarperCollins Canada. I am blessed to have an editor so wise, so insightful, so gentle, and so unfailingly right about everything. She makes my work better every time she touches it, and I love her for it.

Thank you also to Sarah Wight, my copyeditor, who saves me from excessive dialogue tags, among other literary crimes. And thanks to the rest of the team at HarperCollins Canada, including Leo MacDonald, Cory Beatty, Colleen Simpson, Sabrina Groomes, and Natalie Meditsky, who do so much to get my books into the hands of readers.

While writing this book, I spent a lot of time thinking about friendship, partly because I was writing about it, and partly because I was so reliant upon, and so grateful for, the love and help of my friends. They are many, too many to list here, but a few deserve special mention: Brydie Bethell, Naomi Buck, Marie Budworth, Brianna Caryll Valihora, Sari Diamond, Todd Ducharme, Leah Eichler, Bronwen Evans, Bonnie Goldberg, Fiona Griffiths, Reva Katz, Guy Kay, Sarah McEvoy, Stacia Morris, Ira Parghi, Laurie Pawlitza, Alyson Robertson, Jennifer Robson, Reva Seth, Rachel Sutherland, and Cornell Wright.

I am grateful, too, for a wonderful and supportive group of writers in Toronto, whom I think of as the Coven: Karma Brown, Chantal Guertin, Liz Renzetti, Jennifer Robson, and Marissa Stapley.

My books are vetted by a group of beta readers, who see the ugly first draft and help me arrive at a second draft (one that I can show to my editor without shame). Thank you to Leah Eichler, Bonnie Goldberg, Margo Hilton, Judith Lavin, Laurie Pawlitza, Reva Seth, and Maureen Whelton for their heroic service this time around.

Thank you to Evan Kenley, for keeping me company in the editing stage, and for playing research assistant in Buffalo, of all places.

Finally, I thank my family: my sisters, Anne Hilton and Betsy Hilton; my sons, Jack Hilton-Centa and Charlie Hilton-Centa; and my parents, Jim Hilton and Margo Hilton, to whom this book is dedicated. All of you were in my thoughts as I wrote this story about summers at the cottage, and family, and loyalty, and love.